YOU ARE PREY

ARGONAUTS

BOOK TWO

IRIDIUM

PUBLISHING

A DIVISION OF

HOOKE
PUBLICATIONS

BOOKS BY ISAAC HOOKE

Military Science Fiction

Argonauts

Bug Hunt
You Are Prey
Alien Empress

Alien War Trilogy

Hoplite
Zeus
Titan

The ATLAS Series

ATLAS
ATLAS 2
ATLAS 3

A Captain's Crucible Series

Flagship
Test of Mettle
Cradle of War
Planet Killer
Worlds at War

Science Fiction

The Forever Gate Series

The Dream
A Second Chance
The Mirror Breaks
They Have Wakened Death
I Have Seen Forever
Rebirth
Walls of Steel
The Pendulum Swings
The Last Stand

Thrillers

YOU ARE PREY

PREY

ARGONAUTS

BOOK TWO

Isaac Hooke

Text copyright © Isaac Hooke 2017
Published March 2017. All rights reserved.

www.IsaacHooke.com

ISBN-13: 978-1-5207117-1-3
ISBN-10: 1-5207-1171-9

Cover design by Isaac Hooke
Cover image by Shookooboo

contents

*To my father, mother, brothers, and
most devoted fans.*

one

Rade took a seat on the bridge of the *Argonaut*. Around him, the other crew members sat about that circular arrangement of stations known as the Sphinx. There were no actual controls or screens or anything of that sort upon the Sphinx; rather, the crew interfaced with the stations via their Implants.

"How long until we achieve orbit?" Rade asked Lui.

"Another thirty minutes," the ops station operator replied. The Asian American had undergone rejuvenation treatments at the last station stop, wiping away the few wrinkles that had started to form. However the procedure had stiffened some of his facial muscles, making him seem a little robotic. The rest of the crew had made fun of him relentlessly at first, but the automaton jokes had grown old quickly.

"What do we know about Prattein XI?" Rade said.

"Fourteenth planet of the system," Lui said. "Entirely uninhabited. It's similar to Pluto. Basically a big frozen iceberg."

"Sort of like Surus?" Bender asked. The black man was only wearing a few of his gold chains that day. He was cutting back, apparently.

Rade glanced at the alien, which inhabited a

stunningly beautiful Artificial. Behind the collar at the back of her neck, if Rade looked carefully he could see the droplets of mint-colored condensation that signified the Green Phant in possession of the body.

Surus ignored Bender entirely. Rade had been worried her beauty would prove a distraction aboard the bridge, and it had at first. But the crew quickly learned she wouldn't take shit from any of them. She behaved coldly to almost everyone, save Harlequin, another Artificial. For the most part, the crew tried to behave themselves around her, because ultimately she *was* their client and paid the bills.

"The Hellenes haven't set up any mining stations to collect liquid water?" Rade asked.

"No," Lui said. "They've plenty of water on their colony world."

"True enough." Rade turned toward Surus. "This is the last planet. If we don't find anything, is it safe to say your contact was wrong?"

"He wasn't wrong," Surus replied. "If our prey isn't here, we turn back and sweep the system again."

Rade wasn't looking forward to that. They had already spent the past four months in the system moving from planet to planet, waiting in orbit while telemetry drones and Dragonflies scoured the surface for signs of their prey.

"Isn't it possible the Phant already left the system?" Manic said. The moth-shaped port-wine stain above his right eye seemed particular reddish that day. He sat at the tactical station.

"My contact at customs would have sensed him," Surus replied.

She had another Green secretly embedded among the Hellene customs warships at the entrance Gate to the system. Since the officials boarded every outgoing and incoming vessel for inspection, it was the best possible spot for an undercover alien to operate, at least in terms of being able to sense other Phants.

"And he's sure it was a Black?" Rade said.

"Yes," Surus said.

"Remind me of the significance of that color," Shaw said. She sat to Rade's left at the astrogator station. She looked ravishing as always. She had gone back to her brown eyes and dark hair, which she wore in a ponytail much like Surus. But that was where their similarities ended. While they were both beautiful, Shaw was just so wholesome compared to the Artificial. Shaw was tan, Surus was pale. Her eyes shone with joy; Surus' were emotionless. Cute dimples formed in Shaw's cheeks when she smiled, which she did often. Rade had never seen Surus smile even once.

Well actually, there was one more similarity that the two shared... like Surus, despite her looks, Shaw was no distraction to the crew.

"The significance?" Surus said. "The Blacks were the infiltrators and assassins. They were usually the most powerful, psychically, of all Phants. They would often turn the closest associates of their targets into killing instruments, transforming friends and families into weapons of assassination."

"You Phants are just lovely," Shaw said.

"Some of us certainly are," Surus said. "Which is why I hunt them."

The bridge was quiet for a few moments.

"Hey Surus," Bender said.

She ignored him.

"Surus," Bender pressed.

Finally Surus glanced up. "What is it?" The alien seemed annoyed.

"What are you doing tonight?" Bender said.

Surus scowled and lowered her gaze once more.

"I kid I kid," Bender said. "Seriously, I have a question. I've been wondering how the whole possession thing works. What happens to a host robot or Artificial when a Phant takes over? What happens to the AI core?"

"The core remains intact, of course," Surus said without looking up. "When I take over entirely, the AI still functions, but becomes a mere observer, unable to control its own body or even its own thoughts. But it sees, hears, and feels everything I do. This control doesn't necessarily have to be absolute. In fact, I allow Emilia to operate some of the time, but I take over during critical moments of course."

"So who am I talking to now?" Bender said. "Surus? Or Emilia Bounty?"

"Surus, of course," the alien replied. "Since talking to you is a critical moment. I have to keep my guard up."

"I'm honored that you hold me in such high regard," Bender said.

"I want to talk to Emilia Bounty," Manic said. "Let me talk to Ms. Bounty."

Surus turned her head toward the other ex-MOTH. "I'm not some puppet here to leap and dance at your whims."

Manic shrugged. "Could have fooled me." He winked at her.

Rade pursed his lips. He wondered if he was going to have to have a talk with Manic again. The crew *had* been behaving amicably toward her over the past few weeks. He could only attribute their current behavior to lack of action. He had to admit he was certainly growing antsy lately.

"What I want to know," Fret said. "Is what

happens when a Phant touches a human? Why do we go poof?" The comm officer was the tallest present, though it wasn't obvious when he sat at his station. He was also the thinnest, and looked like a stick compared to most of the men.

"The Phant, which exists mostly in the supra-dimension, attacks the human's imprint there," Surus said. "An inter-dimensional reaction occurs, creating havoc on the cohesive elemental particles forming the human's body in this reality, and the molecular bonds simply break apart. The process transpires from start to finish in a matter of picoseconds. Now, if you don't mind..."

The alien returned her attention to her station. Which wasn't saying much, considering the station was empty like all the others. She would be viewing various data elements on her Implant equivalent, of course. Or whatever a Phant did in its spare time while occupying an Artificial. Perhaps communicating with the host.

"I've placed us in orbit," Shaw said after a few minutes.

Rade nodded. "Lui, how does it look down there? Any obvious signs of habitation?"

"Nothing obvious, no," Lui said. "Though it's tricky, because a lot of the surface is composed of methane and nitrogen penitentes."

Rade zoomed in on the video feed from the external camera, and saw the blade-like spires that Lui referred to, so-named because they looked like a bunch of kneeling penitentes. The spires were packed closely together, with some rising several hundreds of feet, others several thousand, depending on the region.

"All right," Rade said. "Launch the telemetry drones. Let's hope we can scare up a Phant this time. I'll be in my office."

Rade stood up and retired to his office. All they could do now was wait.

Shaw joined him a while later, and took the chair across from him, next to the cramped desk.

"So, how's my favorite warrior doing?" Shaw asked.

"Excellent, now that you're here," Rade said.

Shaw smiled that dimpled smile of hers. "Did I give you enough time to cave out?"

Rade nodded. "Yeah. I suppose."

"The counseling sessions with Bax have been going well?" Shaw said.

"They have," Rade said.

"That true, Bax?" Shaw asked.

The disembodied voice of the *Argonaut's* AI answered immediately. "Rade has been attending his sessions, yes. He seems to be deriving some small benefit from them, though he still argues with me on almost every question. As far as the results of our sessions, he still experiences the occasional bout of lost time as far as I can tell. Usually when he is alone in his office."

"Which is exactly why I try to check in on him as often as I can," Shaw said.

"That is certainly a good thing," Bax said. "Because he has ordered me not to notify you when he zones out."

"I wonder if I should change that order," Shaw said.

"No, Shaw," Rade said. "I need the time."

Shaw sighed. "All right. You've been getting better, as far as I'm concerned. And I knew you would."

Rade inclined his head. Truthfully, he didn't know if he was or not. He liked to think he was. But he still needed his cherished alone time.

Shaw flashed a nervous grin. "All right then. Now that we've gotten that out of the way. So... I've been thinking..."

"Oh oh," Rade said.

She laughed. "Yes, I know, end of the world. But, well..." She took a deep breath, and then let her next words out all at once. "What would you say if I stopped taking contraceptives?"

"Ah, no," Rade said. "No no no. I'm not ready to be a father."

"Why not?" Shaw said. "We'd be fulfilling our biological purpose. It could be fun."

"Fun?" Rade said. "I can only imagine what a kid will do to my alone time. And there's nothing like a crying baby waking you up every fifteen minutes when you're trying to get in some sleep before a tough mission."

"That's what nursing robots are for," Shaw said.

"Yeah," Rade said. "I can see it now. Repurposing our expensive combat robots to act as wet nurses. Very nice."

She shrugged. "I don't see anything wrong with it."

"Well I do," Rade said. He leaned forward, his hands balling into fists. "Listen. It's a cold, harsh universe out there. And I won't be bringing a child into it, especially not while we're out here taking on clients and hunting Phants. It's the most ridiculous thing I've ever heard of. Raising a child on a ship... you really want that?"

"Why not?" she said.

"Because it would be a terrible life for the kid, for one," Rade said. "Trapped aboard a ship, with no knowledge of what the real world is like. You'd be dooming our boy to a cramped world of steel bulkheads, overheads and decks."

"Who says it would be a boy?" Shaw said. "And anyway, we could set aside a full body VR area. Assign some AIs to babysit our child while we're working."

"Uh, no," Rade said. "Can you imagine how damaged our child would become? Raised by AIs into a closet psychopath."

"I'm glad you have so much faith in AIs," Shaw told him. "Anyway, I never said we'd let the robots raise our kid full time. It would only be when we're on duty."

"And what about when we have to go planet-side, on missions?" Rade said.

"You usually make me stay behind anyway," Shaw said.

"No I don't," Rade replied.

"So what, you're saying you're going to let me come with you if we find something on this dwarf planet?"

Rade hesitated.

"That's what I thought," Shaw said.

"It could be dangerous..." Rade said.

"Don't give me that," Shaw said. "You know I'm capable of fighting just as well as anyone else. Especially if I get a Hoplite."

He knew she was right, of course. Moments ago he had been telling himself that the biggest reason she had gained the respect of the crew was because she could hold her own in battle. Still, that didn't mean he wouldn't worry about her.

"But we'll need someone to watch the ship," Rade said.

"Really..." Shaw said. "You do remember what happened the last time you made me stay aboard the ship alone, don't you?"

"How could I forget," Rade said, lowering his eyes

guiltily.

"Besides, Bax is more than capable of watching the ship," Shaw said. "Right, Bax?"

"That is correct," the *Argonaut's* AI replied. "Leave me a full complement of Hellfires and a few Centurion combat robots for anti-boarding purposes, and I guarantee you no unauthorized personnel will ever come aboard. Pirates will rue the day they ever crossed paths with the ruthless tactician known as Bax."

"Okay Bax, give us some privacy," Rade told the AI. "Stop listening in."

"My apologies," Bax replied. "I can't help it. You'll have to engage your noise cancelers and disable the cameras if you truly wish privacy."

"Disable my office cameras," Rade ordered the AI. Then he raised his noise canceler around Shaw via his Implant. "Where were we?"

"Talking about how we're going to have kids," Shaw said.

"*Not* have kids, you mean," Rade said. "I wasn't joking. Kids are something for when people retire after two hundred years."

"You want to have kids when we're two hundred?" Shaw said. She definitely sounded incredulous.

"Why not?" Rade said. "That's a good enough time as any. Keep taking your contraceptives, save your eggs until then, and we'll have as many kids as you want."

"You know there's a danger of ovary fatigue, right?" Shaw said. "I've seen it happen, women who stop taking their contraceptives after decades, only to discover the drugs rendered them infertile. And anyway, human life expectancy is only two hundred and fifty, even with rejuvenation treatments. I want to be with our children a little longer than fifty years."

"Fifty years is good enough for me," Rade said, his mind filling with crying babies once more. "Besides, I intend to live until four hundred."

"Good luck with that," she said. "Seriously, though, what are you afraid of? It's not really because you're scared of losing your precious quiet time, is it? Because you know you can still have that."

Rade looked her, but hesitated. He hated revealing his vulnerabilities to anyone, even for someone as close to him as her.

She peered back at him, smiling very slightly in understanding. Then her features relaxed, became serene. "Come on, if you can't tell me, who can you tell? The AI isn't listening anymore. No one is. We're speaking in complete confidence. You don't have to worry about looking bad in front of the team."

Rade sighed. But he still couldn't say anything.

"Is it because we're not married, is that it?" Shaw said.

"Not at all," Rade said.

"Then what is it, then?"

Rade gazed at his hands. He realized his fingers were still squeezed into tight fists, and he relaxed them.

Shaw's hand found his. "Tell me. Please. I need to know."

Her touch relaxed him further and reminded him who she was. He could trust her with all of his secrets. No matter how dark, and how ashamed of them he was.

"Honestly?" Rade said. "I'm selfish. I want to be the center of your life. Your world. If we have a kid, I won't have that any more. I'll have to compete for your attention."

Shaw pursed her lips. "Well, that's probably true.

You *will* have to compete for my attention, at least for the first ten years or so. Until we have our next kid."

Rade almost rolled his eyes. "She wants more than one... this woman is going to be the end of me."

"Rade, if I could have my way, I'd have ten kids with you," Shaw said.

He pulled his hand away from hers and folded his arms over his chest. "I'm not sure you understand what a commitment kids are, even with VR and babysitting robots..."

"Oh I do," she said. "I truly do. We won't have more than one or two while we're aboard the *Argonaut*. But I'd like to have a few more when we retire from consulting. Before I'm a hundred."

"Yeah, I don't know about that," Rade said. "Tell you what. When we're done catching the Phant in this system, I'll think about it."

"All right," Shaw said. "But just so you know, I'm not going to let this go. I feel like now is the time."

"Okay," Rade said.

She got up, kissed him on the forehead, and departed.

Rade heaved a huge sigh of relief when she was gone.

Well that was a can of worms I didn't want opened.

two

The next day Rade scheduled an early workout in the *Argonaut's* onboard gym, taking only Tahoe with him. The telemetry drones had so far discovered nothing of note on the dwarf planet, though there were still another three days before the drones completed their LIDAR scan of the dark side.

Rade and the big Navajo were taking turns doing weighted pull-ups. Rade finished his set, removed the belt from around his waist and lowered the weights hanging from it.

"How did Tepin convince you to have your first child?" Rade said. "While we were still in the military?"

"She didn't have to convince me," Tahoe said.

"You mean you wanted it?" Rade said.

"Not exactly," Tahoe replied. "It happened accidentally."

"She stopped taking her contraceptives?"

"We thought she didn't need them," Tahoe said. "She never had any periods. And where we were from in those days, there was no access to medical treatments, so we just shrugged it off. Anyway, later we found out she was just a late bloomer, at least in that department, according to the Weaver who helped deliver the girl."

Tahoe accepted the belt and did his sets.

"What about the second and third kids?" Rade said when Tahoe was done. "You would have known by then that she wasn't infertile. So why didn't you start on the contraceptives?"

"We did know, yes," Tahoe said. "But we didn't want to risk infertility, not after all those years of shooting blanks on my part. Besides, I didn't mind populating the world with a few more miniature Tahoes and Tepins."

Rade accepted the weight belt, but didn't put on the thing immediately. "It didn't scare you, knowing that you might die at any time while on a deployment, leaving your kids back home without a father?"

"It terrified me," Tahoe said. "But it also helped me, believe it or not. Gave me something to fight for. I can't tell you how many times I was on a mission, and the only thing that got me through, and prevented me from giving up, was the thought that I wouldn't see my kids ever again if I died. I had to see them one last time. Just once more. And that's what spurred me on when things got really bad. That and the fear of leaving them fatherless, like you said.

"Those were my two big fears, my brother. And I still haven't overcome them. Even today, with my kids being older, and given all the time I've spent with them, and all the messages we exchange daily, I still fear those things, especially when we have a drop coming up. It's why a part of me kind of hopes we never find that Phant we're hunting."

"You know you don't have to do this, right?" Rade said. "You can resign any time. I'll buy out your shares, give you a bonus, and you can go your merry way."

Tahoe chuckled. "When I said a part of me hopes we never find the Phant, I meant it. But another part wants to hunt that bitch down and bag it more than anything. I live for this, bro. I can't go back to living an ordinary life. I love my kids, but I love my work just as much. What am I supposed to do? Go back to Earth and live on veteran's and basic pay, bored out of my ass? Before you came to recruit me to the Argonauts, I sat at home all day, drinking, shouting at Tepin and the kids when they bothered me. I'd load up VR and drunkenly engage in online war games, looking for something, anything to shoot. I was literally driving my wife crazy. And then you came along and offered me a chance to put that all behind me, and return once more to the only brotherhood that has ever truly meant anything to me. You saved me. Family is one thing, yes. But good work, with brothers you would die for, well, all I can say is my place is right here at your side. As it always will be."

Rade rested a hand on his shoulder. "Thanks, Tahoe." Rade did his set, then gave the belt to Tahoe.

"Why do you ask, by the way?" Tahoe said.

"Ask what?" Rade said.

"About Tepin and me," Tahoe said. "And how she got pregnant."

"Oh," Rade said. "No reason."

Tahoe looked him squarely in the eye. "Shaw wants a baby, doesn't she?"

"No. Not at all."

Tahoe cracked a wide grin. "Yeah yeah. Shaw wants a baby and you don't. That's it, isn't it?" He lowered his voice as if trying to sound like a dumber version of Rade. "Hey Tahoe, how did you knock up Tepin? Oh, I'm asking cuz I wanna know if I should knock up Shaw, but I'm kinda afraid to. Maybe my cock won't work."

Rade looked at his friend. "I can't hide anything

from you, can I?"

"Seriously man," Tahoe said. "Does Shaw want a baby or not?"

"Yes," Rade said.

"And what did you tell her?" Tahoe pressed.

"That I'm not ready."

Tahoe nodded. "Sounds about right. I wouldn't want to have a baby on this ship, either. So what did she say?"

"She agreed to hold off until we're done our latest mission at least," Rade said. "Then she plans to bug me again."

"Yeah, I can't see you raising a kid on this ship," Tahoe said. "It's far too cramped. And there's way too much testosterone."

"Maybe I should get you to talk some sense into her," Rade said.

Tahoe raised his palms in surrender. "Don't involve me. She'll bite my head off."

"Why not try?" Rade said.

"This is something you have to handle," Tahoe said. "But at least she gave you some time to plan your next defensive. Better start strategizing, bro." He patted Rade commiseratively on the shoulder.

"Unfortunately, I don't think there are any strategies left to me," Rade said. "Once Shaw sets her mind on something, nothing can stop her."

"That's true," Tahoe said. "Look at her relentless pursuit of you." He smiled profusely, then did his set.

THE NEXT MORNING Rade took his place at the bridge. He had trouble sleeping the night before and he felt extremely tired. Shaw had sensed his tossing and turning, and she made love to him hoping to settle his mind and body; it had helped a little. Even so, he definitely wasn't in the mood for command.

He barely listened to Lui's status report before excusing himself to his office, and once he had plunked himself down at his desk, it was all he could do to resist the urge to lower his head and take a nap. He opened up one of the drawers, found a sonic injector, and applied a stimulant. That was better.

He was about to go to the bridge, but something stopped him. He didn't feel quite ready to surround himself with people again. The thought was suffocating. Instead, he found himself staring at the hatch, unable to will his body to rise. His mind began to drift.

The sounds of explosions and missile launchers going off filled his hearing. He fought in a desert. His mech was buried to the knees. He was hidden behind a transport carrier.

"Rage!" someone said, using his wartime moniker. "Can you get your team around to the right? See if you can outflank them?"

"I'll see what we can do," Rade returned.

The incoming missiles intensified. The dunes around the transport carrier began to shift and writhe, with black tentacles rising from the surface.

"They're all around us!" someone sent.

Rade swung his weapon toward the sand and began to open fire.

He snapped to attention when a call indicator lit up in the lower right of his HUD. It was Lui.

Rade glanced at the time. An hour had passed.

He shook his head and answered. "What's up, Lui?"

"We received a LIDAR ping," Lui said. "One of the telemetry drones detected what looks like the entrance to an unnatural cave system."

"All right, thanks Lui," Rade said. He tapped in Surus, who had yet to report to the bridge. "We found something."

"Roger that," she replied. "I'll be right there."

When she arrived at the bridge, Lui shared the three-dimensional rendering of the cave entrance with their Implants.

"It looks fairly deep," Lui said. "Preliminary scans report an initial depth of at least thirty meters. Do you want me to schedule a Dragonfly launch and dispatch some robots and HS3s?"

"Hmm." Rade rubbed his chin. He glanced at Surus. "If our prey is present, he could easily possess one of those. Considering that we haven't fitted the suits with anti-Phant measures yet."

"Yes," Lui said. "And HS3s can't even wear suits."

"If he's inside those caves, our best bet is to get down there ourselves," Surus agreed. "If we send in the HS3 scouts, there's a good chance he'll run. We have no idea how deep these caves are, or if they surface again."

"Which is why it might be better to send in the HS3s first," Lui said.

Rade considered for a few more moments, then made up his mind. "I agree with Surus. I think we're better off deploying directly."

"Should we bring the mechs?" Surus asked.

"Yes," Rade said. It was an easy decision, considering that she was paying for it. "The best option is to send down the Hoplites, with a few robots to provide extra ground support and carry the containment device."

"I'll meet you in the mech bay for deployment," Surus said, and departed.

There was a good chance the team might not need the mechs down there. The cave might be empty— they had encountered their share of false alarms in the system so far. In leaner times, Rade would have been tempted not to deploy the units at all: it wasn't cheap to dispatch mechs to a planetary surface after all, even if that planet was a dwarf. But again, since Surus was covering the deployment costs, it was better to bring the Hoplites along.

Rade activated the main circuit: "All right Argonauts, it's time to get busy. Surus, Manic, Fret, Harlequin, report to the hangar bay for shuttle departure. Everyone else meet me at the mech bay."

"Everyone else" included Bender, Lui, TJ, Tahoe, Shaw and Rade. The four career mercenaries Surus had originally hired were no longer present: she had handed them off to another Green engaged in a hunt in a different system.

Rade deactivated the main circuit. "Bax, have six Centurions join Surus and the others in the hangar bay. I want them suited up like everyone else on foot—let's keep any watchers from picking out our humans from our robots. The remaining Centurions are to remain aboard to protect the ship. The *Argonaut* is yours."

"Understood, boss," Bax said.

By the time he had finished giving all his orders, everyone had already deserted the Sphinx. He squeezed past the curved stations to the exit hatch, and made his way through the passageways and down the scuttles toward the mech bay deck.

He entered the bay and the airlock sealed behind him. Inside, the six Hoplites were spaced close together. The team had retrieved the two and a half meter tall battle suits from the colony of Lang after the completion of the last mission. It had been tricky, considering that the colony was still populated by four fearsome bioweapons at the time. The team had to sneak inside the city, retrieve the mechs, and then kill the bioweapons. The extract was complicated by the swarm of killer drones they had to deal with: Perdix models, laser-enabled and vacuum-capable.

TJ had captured one of the drones during the fighting and used it to remotely reprogram the others. Rade ended up using the reconfigured swarm to terminate the last bioweapon. Now if only his team had been able to do all that the first time they were on that despicable planet.

The Persians had paid Rade and his team a bonus for clearing the colony of the bioweapons, and Rade used the money to pay a lump sum against the *Argonaut's* loan. He asked Surus if she was willing to help with the remainder, and the alien said sure, as long as she became part owner of the company. Rade declined.

He would have liked to have more than six mechs, but first of all he didn't have the holding space aboard. And second of all he didn't have the funds. He tried to convince Surus to finance an expansion to the mech hangar, as well as procure a couple more mechs, perhaps more advanced models, but once again the alien refused to bite. In typical Surus fashion, the alien said: "Six Hoplites should be more than sufficient for our purposes. And if not, then ten certainly won't be. Let alone upgrading to models such as the Zeus or Titan."

Rade went to his locker and removed the fatigues he wore while on duty, replacing them with the cooling and ventilation undergarments necessary for a jumpsuit. Shaw's locker was beside his own, and it was the closest to the bulkhead, allowing her to change behind her open locker door without anyone watching her—except Bax of course. Manic and Fret had tried to take a peek, once, when Rade wasn't there; after the black eyes Shaw gave them, they never tried again.

"Hey sexy," Shaw said quietly, peeking past the rim of her locker at him.

"Hey," Rade said. He was feeling good about his body. He had kept in good shape since the end of the last mission. Though he didn't train as hard as he had after Shaw was taken, he had maintained his diet and exercise regime, and still had one of the flattest bellies he'd ever had. When he got up in the morning, he could see the veins and striations on his abs.

"I almost wish you walked around like that all day," Shaw said.

"I could say the same about you." Rade nodded toward her bra.

Shaw realized she had stepped too far out from behind the cover of her locker door, allowing Rade, and potentially the others, to see her half undressed. She reddened and quickly vanished from view.

Rade shook his head, smiling slightly. He was glad he had decided to let her come along. After what had happened the last time he had kept her aboard, he decided that the safest place for her was at his side. Always.

He finished donning the undergarment and began attaching the jumpsuit pieces. He clipped the internal strength-enhancing exoskeleton to the hardpoints that protruded from his skin at the joints of his body—wrists, elbows, shoulders, hips, knees, and ankles. Those hardpoints improved the interface between his neurons and the suit, giving him a faster movement speed. It wasn't enough to match, say, a robot or Artificial, but it was a definite improvement. And Rade was all about eking every last ounce of performance from his gear, because he knew that even the smallest gains could make the biggest differences when it came time to fight. Even if those gains required him to augment his body with a few metallic protrusions.

He attached the final piece, the helmet, and the suit pressurized. At the same time, an accelerant injected into the dorsal venous network of his right hand, shortening his acclimation time to the new environment from an hour to a few seconds.

When he bent his arms and legs, the suit fabric felt slightly stiffer: because of their target's presumed psychic abilities, Surus had prepared a special anti-psi coating for the jumpsuits. She had placed it throughout the lining, and covered the inside of the glass with the molecular spray. No one else in the United Systems, civilian or military, had anything like it. And if the upgrade gave them all slightly less resilient suits, well, that was a small price to pay for protection from mind blasts.

Rade approached the mech named Electron. Surus had upgraded the Hoplites themselves, designing and fitting special EM-emitters around the AI cores, which would protect the units from physical Phant possession by repelling them. A similar emitter protected the *Argonaut's* AI. Unfortunately, the jumpsuits the team members wore didn't currently offer similar protection. While those suits would prevent remote psi attacks from their targets, if a Phant actually touched them, they were screwed. Surus' advice had been: don't leave the mechs.

"Lui, what's the status on the holographic

generators?" Rade asked as he opened the Hoplite's storage compartment.

"Already loaded into the storage compartments of the mechs," Lui said.

Rade saw the devices in question. "You're two steps ahead of me."

He closed the compartment and climbed the rungs to the cockpit.

Beside him, Bender took Juggernaut, and Shaw took Nemesis.

When Rade entered the cockpit, the hatch sealed, surrounding him in darkness. The internal actuators activated, wrapping him in a metal cocoon and hoisting him into the center of the cockpit. The video feed from the external camera filled his vision, and when he lifted his arm, the actuator translated the action to the Hoplite, which mirrored his movement.

"Welcome aboard, Rade," Electron said. "It's good to work with you once again."

"Thanks, El," Rade said. "It's good to be working with you, too. Run a systems diagnostic and display the prelaunch checklist."

The diagnostic returned one hundred percent, and the checkmarks beside each item in the prelaunch list indicated that the mech was ready to drop.

"Perfect," Rade told the local AI. "If you don't mind, I'd like to confirm a couple of those items for myself."

"Of course," Electron said. "You're the boss."

Rade lifted his left leg, then his right, walking in place. There wasn't much else he could do in the tight confines with those other mechs packed in beside him.

"Still worried about actuator sensitivity?" Electron asked.

"You caught me," Rade said.

"It should be within expected operational parameters," Electron replied.

Rade tried a few more tentative stomps with each foot.

"Seems fine," Rade agreed.

When Tahoe had retrieved the unit after the last mission, the left leg had proved far more sensitive than the right. Tahoe had to take hobbling steps inside the cockpit just to walk normally. After returning to the ship, a Centurion running a tech program had looked at all the mechs, making fixes as necessary. The repair charts showed that everything was in working order, and the test drives had gone well. Still, Rade always liked to double-check.

Judging from the similar, tentative movements of the mechs around him, he wasn't the only one. His team members were smart people.

He examined the stats on the cobra weapon systems, one per arm. The lasers were fully operational. The grenade launchers underneath each laser were loaded with frags, flashbangs, electromagnetics, and smokes. He confirmed that the Trench Coat anti-missile countermeasures were fully stocked. He extended and retracted the anti-laser ballistic shield in his left arm.

When he was satisfied, Rade said: "Everyone ready?"

He was answered by a chorus of ayes.

three

R ade gave the order to drop. The hangar bays opened and the Hoplites stepped out one by one.

There was no atmosphere on the planet, so the team hadn't packed the aeroshell heat shields.

Below, the surface was a dark mass. The light from the suns didn't penetrate to this side. But because of the local-beam LIDAR his mech emitted, he was able to discern an outline of the distant topography, which overlaid his vision.

As he neared the surface, Rade fired the aerospike thrusters in his feet. He didn't bother to deploy the air brakes of course, which would be useless without an atmosphere.

He landed on a flat plain of methane and nitrogen snow between two towering penitentes, whose outlines were visible only because of the LIDAR. The black blobs composing the blade-like spires blotted out the stars to the north and south.

The other five mechs landed nearby, their positions showing up on the overhead map. Three kilometers to the east the six booster rockets had landed; those would be used to launch the mechs into orbit.

The Dragonfly containing the robots, HS3 scouts, and the rest of the crew landed two kilometers to the west.

"Headlamps, on," Rade said. "Rendezvous with me, Argonauts."

There was no point leaving the headlamps turned off. If any enemy units were tracking the party out there, the mechs would be readily visible, thanks to the thermal radiation the battle suits readily emitted in the void: these particular Hoplite models didn't employ thermal-smearing camouflage, which would have helped offset the heat signatures.

Bright lights appeared in the darkness as the Hoplites and ground troops activated their headlamps. The shuttle proved brightest of all, with the red and green lights on each of its four wings.

Rade turned on his own headlamp and swung the illumination in a full circle; it felt like he stood atop a lighthouse in a frozen sea. The white snow surrounded him on all sides; small particles floated in the cone of light, oddly reminding him of dust.

"Looks a bit dreary, doesn't it?" Rade said.

"It does, boss," Electron replied.

"We've been in worse," Tahoe said.

"But not by much," Rade told his friend.

"It does rank near the bottom of the drear scale," Tahoe said.

"El, what are those particles I'm seeing floating in the light beams? Is that dust of some kind?"

"Those are particles of snow thrown up by your original impact that haven't settled yet," Electron replied. "There is less gravity on this planet. Particulates can take quite some time to descend."

"And I suspect this particular mix of methane and nitrogen behaves differently than the snow we're used to," Tahoe said.

Rade waited for the rest of the team to gather. The Hoplites arrived first, followed by the rifle-toting ground troops and combat robots. Of them, only Surus carried the specially-designed electrolaser that would allow her to stun their prey. Said electrolaser looked indistinguishable from an ordinary rifle, and was equipped with sound dampening tech specifically developed by Surus to reduce the sonic profile the weapon produced to a muted crackling.

"Harlequin, load up in Bender's passenger seat. Surus, you're with Shaw. Fret, take TJ's seat. Manic, with me. Units A and B, load up with TJ and Lui respectively. Other units, remain on foot. C and D, continue to port the Phant trap."

Rade knelt so that Manic could more easily load into the passenger seat, located in the upper back region above the jumpjets of Rade's Hoplite; once Manic had strapped in, Rade stood the Hoplite to full height. When the other ex-MOTHs, Artificials and combat robots had boarded the passenger seats of their designated mechs, Rade spoke again.

"I'm highlighting the cave entrance on the overhead map as Waypoint One," Rade said.

A flashing green dot appeared on the map two kilometers away to the west, at the base of a rather large penitente.

"Bender, I want the HS3 scouts on point fifty meters ahead," Rade said. "The rest of you, traveling overwatch."

Tahoe arranged the two fire teams, and the first three mechs proceeded forward in a zigzag formation, followed by the next three thirty meters behind.

The gravity was about one twelfth that of Earth, and the heavy mechs easily advanced along the surface, taking long, bounding steps. They left deep footprints in the methane and nitrogen snow. The two Centurions porting the glass container, or "Phant trap" as everyone called it, kept up, though they had to bound at twice the speed to compensate for their far shorter legs.

The airborne HS3s arrived at the cave opening in about twenty minutes.

The three Hoplites of the lead fire team reached them shortly thereafter.

Rade called a halt to his fire team, and Shaw and Manic assumed defensive positions in the snow beside him. The porters took cover behind them.

Rade switched to the POV of one of the HS3s. Its headlight illuminated a cave entrance that was easily tall enough to fit a Hoplite, and wide enough to fit two Hoplites abreast at the same time. The tunnel inside was circular, the walls smooth, as if carved by a giant drill or laser of some kind. Definitely not natural.

"Okay, send in the HS3s," Rade said.

The three HS3 scouts swerved inside. The cave retained its same dimensions as the drones advanced.

According to Surus, it was very difficult for a Phant to assume control of aerial drones like HS3s because of their flying nature. The aliens had to touch the AI cores, usually seeping in from the ground into the feet assemblies and making their way up to the torso to where the core resided. For a robot that didn't touch the ground, like an HS3, a Phant essentially had to drip down from the ceiling onto the passing device, which was a difficult action to time. So Rade wasn't overly worried about the Phant possessing any of the HS3s.

The signal began to distort and pixelate.

"The interference is fairly bad in there," Bender

said. "We might have to send in some of the Centurions to boost the range."

"Units A and B," Rade said. "Get down from the passenger seats and enter that cave. Spread out as necessary to boost the signal."

On the overhead map, he watched the two robots join the three HS3s. The units halted in turn as the need to place repeaters arose, until only a lone HS3 was continuing on point. So far, the cave hadn't yet branched in any direction, and it continued in a straight line that trended ever downward.

Finally Bender said: "That's as far as it can go before losing signal. What do you want to do?"

Rade considered sending the HS3 forward to scout on its own, with instructions to return if it spotted any signs of Phant activity, but thought it best to simply stay within signal range.

"TJ, Lui, Bender, go inside and string out," Rade said. "Act as repeaters. Boost the range. Everyone else, assume a defensive position at the cave entrance."

Rade and the other members of fire team two bounded toward the entrance as TJ, Lui and Bender took their mechs inside. Once there, Rade assumed a defensive stance at the opening, keeping his cobra pointed toward the ice plain behind him, while Shaw did the same. Tahoe meanwhile aimed his cobra into the tunnel. The jumpsuited individuals in the passenger seats followed the aim of their respective rides. Rade kept his video feed from the scout on point active, though he had reduced it to a quarter of his vision and repositioned it in the upper right of his HUD.

"Surus, do you sense our prey?" Rade said.

"No," Surus said. "If the Phant was here, it's long gone."

The robot line moved forward when TJ, Lui and

Bender arrived. Bender was the first to halt, allowing Lui and TJ to continue forward. Before those two mechs had to separate to further boost the signal, the lead HS3 arrived at a chamber.

Rade watched from the scout's POV as the tunnel gave way to a small, circular ovoid carved into the ice. The chamber was empty, save for a wide disk situated in the middle of the floor. The metal surface was engraved with Fibonacci spirals.

"I was afraid of this," Surus said, obviously viewing the same feed.

"What is it?" Rade asked. Though he had a very good idea already. That disk looked similar to something he had seen once before, a long time ago.

"An Acceptor," Surus said. "The teleportation device used by Phants."

"How do these work again?" Lui said. "They're restricted to teleportation to the same system right?"

"No," Surus said. "The range is galaxy-wide. The technology is similar in concept to the Gate and Slipstream pairs you humans use to transport between systems, except that Acceptors form micro-Slipstreams in realtime between the source and destination disks."

"How did it get here?" Fret said.

"Our prey placed it here, of course," Surus said.

"Why here?" Rade said. "Why would the Phant wait all this time to deploy it?"

"The physics of the involved micro-Slipstreams are very specific," Surus said. "And follow narrow rules. A big one: when drawing a straight line on the galactic map from the source system to the destination system, there can be no black holes within a radius of two thousand lightyears of the target system. If the target system happened to be on the far side of the galaxy, directly opposite human space, it could be occluded by

29

the massive black hole at the center of our galaxy. By coming to this border system, our prey was able to circumvent that black hole, and find a clear path from here to the destination system."

"Can you tell us where it leads?" Rade asked.

"Not with any certainty, no," Surus said. "My best guess: a world destroyed by the Phants."

"What about one of the motherships?" Tahoe said.

"It's not possible," Surus said. "The Phant would not know the link codes to any other motherships. While the hives trust one another to some extent, their trust does not extend that far. It would be far too easy for one hive to invade another, otherwise. And since the mothership our prey came from was destroyed, I conclude that the destination cannot be a vessel."

"So a conquered world..." Rade said.

"Yes," Surus continued. "The Phant would know the codes to target Acceptors placed on the worlds its hive had conquered in the past."

"What exactly could we expect on a conquered world?" Lui said. "A bunch of Phants?"

"Very likely it will be completely devoid of Phant life," Surus said. "I would expect some remnants of the local population, however. Traditionally, before the Phants destroy a world, they usually spare a small portion of the indigenous inhabitants, usually around one percent, to be used as breeding matter for future geronium production on the destroyed world, for entertainment, or to supplement the ranks of those who fight for and defend the hive. But once the Phants move on, that world is typically forgotten. Individual Phants may occasionally teleport back to check on the local population, but there is no real need."

"So when our prey reaches this destroyed world,"

Lui said. "Any Acceptors he finds won't lead to other motherships?"

"That's correct," Surus said. "Each hive is given control over one conquered world. If our prey does find an Acceptor, it will only point to another destroyed world."

"So why don't we just destroy the Acceptor on this side, and trap the Phant on the other side?"

"Normally I would agree," Surus said. "In fact, while helping the Sino-Koreans trap the surviving Phants from Tau Ceti, I encountered many Acceptors, and destroyed them. However, my fear is that I didn't get them all. Our prey may have leaped to the conquered world to retrieve some artifact, with no intention of ever returning to this Acceptor, but to another in Tau Ceti that I missed. Using the same target Acceptor waiting on the other side of this one."

"Why go through all that trouble?" Rade said. "Why not use the Tau Ceti Acceptor to travel to the conquered world and retrieve the artifact directly?"

"I don't know," Surus said. "It could be that my hunter killer units forced the Phant to flee before then. Either way, I won't take the chance. We must travel through, capture, and interrogate our prey to discover the truth. Then we will return, and destroy this Acceptor. Let us enter, so I may determine whether the link remains intact. Because if not, this entire discussion is moot."

Rade instructed two robots to remain behind to protect the cave entrance.

"You'll stay here for the duration of the mission," Rade told the Centurions. "Protect this tunnel until we return. I want you to rig charges near the opening, and collapse the tunnel if you're attacked with overwhelming force. It'll take us some time to dig out when we return, but it's better than finding ourselves trapped on the opposite side of the galaxy without an Acceptor to return to at all."

"If you do use charges, make sure that they are restricted to the opening," Surus told the robot. "If debris of any kind falls onto the Acceptor, it will be blocked, and we cannot use it to return."

"Understood," Unit F said.

The group proceeded into the tunnel.

The mechs and combat robots gathered near the opening to the ovoid chamber, standing in single file to allow Shaw's Hoplite, and her passenger Surus, to walk past and proceed inside.

Shaw halted Nemesis next to the disk. It was big enough for only a single Hoplite to stand on.

"The link is intact," Surus announced a moment later. "Come inside one at a time and step onto the teleporter. I will activate it by modulating the micro-Slipstream. I must go last, of course, since none of you have the ability to operate the device."

"Maybe you should go first," Rade said. "And come back once you confirm it's safe on the other side."

"All right," Surus said. "Shaw, if you don't mind?"

For a moment Rade was about to tell Shaw to stop in her tracks; he had actually intended that Surus dismount and go alone. But he clamped his mouth shut. Shaw would never let him live it down if he stopped her now in front of all his men. He saw the wisdom in providing a Hoplite as escort, of course, but he just wished it didn't have to be *Shaw's* Hoplite.

Shaw seemed to sense his concern, because she moved the mech quickly, as if worried Rade would change his mind. In a moment she was on the disk.

Rade raised his hand then, indeed having had a

change of heart and wanting to transfer Surus to another Hoplite, but then Nemesis vanished.

Rade stared at the empty disk. Long moments passed. He shifted from foot to foot, willing her to return.

Ten seconds passed.

Twenty.

Nothing appeared on the disk. Rade stared at it nervously.

What the hell is taking so long?

Thirty seconds.

Forty.

"Where the hell is she?" Fret said. Even the others were getting worried.

Fifty seconds.

Sixty.

"This isn't good," Bender said.

"Damn it," Rade said. He flexed his fingers into a fist, but somehow resisted the urge to punch the ice wall beside him.

Another tense minute passed, and finally Nemesis reappeared. Surus was strapped into the passenger seat, and the status indicator showed that Shaw was in the cockpit. Her vitals were completely green, and the mech appeared unharmed.

"You were supposed to come straight back," Rade said.

"We decided to clear the area while we were there," Shaw said.

Rade growled softly to himself.

Shaw walked Nemesis off the Acceptor.

"So is our prey there, or not?" Rade asked.

"I believe so," Surus said. "Shaw and I emerged from a cave mouth near the top of a mountain and observed a vast plain before us. I detected a very faint

Phant presence on the far side of that plain."

"All right," Rade said. "Guess we're good to proceed, then. Bender, send the HS3s forward please."

The three HS3 scouts flew above the disk and disappeared.

"Bender, go!" Rade said.

Bender moved Juggernaut onto the disk. As soon as the mech stood still, it too vanished.

"TJ, go!" Rade said.

And so the party members walked one at a time onto the Acceptor and disappeared in turn.

When all the mechs save Electron and Nemesis had gone through, Rade instructed Units C and D to carry the glass tank onto the device.

When they were gone, he glanced at Nemesis.

"After you," Shaw said.

Rade took his place on the disk.

four

A moment later the ice walls winked out around Rade, replaced by black stone. A rocky passage lay before him, ascending to a sunlit opening. His headlamps illuminated the robot units ahead of him in the passageway: the two Centurions carrying the glass Phant trap between them and scaling the slope toward the cave mouth. Beyond the pair he caught a glimpse of another mech before it moved outside.

Underneath him resided another flat metal disk, covered in Fibonacci spirals, a twin to the one he had just left behind.

Rade stepped off the Acceptor. He noticed the heavier gravity immediately.

"What are the Gs, El?" Rade asked his AI.

"A little more than Earth gravity," Electron answered. "At one point oh three."

On the disk, Nemesis materialized.

Rade glanced at the overhead map. The HS3s had assumed positions outside the opening, and mapped out what appeared to be a rocky outcrop overlooking a plain.

Rade climbed the passage, following the robots to the opening. He stepped through. He indeed stood at a cave mouth, though it was situated upon a mountain. Below, a vast black plain spread out before them. The sky was gray, cloudless. Above resided a red and blue gas giant similar to Saturn, though it had four large ring systems. The giant was about the size of a human head in the sky, while the rings spread out to three times the radial length.

The other Hoplites and robots resided on a ledge next to the cave. Rade stepped aside to make room for Nemesis.

He continued to gaze at the sky and spotted a blindingly bright blue dot to the left of the gas giant, obviously the system's sun, or suns. When he looked directly at it, his photochromatic filters muted the brightness automatically. He zoomed in, curious if he could discern more than one star, but even at the stabilized 183x zoom, it still appeared as a lone sun.

He reset his zoom.

"My guess is this is a moon of some kind," Lui said.

"I'm assuming there is atmosphere?" Rade said. He noticed that the rotors on the HS3s were spinning.

"Yes," Lui replied. "The air is mildly toxic, but we could breath it for a couple of hours if we had to. The oxygen content is thirty percent: similar to Earth during the age of the dinosaurs. We can expect bigger lifeforms, should we encounter any. And also bigger explosions."

"Hell ya," Bender said. "The bugs are going to fry."

"Too bad we have no incendiary throwers," Fret said.

"I'd say this is the closest to an Earth analog we've ever seen," Lui said. "I can only guess how far away this system is from our own solar system. It's probably at least on the far side of the galaxy, like Surus suggested. Or it could be in another galaxy entirely."

"I assure you, we are in the same galaxy," Surus said. "Even the Phants don't have the technology to traverse galaxies. Not like the Elder."

"You talk as if the Elder were still alive," Tahoe said.

"Perhaps they are," Surus said. "But back to the matter at hand: look there."

Rade turned toward Surus, who was standing in Shaw's passenger seat and pointing behind them.

Rade pivoted around, and saw black peaks in the distance beyond the summit of the current mountain, thrusting past it to poke into the lower atmosphere.

"Do you see that east-west trending ridge in the distance?" Surus said.

"That's not a ridge," TJ said. "That's a bunch of Mount Everests clustered side by side."

"I was right," Surus continued. "This is a conquered world. Those are the remnants of geronium feed piles; the raw elements were digested by Phants and deposited on the surface to form those mountains, likely an eon ago. The crust of this planet has been completely transmogrified by the Great Formers: those creatures known as slugs and crabs that you once fought. And the Phants have sapped it all."

"You mean they're here?" Bender asked.

"No, the moon is spent," Surus said. "The crust cannot be converted further. The hive that did this would have departed an age ago. There is a chance we may find a colony of the former inhabitants somewhere ahead. Likely bioengineered to withstand the atmospheric changes produced by the Formers: the 'toxic elements' that Lui mentioned. If we do find a colony of survivors, they will have no knowledge of their true history, and likely will have forgotten their Phant conquerors. Typically, after the cleansing, cultural archives are lost, and the survivors devolve into a caveman level society, early Tech Class I on the developmental scale. Sometimes preservation depots are left behind by the Phants, and the survivors can find these and rediscover some of their lost technology, but such depots are the exception rather than the norm, created at the whim of the conquering hive. When the Phants leave, usually the former inhabitants rarely bounce back to anything beyond a preindustrial phase, or late Tech Class I, even with the presence of preservation depots."

"I can see why," Tahoe said. "With the crust destroyed, there is no way to grow crops. No natural resources. No oil or gas for industrialization. No iron for building. Only the hardiest races could survive this. It's like being trapped in the dark ages without any food sources."

"You're mostly right," Surus said. "Though there are usually sparse natural resources scattered about. And small plots of land capable of supporting crops. But even so, such resources are an island amid a wasteland sea, definitely not enough to support more than a few thousand inhabitants. It is why races rarely survive when a hive departs, unless they are bioengineered to endure, perhaps as part of some deal struck by the conquered with the hive in exchange for not resisting the initial invasion."

"Mmm," Rade said. "I seem to recall the Phants making a similar offer to humanity."

"It was a good thing you refused," Surus said.

"Yeah," Rade said. He returned his gaze to the black plains before him. "So before we teleported here, you told me you had a faint reading on our prey?"

"Yes," Surus said. "It's coming from the north. There is a hillock there. I'm highlighting it on our shared displays."

Rade stared at the horizon. A green triangle appeared above it. There, a tiny bump protruded from the otherwise flat plains in the distance. He zoomed in and realized the hump was indeed a hillock, black and pocked with holes. "Looks like a big termite mound."

"Or a piece of green cheese gone bad," Bender said.

"So that's what you keep in your pants," Manic said.

"Har," Bender replied.

"They never cease bantering," Surus commented.

"I know," Shaw said. "Sometimes I feel like a teacher herding her school kids on a field trip. But when the fighting starts, I promise you, these are the men you want at your side. And the interesting thing: you can also use their classy banter as a gauge for how bad the fighting is."

"How so?"

"Well, when things get bad, let's just say you're going to hear a lot of inappropriate comments."

"More inappropriate than what I've heard already?" Surus asked.

"Ma'am," Bender said. "Trust me. You haven't heard anything inappropriate yet."

"Lui, what exactly are we looking at?" Rade said, trying to steer the conversation back to the hillock.

"If I had to guess, I would say it was an alien nest of some kind," Lui said. "Maybe created by the former inhabitants of this colony, as Surus was suggesting earlier."

"I believe that is exactly what it is," Surus said.

"Inside, we'll likely find a pre-industrial civilization harboring our prey."

"Will this civilization be dangerous in any way?" Tahoe asked.

"It's hard to say at the moment," Surus replied. "But I think it would be safe to err on the side of caution."

"Our prey knows you're here, right?" Rade said.

"He can sense my presence equally, yes," Surus replied.

Rade glanced directly down at the mountain. A path wound its way to the plain below. "All right. Well. We can talk about this all day, or we can start making our way toward that hillock. I elect we do the latter. Units C and D, stay behind and guard the entrance to the Acceptor. Notify us if you spot any incoming tangos."

"Are we authorized to engage these tangos?" Unit C asked.

"You are," Rade said. "Protect the cave at all costs. Units A and B, take over the portage of the Phant trap. Tahoe, bring us down."

Tahoe organized the group into two fire teams, and the Hoplites descended the winding path in traveling overwatch. One HS3 led the way, the other two dispersed down the mountainside and made directly for the plain below, where they would wait for the others. The two robot porters brought up the rear, carrying the Phant trap. Rade could have had a single Hoplite port that glass container, but he wanted to keep every last one of his six mechs combat ready.

The winding route proved treacherous, and very often the way became so narrow that the Hoplites were forced to hug the rock wall and proceed crabwise, one foot at a time, toes pointed outward.

They had to use their jumpjets to cross sections of the path that had fallen away entirely.

"Why would the Phants who conquered this world place their Acceptor in such an inaccessible place?" TJ said when the squad finally reached the ground.

"My guess is they wanted to keep it away from the inhabitants," Fret said.

"That would make sense," Tahoe said. "Except that only Phants can activate the teleporters. So Surus, why?"

"It could be they simply wanted a place that was near to the geronium feed piles," Surus said. "That way they could teleport here from the mothership, feed, and then return when they were glutted."

"Sound like lazy bastards to me," Manic said.

"Your kind of people, huh Manic?" Bender said.

Rade surveyed the plain. "All right. Bender, activate the holographic emitters on the HS3s and send them out to survey the north, east and west. I want them to continually increase their altitude at the same time, until they reach a height of ten K. I'm expecting to get some good reception, considering that this is a preindustrial race."

He pulled up the signal pollution graph on his HUD. Sure enough, it was empty save for the spectrum produced by his team.

A moment later the HS3s disappeared. They hadn't even begun to move, yet. He glanced at his overhead map. The dots showed that the HS3s were still there, heading in the indicated directions.

The vanishing act could be explained by the fact that all three HS3s were fitted with holographic emitters, using tech designed by Surus to decrease the weight, allowing the drones to still fly despite the load. It was apparently tricky to hide the motion of the four rotors each drone used, but Surus had found a way. It was tech that not even the military had.

When Rade asked why she hadn't yet patented it, Surus replied: "You think I'm going to give humanity my best kept secrets?"

"If she doesn't patent it, then I will," Bender said.

"You'll do no such thing," Rade told him. "This is for us, and us alone. For the Argonauts."

The illusion would only work against primitive races of course, as modern tech would easily see through the ruse, via LIDAR and thermal vision for example. And if the members of the current preindustrial species were able to see on the thermal band, then it wouldn't work at all.

Rade considered that at the height the drones would be flying at, the HS3s wouldn't have been visible to ground observers anyway, not unless these aliens had something like a primitive telescope.

"What if our prey has installed advanced sensory tech around the nest?" Lui said. "Sensors beyond the current Tech Class of the aliens?"

"I guess we'll find out soon enough," Surus said. "Though I'm hoping our prey hasn't had time. He would have arrived somewhere around four to six weeks ago."

"And you said he already knows we're here?" Lui said.

"That's right," Surus said. "We must keep a watchful eye for any incoming search parties."

The HS3s separated, with one moving north to scout the plain, and the other two east and west to follow the mountain range. All three shot upwards, too, rapidly increasing their altitude.

Rade was able to receive clear reception from the drones out to ten kilometers in the north, east and west directions. Each of those scouts also hovered at a height of ten kilometers, giving him a clear picture of the plains and mountains. There were no tangos out there. Not a one. The black plains continued to the north to infinity, with only that lone hillock interrupting the otherwise flat terrain. Behind the squad, the east-west trending mountain range continued to the horizon on either side, and to the south, the mountains grew higher and higher until they did that thing of biting into the sky and piercing the lower atmosphere.

"Bender, have the HS3s maintain their current separation from the squad as we advance," Rade said. "Units A and B, watch our six. Tahoe, take us forward."

Once more Tahoe formed two fire teams of three mechs each and had the Hoplites advance in traveling overwatch. The HS3s maintained their ten-kilometer gap to the north, east and west.

Wish we could have brought the Raptor along, Rade thought. Though he supposed that the HS3s were proving to be a great eye-in-the-sky alternative.

The mechs advanced at a moderate pace, though it seemed slow compared to the dwarf planet with its lower gravity. The best description of the ground below was of a packed, gritty mixture of soot and sand, as if thousands and thousands of pounds of shale had been pulverized to form this black sand-like grit. The grit swallowed the feet of the mechs, but underneath that loose layer the particles seemed compacted, and hard. Meanwhile, the two robot porters sunk into the black sand up to their calves with each step.

The loose particles quickly refilled the footprints the Hoplites left in their wake, so that the depressions the squad made were much smaller than the size of their steel extremities. There were no such depressions in front of the Argonauts to follow, which told Rade dust storms occasionally swept the landscape clear. Unless their quarry had brought some air-capable vehicle through the Acceptor, such as a small air stallion, and used it to cross these plains.

The lower legs of the mechs soon became covered in the black dust they kicked up, and it interfered with the camouflage ability—though since the rest of the mechs were colored black by the camouflage skin to match the surface anyway, it didn't really matter.

In about an hour, the lead HS3 had flown close enough to the hillock to determine its size: it was about a kilometer high, and roughly circular in shape, with a radius of twenty kilometers. Rade sent the HS3 down to explore the pock marks he had seen from afar, and invariably they proved to be small tunnels that ended in a blockage only a few meters inside.

"So, Surus?" Rade said. "What do you think?"

"Our prey is definitely somewhere inside there," Surus said. "I'm getting the strongest sense of him than ever before."

Closer to the bottom of the hillock, the HS3 discerned two large forms residing near the opening of one of the pockmarks. Rade instructed the HS3 to keep its distance from those forms for the moment.

Rade accessed the HS3's viewpoint and zoomed in on the entities.

The creatures looked vaguely similar to beetles with those bodies segmented into heads, thoraxes and abdomens. The abdomens were bulbous, and covered in a thick, rainbow-hued carapace. Each of them had six jointed legs: two pairs emerged from the abdomen, with the final set attached to the thorax. The limbs were covered in large hairs, as well as several talon-like, downward-curving spurs. The front right forelegs were wrapped with what looked like red fabrics near the top, with two dangling balls of silver hanging from them. That was the only "clothing" the creatures wore.

On the dark, rainbow-hued head, which was elongated like an alligator's, several small dots arranged in a diamond shape could have been eyes. Two long antennae protruded from the head above those eyes. A pair of thick mandibles composed the maw region; beyond, what looked like part of an esophagus could be seen—it was covered in small white hooks or teeth. Two forward-faced prehensile limbs emerged from the thorax underneath the head, reaching past the mandibles. The multiple pincers at the tips looked capable of operating tools.

On the dorsal area of the thorax, several fist-sized tubules pointed skyward. From the way the tips expanded and contracted, Rade guessed those were used for respiration.

"Well well well," Bender said. "We gots ourselves some classic bugs."

The opening the pair guarded appeared darker than the surrounding pockmarks, and Rade suspected it wasn't plugged like the rest. The speakers on the HS3s picked up a very soft chittering, which coincided with one or another of the alien sentries rubbing their mandibles together.

"What do you think about sending in the HS3 for a closer look, Surus?" Rade asked.

"I wouldn't recommend it," Surus said.

"I agree," Tahoe said. "Look at how small those eyes are, if they're even eyes. My guess is they have very poor eyesight. Especially if they dwell in caves, which is what it appears they do."

"Well that's better for us, then, isn't it?" Fret asked.

"No," Tahoe said. "Because if those things lack proper vision, they'll compensate with hearing. Look at the size of those antennae. I have no doubt they use them to detect sound waves, in addition to directly feeling out their surroundings."

"Okay, but how is that going to help them 'see' our scouts?" Manic said. "Especially when our HS3s are completely silent when operating in stealth mode."

"Do you see how the creatures occasionally rub their mandibles together, making that grating sound picked up by the HS3s?" Tahoe said. "It has to be a form of echolocation. If that's the case, if we get close, they'll 'see' through our holographic emitters immediately."

"Maybe they're just chatting to pass the time," Fret said.

"Doubt it," Tahoe said.

"I agree with Tahoe," Surus said. "Before we dispatch the HS3s, I will need to modify the emitters to transmit canceling sound waves to mimic the surrounding environment. The same principles apply, except instead of only light, the units will produce sound as well. I prepared for this contingency by installing tiny speakers in all of the units. So we're halfway there already. I just need to program them."

"Fine," Rade said. "But how long will that take?"

"Not more than ten hours in total. Five, if TJ and Harlequin assist me. Most of that time will be spent experimenting on a single unit. Once the changes are complete, it's a simple matter of uploading a patch to the remaining units, and our emitters will become both light and sound masking."

"Well," Rade said. "Looks like we have five hours

to burn. Recall the HS3s, Bender. Argonauts, open up your storage compartments and crack out the secondary emitters, as we'll want to update those, too. TJ, Harlequin, assist Surus. Then it's time for some Phant hunting."

five

R ade resided somewhat apart from the others while he waited. He had Electron open up the hatch, and he sat on the edge of his cockpit in his jumpsuit, his feet dangling down into midair.

He stared at the gray sky, watching it slowly darken as the bright point of the sun crossed beneath the horizon. He occasionally glanced at the overhead map to confirm that the red dots representing the creatures remained at the hillock. About an hour ago, two more of the beetle-like aliens had emerged to relieve the original sentries. They carried the same red bands wrapped around their upper right forelegs. Rade deduced that the silver balls hanging from those bands were actually bells, judging from the ringing sound the ornaments produced during the shift change.

The Argonauts were talking about the entities at that very moment. Rade listened idly.

"The Arthropoda phylum obviously dominated this world," Lui said.

"Don't be assigning Earth classification systems to these bugs," Bender said. "Just because they breathe air, don't make them related to us in any way."

"He's right," Surus said. She had one of the HS3s resting on the knees of her jumpsuit, with a small wire running from the drone to the helmet interface of her suit. "Their DNA will be completely different. While some of their phenotypes will be similar in many respects to the external characteristics of many lifeforms on Earth, they will require their own taxonomic classification system. In the past, what my species has done is assign a separate overarching Kingdom for each planet, and then create individual phyla from there."

"They look so... well, insect-like," Fret said. "I was expecting something a bit more alien."

"They're alien enough for me," Shaw said. "Like big cockroaches with alligator heads."

"At least they don't look human," TJ said. "I always love it when I'm reading a science fiction novel or watching a film, and then the aliens show up, looking like humans with fluffy ears or a couple of bumps on their heads, and of course they speak English right off the bat. It's silly beyond comparison."

"I think those books are called fantasy," Manic said. "Not science fiction."

"They should be," TJ agreed. "Slash begin rant: but have a look at the virtual shelves sometime. Eighty percent of the books stocked as science fiction are *not*. They have aliens coming to Earth, aliens speaking English, aliens wanting to eat humans as food. If anyone else can't see how ridiculous any of that is, well, I won't comment further. Actually I will. First of all, why would an alien race capable of interstellar travel even *need* to travel to Earth for food? Surely they would have solved resourcing problems long ago. They could grow compatible cattle in their own backyard at a far cheaper energy cost, but noooo, they're going to expend billions of kilojoules of precious energy to travel to Earth so they can eat a few humans. Slash end rant."

"The Phants essentially attempted the same thing in our space," Tahoe said. "Except they wanted to convert us into food, rather than eat us directly. Or convert the crusts of our worlds, anyway."

"Yeah, but that's different," TJ said. "They don't look human, for one. And it took them some time to learn our languages. And like you said, they don't eat us directly."

"Well you know," Lui said. "While I agree with you that aliens should actually *look* alien, and not speak Earthling, at least not right away, I actually have nothing wrong with an alien eating a human in a sci-fi themed work. To me, it seems feasible. I'm not saying the alien would actually survive the digestion process, and if it did, that it would actually absorb any compatible nutrients from the human. But I do say it's possible, and definitely not in the realm of fantasy."

"Yeah, I guess I can see your point," TJ said. "I'd be okay with an alien dying after it eats a man. Or having a bad case of indigestion. Then I could still call that sci-fi."

"Well wait, getting back to the Phants," Tahoe said. "Don't you think it's a bit fantastical how they can possess our robots and Artificials?"

"No of course not," TJ said. "Just because we don't understand the science behind something, doesn't make it magic. That's like saying Slipstreams belong in fantasy novels. They're purely sci-fi."

"All right," Tahoe told him. "If you say so."

"I do," TJ replied.

"Then what about psi powers?" Lui said. "That's straight from fantasy. And yet we face an enemy who may use such abilities against us."

"Psi powers aren't fantasy!" TJ said. "Get with the

program. Again, just because you don't understand something, doesn't make it goddamn magic."

"Wait, why does it matter whether its sci-fi or fantasy at all?" Shaw said. "If the story is engaging, gets to you emotionally, and you really feel for the characters, then what difference does it make?"

"All the difference," TJ said. "If you're finding yourself distracted by things that are just too implausible, you lose that whole suspension of disbelief, and it can be hard to keep watching or reading. When you're constantly laughing at the absurdity of it all, then there's something wrong."

"Hey TJ, aren't you supposed to be helping Surus and Harlequin?" Fret said.

"I am," TJ replied. "Taking a short break, that's all. That all right with you?"

"No it's not," Fret said. "Don't make me climb down from here."

"Pfft," TJ said. "Like anyone is scared of your skinny ass."

"You should be," Fret said. "Remember what I did to Skullcracker that one time..."

"What time?"

"You don't remember?" Fret said. "When you came into his bunker and you saw him sucking his thumb?"

"All right," TJ said. "That's it. I'm going to call Skullcracker when we get back, and tell him you've been dissing him."

"No wait, I remember," Tahoe said. "He wasn't actually sucking his thumb. He was trying to hold his tooth in."

Fret started laughing. "Yeah man, see? Someone remembers. I clocked that boy out cold."

"Yeah, but he clocked you back the next day, bro,"

Tahoe said. "I seem to recall having to splash water on your face to wake you up."

"Sounds like I really missed out on life at your base," Shaw said.

"Well, life can get prettttty slow when you're between deployments," Lui said. "Sometimes there were long stretches with nothing to do but beat each other up."

"I don't know how you manage not to smear the bulkheads with each other's blood during our long space voyages," Shaw said.

"We're getting old," Lui explained.

"Speak for yourself," Bender said. "I been smearing the bulkheads with Manic's blood, don't you worry."

"You wish," Manic said. "That's your blood, not mine. Your period blood."

"*What?*" Bender said. "I don't got period blood, bitch. The only period blood on me is from your pussy."

"So that's what you call Manic's ass now, is it?" Shaw said.

"Yup, I take him every day," Bender said. "And I close my eyes and pretend it's Surus."

"All right, that's enough," Rade said. He drew the line at insulting the client.

Surus worked away quietly, pretending she hadn't heard.

"Sometimes I miss the Teams," Fret said. "What we have here, it's a nice microcosm of what we had back then. But I do find myself yearning for the old days. Not the wars, mind you. While I don't regret fighting, I also wouldn't do it again. Fight those damn, damn wars. But the camaraderie, the whole team atmosphere, the brotherhood, that's what I miss."

"Like you said, we have that here," Tahoe said. "And it's not a microcosm. It's the real deal."

"Well sure," Fret replied. "But what I mean is, we don't have everyone we had then."

There was a moment of silence among them.

"We lost a lot of good people," Tahoe said. "To those wars."

"We didn't lose everyone," Lui said. "Others simply retired."

"But that still counts as a loss, doesn't it?" Fret said. "They're not here with us anymore."

"You never know," Lui said. "When they see how much fun we're having, some of our old friends might be coming back sooner than you think."

"So, the mood is getting a bit dark, me thinks," Fret said.

"Well that suits you, doesn't it?" Manic said. "Mr. Doom and Gloom."

"Don't call me that," Fret told him. "Okay, fine, maybe I'm negative sometimes. But anyway, as I was saying, to lighten the mood... so, Shaw, you think these aliens look like big cockroaches with alligator heads, huh?"

"That's right," Shaw replied.

"There's got to be a cock joke in there somewhere," Manic said.

"I'm sure there is," Fret said. "But I was thinking about what we could call these bugs. How about gatorbeetles?"

"Gatorbeetles?" Bender said. "That's a ridiculous name. I think I should be the one to name them."

"All right, what would you call them?" Fret asked.

Bender was quiet a moment. "Bulbous-ass bugs. 'Cause their asses are bulbous, see?"

"And he says my names are ridiculous," Fret said.

"Bender, look. I'll cut you some slack because you take apart and rebuild robots, and you hack into governmental databases for fun, but seriously bro, bulbous-ass bugs? You're a moron. I'm going to continue calling them gatorbeetles."

"Fine, and I'm going to keep calling them bulbous-ass bugs," Bender insisted. "Or bulbies for short."

"You go right ahead," Fret said.

Rade muted the comm, shaking his head. He wasn't in the mood for their chatter.

After a few minutes, he sensed motion to his right. It was Shaw, in her jumpsuit. The mechs were arranged in a fairly tight circle, allowing her to leap from Hoplite to Hoplite without touching the black dunes. When she reached Electron, she clambered down to his cockpit and took a seat beside him on the open hatch, dangling her leg assemblies over the edge.

By then, night had completely descended on the moon. Foreign constellations filled the sky.

Shaw tapped in. He accepted.

"Think we'll get him?" Shaw asked.

"Our prey? Of course."

She wrapped a gloved hand around his. "Wish we didn't have to wear these."

"I know," Rade said, yearning for the electric touch of her skin against his own, rather than simply the pressure of her glove.

"The air is breathable..." Shaw said.

"You'd risk contracting a potential contagion?" Rade said.

"If it meant holding you for real one last time, yes," Shaw said.

Rade frowned. "You talk like you don't think we'll survive."

"Sorry," Shaw said. "I get this way before missions

sometime. All dour, like Fret. Convinced I'm going to die."

Rade chuckled softly.

"What's so funny about that?" Shaw said.

"Nothing," Rade said. "Just that, I'm the same way sometimes before a mission." He paused, then amended: "Most of the time."

"Great minds think alike," Shaw said.

"I'm not sure that's a sign of greatness."

"It's a sign of humanity," Shaw said. "A sign that we understand our human frailty, and our mortality. I've been thinking about that a lot, lately. Human mortality. It's why I've been pressing you about kids. Sorry, I know you don't want to talk about that."

Rade nodded slowly. He gazed up at the stars, and was quiet for several moments. "We're not going to die here, Shaw. It's not our destiny."

"I hope you're right," Shaw said.

Rade kept his gaze on those stars. Fret's earlier words had stirred long suppressed memories. "Do you ever think about the brothers we lost?"

"All the time," Shaw said. "Brothers and sisters, for me."

"I like to think they're watching over us," Rade said. "That those stars, they're our fellow warriors."

"It's a nice thought." Shaw squeezed his hand tighter.

"But then I remember what Tahoe told me once about those stars," Rade said. "And my rational mind takes over."

"What did Tahoe tell you?" Shaw said.

"Stars are merely giant balls of compressed hydrogen and helium whose temperatures and pressures are sufficient to generate runaway nuclear reactions. There's nothing spiritual about them."

"I see," Shaw said. "But I'm sure you knew that already."

"I did," Rade agreed. "But it only reinforces the fact our friends, well, they're merely dead."

"While that may be true," Shaw said. "I do believe they're watching over us in some way or form. The Phants claim when we humans die, we leave behind residues or imprints in the supra-dimension. I'd like to believe that. Hell, they destroy planets because *they* believe it, so there's probably a good chance it's true. But either way, whether our lost friends are watching over us or not, we have each other now. We always will. And no one can take that away from us."

Rade leaned against her spacesuit and touched his helmet to hers.

RADE AND SHAW lunged across the black plain. Behind them, a blackness swallowed up the land to the horizon, an impossibly large amorphous mass, the tendrils along its edges flowing toward the tiny fleeing humans.

Neither Rade nor Shaw wore jumpsuits. Each step in the sand buried them to the knees. The grit scratched at Rade's skin, drawing blood. But there was nothing he could do but hobble on, moving as fast as the thick sand allowed.

The darkness reached them and wrapped around their ankles.

Upon contact, Shaw spun toward him and clamped her hands around his neck, choking him, pulling him toward the rising darkness.

"Shaw—" He managed before she cut off his air

flow entirely.

Shaw grinned like a madwoman, squeezing tighter. The darkness flowed upward, enveloping her upper body entirely so that she was merely a glistening, black, faceless humanoid shape.

As the life slowly ebbed from him, he heard a distant laugh. It sounded strangely mechanical.

Rade was awakened from the nightmare by a beeping on his HUD. Surus was requesting he re-open communications.

Rade unmuted his comm device. "What is it?"

"I have completed the noise masking changes ahead of schedule," Surus replied.

Rade glanced at the time. Only three hours had passed since she had begun. She'd finished two hours ahead of her previous estimate.

"Thank you," Rade said groggily. He had his suit inject a stimulant, then spoke over the main comm. "Wake up, everyone."

Rade had allowed the Argonauts to sleep in their cockpits or passenger seats while Surus, Harlequin and TJ worked at modifying the emitters. Meanwhile the Hoplite AIs and two combat robots had remained on watch.

"I don't suppose I can take a nap?" TJ said.

"Go ahead," Rade said. "Set your timer for twenty minutes and put your AI in control of your Hoplite in the meantime."

"Thanks boss," TJ said.

When everyone else was up, Rade turned toward Bender's mech.

"Activate the emitters on the HS3s," Rade said.

The three drones vanished from view.

"Lui, status on the noise cancelers?" Rade asked.

Several clicks emitted from the external speakers

of Lui's Hoplite.

"They're functioning as expected," Lui said a moment later. "I'm not detecting the HS3s on echolocation. Surus has done a bang up job."

"All right," Rade said. "Bender, send a single HS3 forward. Take it past the sentries and into the cave. Very very carefully."

"Roger that," Bender said.

"Assuming that's actually a cave," Fret said. "And not an alcove."

"If it wasn't a cave," Harlequin said. "Where did the relief sentries come from?"

"Maybe there's an Acceptor inside the alcove," Fret said.

"I somehow doubt that," Manic said. "Given the tech levels we've seen so far. Those aliens are wearing bells. *Bells.*"

On the overhead map, the dot indicating the designated HS3 moved toward the hillock. Rade switched to the video feed from the scout and watched it approach. The two alien sentries appeared invisible against the dark wall of rock. Rade switched to the infrared channel, and the creatures stood out from the night, their outlines filled with varying shades of green that represented the different levels of body heat. The pair seemed oblivious to the approach of the scout.

The sentries continued to rub their mandibles together now and then, and the chittering produced by that action became louder as the HS3 approached.

The scout closed to two meters away, and still the gatorbeetles did nothing.

One meter.

six

R ade held his breath as the HS3 edged past the twitching antennae of both gatorbeetles.

"Careful," Rade said.

Rade knew that the individual rotors on the craft generated an outflow of air. These military grade variants produced very little current, but still Bender had to be careful to take what little was produced into account. If he got too close to those probing antennae...

One of those antennae stiffened, as if the sentry it belonged to had sensed the slight puff of air produced by the HS3.

But then the scout was past and moving into the cave beyond.

Rade switched to the rearview camera on the HS3 and saw that the two sentries were searching the space just in front of the cave mouth, as if they had definitely detected an air current. After several tense moments, they finally returned to their previous stances, as if concluding that what they had sensed was merely nothing.

Rade exhaled in relief and switched to the forward camera on the HS3 once more.

It was too dark to see anything inside the tunnel,

even on the infrared channel.

"Bender, halt the scout," Rade said.

"Done," Bender replied.

"Is the local-beam LIDAR still active?" Rade asked. That was what the drone used for collision detection.

"It is," Bender replied.

"Good," Rade said. That meant the gatorbeetles couldn't detect LIDAR.

Rade activated the LIDAR overlay, which projected a three dimensional wireframe over the tunnel, filling out the dark areas. The drone was hovering next to the ceiling.

"Continue forward," Rade said.

The drone proceeded ahead, following the downward slope of the tunnel.

The HS3 had only traveled a few meters before the video signal began to pixelate and freeze.

"I'm getting severe signal distortion," Bender said. "This is about as far as I can go. Unless you want to send the other HS3s in to act as repeaters."

"Do it," Rade said.

He waited for the other two to stealthily fly past the sentries and enter the cave. Each time the sentries became agitated, and searched the entrance. The third time, Bender had to send the last HS3 deeper as the gatorbeetles proceeded a short way into the tunnel to explore.

When the HS3 stopped transmitting, Rade said: "Tell me that those aliens didn't find our scout."

"No," Bender said. "It passed beyond signal range. I gave it instructions to return to the entrance when the threat passes."

Several moments passed.

Finally the video feed returned.

"The HS3 is back within signal range," Bender announced.

"I see that," Rade said. On the feed, he saw that the gatorbeetles had given up and returned to their posts.

The final drone remained close to the entrance to maintain the signal while the other two proceeded deeper.

Rade switched his viewpoint to the lead HS3 and watched the progress from there.

The tunnel sloped downward for several minutes before reaching a crossroads. Two tunnels branched away to the left and right, while the main continued forward. Vertical glow bars placed next to each opening provided dim light.

"Do those glow bars look like something a preindustrial society would make?" Tahoe asked.

"No," Manic said.

"Evidently, they've recovered some of their ancient technology," Surus said.

"Either that, or our Phant has been feeding them tech," Shaw said.

"Well," Lui said. "It's looking like they rely on a combination of both sight and sound to navigate the cave environment at this point."

The HS3 revolved to observe each of the three different branches, sending its LIDAR beam down each tunnel in turn. They all seemed much the same.

"Do you want me to follow the right-hand rule of mazes?" Bender asked. That was the rule to take the rightmost branch every time, retracing one's steps and taking the next right-hand branch after reaching a dead end.

"No," Rade said. "Let's go straight on this one. Squeeze as much range from our repeaters as we can.

Unless Surus has a suggestion?"

"I won't be able to give you any further directional information regarding our prey until I'm actually inside the nest," Surus said. "So straight ahead is as good a choice as any."

Shortly after passing the crossroads, the video began to distort once more.

"I'm retreating a few meters," Bender said. "And then leaving an HS3 here to act as a repeater."

The video became crisp again. The HS3 continued downward alone, reaching another crossroads. After the scout turned to scan each direction in turn, once more Rade instructed Bender to move forward.

A distant chitter echoed from the cave walls. In moments a lone gatorbeetle appeared ahead, scampering toward the HS3 in the center of the tunnel. According to the three dimensional image produced by the LIDAR, the alien's antennae were outstretched and constantly feeling out the wide walls. The HS3 flew directly above the V shape formed by those antennae.

The creature paused for a moment, as if puzzled by the slight gust of air it must have sensed from the HS3 as the scout flew past, then it momentarily flicked up its abdomen in what must have been the alien equivalent of a shrug and continued on its way.

"If we have to go in there, it could be tricky navigating those tunnels while gatorbeetles are wandering around," Tahoe said. "Especially if we have those antennae to contend with."

"Look at the distinct V the feelers form," Shaw said. "Assuming we penetrate the nest in our jumpsuits, full stealth mode, and when a gatorbeetle comes along we all curl into a ball and hug the edges of the walls as they pass, the aliens won't even notice we're there. We don't produce any gusts of air, after all."

"I don't know..." Tahoe said. "It's still going to be dangerous."

The HS3 reached a subterranean T intersection and rotated first to the left, then the right. Both passages seemed the same, in that each descended for fifty meters before sloping out of view.

"Who wants to bet our feed is going to drop out momentarily?" Fret said. "As in, when we take either of those bends?"

No one took him up on the bet.

"Bender, take the right hand branch," Rade ordered.

The HS3 moved into the designated corridor. After traveling only a meter, unsurprisingly the feed began to distort badly.

"I'm losing connection," Bender said. "And backtracking the HS3 to the T intersection."

The connection restored a moment later.

"Looks like we've gone as far as our HS3s can take us," Rade said.

"Time to get our boots dirty?" Bender said.

"Not yet," Rade replied. "We stay in the Hoplites for the moment. Tahoe, take us forward. Stealth mode. Halt three klicks from the hillock: like someone said, those antennae look extremely sensitive. Let's not take any chances."

Stealth mode meant the slowest possible speed, with noise cancelers active throughout the mech body; though even at that pace the Hoplites wouldn't be entirely quiet.

At that speed, it took half an hour to reach the designated waypoint three kilometers from the hillock.

"All right, now it's time for the dirty boots," Rade said when they arrived. "Dismount, Argonauts. And break out the secondary holographic emitters."

Those secondary emitters were stowed in the storage compartments of the mechs. Surus had developed a way to use the emitters not only with the HS3s, but also in conjunction with the camouflage tech of their jumpsuits as well, allowing them to completely blend in with the background. Once again, it was tech that not even the military had—soldiers relied on their dynamic camouflage alone. And with the recent sound-masking patch that Surus had uploaded, it would hide them from echolocation, too. Similar to the HS3s, the jumpsuits would still appear on any LIDAR and thermal bands of course, but it was apparent by now these gatorbeetles didn't utilize either.

While in theory the Hoplites themselves could squeeze between the two sentries and fit inside the tunnel beyond, unfortunately the tech didn't work with the larger mechs. It was restricted to the jumpsuits, the HS3s, and the Phant trap. Even if Surus could get it functioning with the Hoplites, the minimal hum produced by the servomotors even under stealth mode would give the units away; to eliminate that would require a complete retrofitting of the noise cancelers across the skin of the mech. Not something she could do at the moment.

"Well this is farewell for the moment, El," Rade told his Hoplite's AI.

"It is," Electron replied. "I'll keep the cockpit warm for you."

"You do that."

The hatch opened and Rade climbed the rungs to the ground. When he stepped onto the black sand, it swallowed him to the middle of his calves.

Rade opened up the storage compartment and

grabbed the triangular-shaped emitters inside. He clipped them to the harness and utility belt of his jumpsuit, using the pattern Surus prescribed. These particular emitters were larger than those Surus had developed for the HS3s, and they couldn't be worn on the jumpsuits while inside the cockpit—the protrusions they formed on the suit interfered with the inner actuators that composed the motion cocoon.

When he had finished attaching the devices, Rade lifted one of his boots from the sand. Already the gray material was sheathed in soot from the sand. That black dust would probably cover him to the thighs by the time he reached the cave entrance.

"Will this dust interfere with the holographic emitters?" Rade asked.

"Only when you move fast," Surus said.

"What does that mean?" Rade said.

Surus finished attaching her own emitters and turned toward him. "I designed the emitters so the suits would act as a backup, in case there was an error in the occlusion calculations that caused the holograms to momentarily fail in their coverage of the subject inside. These errors in emitter calculations will only occur when a subject is moving faster than usual, for example running. The errors are cumulative, meaning that you could run without issue for a few paces, but after that, portions of the suit would occasionally show through until you slowed. And since the black dust is preventing the suit camouflage from working in the leg region, those portions will be visible."

"So you're saying if we move too fast then they might see our legs?" Bender asked.

"Precisely," Surus said. "But if we *were* moving fast, the sensitive hearing these aliens possess would no doubt give away our positions long before they actually saw us, because moving fast also counters the echolocation masking."

"Don't forget to bring along some frags, smokes, and charges, people," Rade sent.

Listening to his own instructions, he unloaded a few frag and smoke grenades from the launcher of his Hoplite and secured them to his harness. He grabbed a couple of explosive bricks from the storage compartment of the mech and similarly attached them.

"Nothing I love better in this life than sneaking into an alien nest," Bender said while retrieving several grenades from Juggernaut. "And I ain't joking. Well actually, that's not entirely true. I do like something just a little bit better. And that's sneaking into an alien nest with guns blazing."

"I'm sure your girlfriend wishes the same thing when you visit her alien nest," Manic said.

"Har," Bender replied.

"Switch to stealth mode," Rade said. Unlike the Hoplites, the local noise cancelers installed in the suits and robots would ensure that stealth mode muted every sound.

"Hoplites, assume guard positions," Rade instructed the mechs. "Argonauts, activate emitters."

The Hoplites formed a defensive circle, each of them facing outward to scan the plains.

Meanwhile, one by one the jumpsuited members of the team completely vanished as the emitters took effect.

Rade activated his and walked forward, testing the masking effect. Around him others were doing the same. While the emitters did a good job of hiding the suits themselves and the disturbances to the ground directly below, the sand-filled indentations left in their wake were somewhat obvious.

"Uh, I'm not sure this is going to work," Tahoe said. "Invisible boots that create visible prints? Even if they're shallow, these footprints are still fairly obvious giveaways."

"Maybe they won't see them in the dark?" Manic said.

"When we get close, I'm sure they will," Tahoe said. "Their eyes have to be adapted for night vision. They live in caves, after all."

"I thought we already decided they can't see the thermal band?" Manic said. "Or they would have swatted our drones down."

"Yes, but I mean like the kind of night vision cats have."

"All right fine, it's a risk," Manic agreed. "But I think it's a reasonable one."

"I'm going to have to agree with Tahoe." Rade zoomed in on the hillock. "Let's approach the entrance at an angle, and climb onto the sloping side of the hillock before we make our way to the entrance. The hillock surface looks free of sand and fairly solid from here. I'm hoping we won't leave any footprints."

"And if we do?" Shaw said.

"Then we cross that bridge when we get to it," Rade said.

"Will our noise cancelers be able to block the sound of our boots scraping across the rock?" Fret asked.

"They should," Rade said. "Tahoe, take us in."

Tahoe organized the squad into a single party, and they advanced in a straight line. Each member stepped in the footprints of the person ahead, with the goal of minimizing the number of depressions they made in the sand. The two robots brought up the rear; the pair no longer ported the Glass container, but dragged it along behind. Or rather, one of them did: the pressure produced by the container flattened out the sand, basically eliminating the footprints the party left in its wake. Of course, the price was that they left a long rectangular depression behind them instead.

"Hoplites," Rade transmitted. "Use your jumpjets and relocate to a new position. Stay low. Move at least fifty meters away from our starting position." If the Hoplites didn't move, the trail the party was creating would lead directly to the mechs.

"Roger that," Electron replied.

Rade glanced at his overhead map. The Hoplites relocated as per his orders. As for the Argonauts, though he couldn't see anyone in front of him as he made his way forward across the sand, he knew where everyone was thanks to the map. He activated the "squad display outline" mode on his HUD, and his Implant overlaid blue silhouettes over his vision, showing Rade precisely where each of his team members were in front of him. Those outlines were three-dimensional, and updated as their individual limbs moved. It was just as good as LIDAR, well actually better, because it made them stand out from the backdrop.

They reached the hillock. As hoped, it was composed of a solid material and free of the sand. The Argonauts made no impressions on the bare rock as they clambered onto the slope and advanced toward the two sentries at the entrance. As Rade had told Fret, the sound of their boots scuffing against the rock was completely suppressed, making their approach absolutely silent.

When Bender, on point, neared the entrance, Rade lowered the laser rifle from his shoulder and said: "Walk extra slow when making the crossing, people.

We don't need the gatorbeetles detecting the vibrations of our passage."

Rade watched the dot representing Bender edge past the closest alien sentry; the dot hesitated at the entrance, then moved inside.

"Watch the antennae at the entrance," Bender sent.

One by one the squad members reached the cave mouth, waited a few seconds, and then proceeded inside. When Rade's turn came, he saw why the individual members were pausing at the opening: while there was a relatively wide gap between the gatorbeetles, enough to fit a Hoplite anyway, those continually twitching antennae routinely swept past the empty area. Rade watched the moving feelers for a few moments to work out the pattern.

He timed it so that the twitching antennae were well away from the opening when he dodged past.

When everyone was in, the squad continued the advance into the tunnels, following the three-dimensional outline of the walls as generated by the LIDAR.

"And so we enter the hornets nest," Manic said softly.

The HS3 that lingered by the entrance had quickly descended deeper, staying within fifty meters of the point man, Bender. This allowed the farthest HS3 to proceed into the right-hand passageway of the distant T intersection.

"Be very careful," Surus said. "While it is well and good you consider yourself hunters, the truth of the matter is, in this alien nest you are the prey. We remain in the shadows at all times until we discover our target. And then we strike. I'm hoping for a surgical-precision type capture, followed by a clean extract. With luck, we'll be gone before the aliens know we were even here."

Rade had to smile at that. Somehow he doubted it would be so easy.

seven

T he walls proved uneven, especially on the tops and sides, though the floor was relatively smooth, likely worn away by the endless passage of aliens across the surface.

A glow appeared ahead, overlaying the LIDAR display. That would be the first crossroads. In moments the squad reached the branching area. Vertical light bars bordered the different passageways that led away to the north, east and west.

"So, Surus?" Rade said. "Left or right."

"Straight ahead."

And so they continued forward, leaving behind the light once more.

As Shaw had suggested earlier, they hugged the walls when any gatorbeetles came past, and crunched their bodies into tight balls, thus avoiding the V-shaped feelers that extended from the heads of the aliens. Not once did the passing creatures notice any of them, or even pause, as the gatorbeetles often did when the HS3s slunk by.

Those HS3 scouts filled out the explored regions on the overhead map, slowly peeling back the fog of war that was the alien nest. By the time Bender reached the T intersection, the lead HS3 had arrived at a small cavern. It seemed to be a trade zone of some kind.

Rade accessed the scout's video feed and switched off the LIDAR overlay because more glow bars in the area provided illumination. Lining the walls, fat gatorbeetles resided in front of individual baskets that seemed woven from silk; the long, boat-like shapes gave Rade the impression that the different creatures had carried those baskets there on their backs. Inside them were various trade goods, Rade thought. One contained golden, translucent cubes that appeared to be made of amber of some kind. Another was full of dyed, bamboo-like pipes, each a different color. The proprietor lingering in front of the latter had several of those pipes stuffed into the air tubules that ran along its upper thorax.

"See that," Manic said. "Even aliens perform body augmentation. It's a sign of a highly-evolved, and highly-developed species."

"That's right, try to defend your dick piercing," Bender said.

Other gatorbeetles moved to and fro among the stalls. One of them approached a basket filled with white, squirming larvae as big as Rade's arm. With a prehensile forelimb, the client gatorbeetle reached into a small pouch hanging below its thorax and produced a thick white crystal. It gave that to the vendor; the recipient promptly grabbed a larva from the basket and handed it to the customer. The patron brought the squealing larva to its mandibles and took a bite before ambling off. A drooping thread of white goo continued to connect the severed portion of the larva to the gatorbeetle's maw; below the head, the throat repeatedly expanded and contracted as if the inner esophagus was crushing or chewing the food.

"Yummy!" Bender said. "Hey Lui, does that sight bring out the foodie in you? I bet you're in the mood for maggot!"

"Is that what you call the snake you keep in your pants?" Shaw said.

"Oh I'm sufficiently aroused all right," Lui replied. "Enough to vomit. On both accounts."

"Surus, do we take that cavern?" Rade asked.

Surus retreated down the opposite turn off of the T intersection, then came back a moment later. "At this point, I don't know. From far away, I can perceive the general direction of a given prey, but as we get closer, it becomes impossible to determine with any accuracy the direction the Phant resides. I suppose we will simply map out the entirety of this nest, if we have to."

"Not sure I'm looking forward to *that*," Manic said.

"It should become obvious where our prey resides, soon enough," Surus said. "At least to me. I will keep you all informed."

The lead HS3 crossed the cavern, heading toward an opening on the far side. In the dim light produced by the vertical glow bars, Rade realized the antennae of most of the buyers were decorated with gold and silver-colored rings near the bases.

"See those rings?" Shaw said. "Looks like even alien societies follow rich-poor hierarchies and power dynamics. This looks suspiciously like elite individuals buying from a poor underclass."

Rade saw two gatorbeetles standing on either side of the exit, wearing the familiar red bands with the small bells around their upper right forelegs. They wore none of the gold and silver rings. More sentries.

The HS3 maneuvered past the searching antenna and into the tunnel beyond. It was wider than the previous passages before the trade zone, with the pedestrian traffic to match. Sometimes two or three gatorbeetles advanced abreast down the middle of the passage; whenever one or more of the insects encountered any of the others traveling in the opposite direction, the gatorbeetles would swerve to the side and let them pass before returning to the middle again. Usually those carrying fewer rings on their antennae deferred to the gatorbeetles that possessed more. However, everyone yielded to the sentries with the red bands.

"Looks like these creatures are nocturnal," Tahoe said. "They're out in their evening finest."

"Keep to the center of the room," Rade said when the Argonauts reached the trade zone for themselves. A clear path ran through the middle of the cavern as the customers browsed the baskets of the vendors set up along the walls.

The squad members moved past the different stalls. Around Rade, the patrons and vendors communicated by producing that mandible-sourced chittering, as well as occasionally touching the tips of each other's antennae together.

"Harlequin, I want you to sample and record all the sounds you hear these aliens using," Rade said. "Look for patterns. Greetings, goodbyes, and so forth. We may need to use small snippets at some point."

"On it," Harlequin replied.

Rade nearly got stepped on at one point as a gatorbeetle backed away from a basket, and he barely dodged to the side.

The squad avoided the searching antennae of the sentries near the exit, and proceeded into the wider, more trafficked tunnel beyond, where they were occasionally forced to halt while waiting for the creatures to defer to one another. One time Fret was accidentally touched by an antenna, but all that did was confuse the involved gatorbeetle, which halted in place, seeming to think it had encountered an obstacle.

The deeper the squad traveled into the nest, the more vulnerable Rade felt. If something went wrong now, they would have a hell of a fight to the surface. He wondered how many of these so-called civilian gatorbeetles would actually participate in the attack, versus leaving the fighting to the sentries and other guards. Probably more than a few would partake: to these creatures, he and his team would be comparable to a bunch of felines running around.

Though the aliens would quickly learn that he and his team were felines with a bite.

Then again, he had no idea how effective the laser rifles would prove against those carapaces. But he somehow doubted those shells were naturally anti-laser.

The lead HS3 reached a T intersection and took the rightmost branch. The other HS3s followed in due time, as did Rade and the others.

In the latest tunnel, smaller corridors almost continually branched away to the left and right. Rade had an HS3 enter one of those corridors, and discovered that it terminated in a moderately-sized chamber. Inside were various objects that could have best been described as furniture and personal belongings, with a gatorbeetle lounging in the center on a patterned mat of some sort, using its prehensile forearms to manipulate a strange object—basically two sticks connected by strands of silk. Rade guessed it was a game of some sort. Either that or some kind of primitive knitting machine. Yeah, he had no idea.

The HS3s explored a few more of the side

chambers, and discovered additional gatorbeetles residing within, sometimes families of two or three. That particular subterranean area appeared to be a residential quarter.

Eventually they reached a dead end and had to backtrack, taking an alternate passageway through yet another residential section.

For the next several hours, the squad wandered aimlessly like that around the inside of the nest, taking right turns until reaching a dead end, then backtracking to the next available rightmost passage. The overhead map continued to fill out, to the point where they had mapped a full fifteen percent of the nest, at least in relation to the size of the surface hillock. They discovered mostly more of the same: trade zones and residential neighborhoods. They did pass by the alien equivalent of restaurants and grocery stores now and again, with gatorbeetles dining or purchasing the familiar white larvae prepared in various manners: half the time still alive, the other half withered. They were often coated in different colored slimes that must have been the alien equivalent of herbs and spices.

The Argonauts occasionally came across bigger, town square-style crossroads, usually decorated with various statues and columns that seemed formed out of stalactites and stalagmites. There was often an object of interest at the center, such as a statue of a gatorbeetle or larva, with a plinth at the based covered in what looked like antennae impressions. Smaller gatorbeetles usually lingered around the central fixtures of those squares. The jobless youth, perhaps, subsisting on the alien equivalent of basic pay.

The HS3s mapped out one crossroads that seemed to be a work in progress. Some gatorbeetles cut into the rock with their mandibles, expanding the extents.

Others were swallowing the refuse matter piled into dark cones beside the walls, their esophagus' pumping; a moment later they would expectorate the material onto half-formed statues or other adornments, slowly adding to the shapes.

"Look at that," Bender said. "These bugs are big, natural 3D printers. Every house should have one."

"We'll have to get you one as a pet," Lui said.

"You could try," Bender said. "But somehow I don't think my 'pet' would survive the first day in my household."

"But it could 3D-print you a pussy!" Manic said.

"And when it does, I'll be sure to call you over," Bender replied.

"Sounds divine," Manic said.

"I'm sure it does."

Eventually they reached a larger tunnel that seemed to have more of the gatorbeetles with the red leg bands on patrol. Those guards would often touch the tips of their antennae when their courses intersected, and then one or the other would promptly turn around. Rade guessed those guards employed some kind of pheromonal signaling, similar to what ants and other hive insects used.

Several side openings in that region led to corridors filled with cells carved into the rock. Inside those cells, larvae undergoing various stages of growth were encased in a translucent yellow substance that reminded Rade of honey.

"This seems to be where they rear their offspring," Tahoe said.

"You think?" Bender replied.

"Could also be where they grow their food," Shaw said.

"Maybe they eat their own babies," Lui said.

"Some of these larvae look suspiciously like the squealing worms we see them eating all the time."

"Why does that thought sicken me?" Shaw said.

"It sickens all of us," Tahoe replied. "But it would make some sense, given how scarce the natural resources are on this world, after what the Phants did to them."

Eventually the lead HS3 arrived at a wide cavern. Multiple passageways led away on all sides. Between them, vertical glow bars provided dim lighting. The cavern itself was empty, save for a pair of sentries flanking a large boulder set into a hole in the far wall. Intricate designs, mostly seeming to represent other gatorbeetles, engraved the surface of the boulder.

"So what now?" TJ said.

"That boulder, and those sentries..." Rade said. "They're obviously guarding something they consider important."

"Maybe it's their equivalent of a governmental center?" Tahoe said. "Or, considering that these aliens are preindustrial, a royal palace."

"That would be a logical inference," Harlequin said. "But the question is, would it be worth our time to infiltrate such a place? In other words, would our Phant reside here?"

"Phants do like to burrow their way into the upper hierarchies of societies," Surus said. "They prefer power, and the trappings that go with it. So there is a good chance, if this is indeed their equivalent of a royal palace, that we will find our prey somewhere inside. And if he is truly searching for some artifact left here by his hive in ancient times, this would be the best place to gather the necessary resources he might need to find it."

As Rade watched, a gatorbeetle wearing two silver

rings on each of its antennae approached the boulder. It was a rather plump specimen, with a swollen thorax. The area surrounding its mandibles and eyes—its "facial" region—was powdered white, as if it wore makeup.

The gatorbeetle rubbed its mandibles together, and one of the sentries chittered in response. The newcomer touched its antennae tips to those of the sentry, then the guard stepped back, chittered something toward its companion, then the two sentries hurled their entire body weight against the boulder, forcing it deeper into the hole.

The HS3 repositioned to get a better view of what lay beyond; meanwhile the silver-ringed creature skittered inside the crack that formed between the hole and boulder. Two gatorbeetles that were apparently waiting inside near the entrance emerged, carrying small yellowish blobs in their mandibles. When all of the aliens were clear, the sentries released their hold on the boulder. The floor immediately beyond it must have been sloped, because when the gatorbeetles eased up, the boulder promptly rolled back into place and sealed the gap.

"That looks like a good place to camp out if we wanted to get inside," Tahoe said.

"It does indeed," Rade said.

He pulled up the video recorded by the HS3 during the moment when the sentries had rolled the boulder inward, and played it back at one-fiftieth the speed and zoomed in. Beyond, it appeared an even more spacious cavern awaited. The floor was uneven, covered in a series of mounds as if past occupants had spent an inordinate amount of time lingering in one place and wearing away the rock before moving onto another section of the floor.

He caught a glimpse of what looked like three gatorbeetles crowded together near the far side of the cavern, their backs to the entryway. And that was all he saw before the boulder descended back into place.

"All right Argonauts, keep moving," Rade ordered. "We make our way to that boulder. Bender, I want you to send the lead HS3 inside the next time a gatorbeetle enters."

"You got it."

But no other alien arrived by the time Rade and company reached the cavern. The three HS3s lingered invisibly by the boulder as the hidden squad members took up positions nearby. Those HS3s kept far enough away from the gatorbeetles to prevent any rotor prop wash from reaching them, of course.

Rade quickly grew sick of waiting, and dispatched the HS3s to begin exploring the different passageways that branched off around them. The scouts moved as far as signal range permitted, but discovered nothing else as interesting as the current cavern. Gatorbeetles occasionally emerged from the various side passageways and into the cavern, but none of them approached the boulder, instead crossing the chamber to take a different exit tunnel.

At the two-hour mark, Rade recalled the HS3s and began to despair that those sentries would ever roll the boulder aside again.

"Surus," Rade said. "Could we modify the holographic emitters to create an illusory gatorbeetle? Like the one we saw gain entrance?"

"Unfortunately, even if I succeed in creating the perfect illusion," Surus said. "And replay the exact same chittering the newcomer used to greet the guard, we have no way to emulate the antennae tips."

"Maybe we can tap their antennae with our

gloves?" Fret said.

"I believe they are not simply touching antennae," Surus said. "There has to be a pheromonal chemical exchange taking place. And we have no way to emulate that."

"It's essentially a biometric scanner, isn't it?" Tahoe said.

"Yes," Surus said.

"I say we camp out in the tunnels and capture the first fat bug that comes passing by," Bender said. "Then we chop off its antennae, come back here, reprogram our emitters, and use our newly acquired goods to get past the sentries. Lopping off the body parts of my enemies is my favorite method of bypassing biometrics, after all."

"The chemical signatures of the pheromones are likely produced by the feelers in realtime," Surus said. "When you touch the dead tips to the antennae, all you'll do is confuse the sentry. No, the best course of action at the moment is to wait."

"We could always shoot them down," Bender said. "Then roll the boulder aside ourselves."

"Yeah, and bring the whole nest down on us," Manic said. "That's a great way to send the Phant fleeing."

"We wait, for now," Rade said.

Finally, shortly thereafter an enormously corpulent gatorbeetle entered from one of the tunnels and approached the entrance. Once again, the facial region around the mandibles and eyes was powdered white, though even more profusely than the previous gatorbeetle. The bottom halves of its antennae were coated in a gaudy layer of rings that clearly restricted the motion of those feelers, judging from the jerky motions the antennae made.

"All right, Bender, send in the HS3s the moment that boulder rolls inward. Everyone else, get ready to enter behind our friend. It might be a while before the next gatorbeetle comes by requesting entry, so if the chamber beyond looks safe, we're going in. Tahoe, organize us into two fire teams for entry on the left and right."

The fat gatorbeetle exchanged chitters with a sentry, and deigned to offer the tips of its antennae. The sentry touched those feelers with its own, then on cue turned around and pushed at the boulder with the second guard.

Rade caught a glimpse of the uneven-floored cavern beyond. He spotted the three gatorbeetles huddled on the far side, ignoring the entrance. Everything seemed unchanged from before.

Only one gatorbeetle was waiting to depart that time.

"Looks clear," Rade said as the waiting creature emerged and the other entered. "Let's go."

The Argonauts ducked between the two sentries and into the crack formed by the boulder and the gap. The first fire team took the left side, the second, the right.

As the last of them entered the cavern beyond, the boulder rolled shut with a resounding thud behind them.

eight

Tantalus very carefully low-crawled toward the opening of the long foraging tunnel. It opened out upon the plains.

There, three hundred meters in front of him, resided the six large metallic objects. Tantalus zoomed in. Yes, he could confirm now with absolute certainty that they were mechs.

Tantalus hated mechs. Their AIs considered themselves a superior breed to his own. They looked down on those such as he, considering him and his ilk inferior, weak in mind and puny in body.

He checked the class in his database. Hoplites.

Ever vigilant, the deadly battle units relentlessly scanned their surroundings. They had cobra lasers mounted to their right arms, ready to fire at any threat that presented itself. They carried long, body-length shields in their left arms. Nozzles surrounding their chests and waist regions indicated Trench Coat launch points, countermeasures that would protect against missile attacks.

Tantalus had only awakened from storage a few hours earlier. The Master had sensed the presence of another of its kind, and asked that Tantalus proceed to the Acceptor to investigate. Tantalus had taken a foraging tunnel to the surface, and when he had emerged he spotted the intruders camped out far away on the plains. He had returned to the tunnel and taken a different branch that led to the current opening, allowing him to emerge much closer to the interlopers.

He wondered which of the mechs contained the Other the Master had spoken of. The Master had cautioned Tantalus to be wary of possession, and warned him not to get too close. Tantalus had no intention of doing so.

Tantalus retrieved the Tech Class IV blaster from his holster. The Master had taken the weapon from the preservation depot not far from the nest; that depot contained several pieces of technology formerly possessed by the space-faring race before they became the Conquered.

When the Master had bestowed the weapon to Tantalus, the description had been very enticing indeed. Tantalus quickly determined that the blaster was capable of readily disabling the neural networks found in the inferior AI cores produced by Tech Class III humans, his former masters. It would not affect manual operation of such machines, unfortunately, so if the Other possessed any of the mechs out there, or any humans were aboard, then his initial offensive would be useless. Which was why he considered what he was about to do more a probing attack than anything else. He had an ordinary laser blaster he could use if the situation turned hairy, plus a hundred of the best warriors from the nest waiting in the tunnel behind him.

The weapon had required modification to work with his body, of course, since it was designed for use by the prehensile forelimbs of the Conquered. The blaster had a biometric lockout mechanism as well, but with the help of the Archive AI assigned to the preservation depot, Tantalus had found the necessary tools required to reprogram it, and adjusted the fitting to suit his human grip. The Archive AI spoke the chittering language of the Conquered of course, a somewhat refined version at that; but Tantalus knew the language thanks to the Master.

He aimed the weapon at the Hoplites and opened fire in rapid succession. Three of them managed to drop to the dunes, hiding behind their shields. Tantalus merely fired directly at the protective devices, knowing his energy bolt would suffuse straight through the metal. In moments, he surmised that he had disabled all the AI cores, given that the mechs had ceased all activity.

That shouldn't have been possible; there should have been at least one Hoplite remaining. That meant the Other was no longer with them. A somewhat troubling thought. Still, it could be a ruse.

Tantalus waited thirty minutes to ensure any human operators weren't simply "playing dead," then he chittered at the Conquered behind him, and, with the special gloves he wore, touched the antennae of the warrior at their forefront, completing the instruction chain with the necessary pheromonal signaling.

The lead warrior led the Conquered out onto the plains.

In moments, the warriors had confirmed that the Hoplites were indeed disabled, and that there were no humans hiding in the cockpits—if there were, the Conquered would have already been attacked.

Tantalus turned toward the distant mountain and pressed the button on his utility belt. The hidden charges he had placed above the cave to the Acceptor detonated. A large plume of smoke billowed skyward near the summit, and he could feel the rumbling even here as the rocks tumbled down in a vast avalanche, sealing the cave.

He remembered the argument that had taken place a few weeks ago between himself and the Master regarding those charges. Tantalus had wanted to detonate them immediately to prevent anyone from following them here.

"No," the Master had said. "We do not want to block off our only escape so readily, not until we determine how amenable these Conquered will be to our control."

"But what about the Hunters?" Tantalus had said.

"Let the Hunters come," the Master replied. "If they dare. And when they do, *then* we will detonate the charges. We will trap them. If all goes as planned with the nest, the Hunters will quickly realize that they are the ones who are Hunted, not we."

Well, Tantalus supposed, the Master would certainly be pleased.

nine

Vertical glow bars clung to the distant walls, dimly illuminating the new subterranean chamber. Rade realized there were far more than simply three gatorbeetles lingering on the far side of the cavern: the boulder had occluded a throng of about twenty of them, which he saw readily now that he was completely inside. Those creatures all had their backs to the entryway and were crowded around something. What it was, he wasn't sure: it appeared an indistinct blur past the limbs and bodies of the gatorbeetles on his video feed.

Rade zoomed in further and tried to focus the area, but the lighting simply wasn't good enough. He checked the LIDAR and thermal bands, but wasn't able to judge anything more about the strange object—there were too many alien bodies in the way. From the way they were bowing and scraping Rade thought they were fawning over it, whatever it was.

"All right, send the HS3s closer," Rade said. "Let's see if we can figure out what holds their attention so rapt. Meanwhile, spread out. Let's not place ourselves in the path of any aliens coming or going from the entrance."

The group took up defensive positions across the

uneven floor while the HS3s moved forward; the scouts captured multiple angles of the throng during the approach.

Rade switched to the viewpoint of the middle HS3 and as it closed he noticed that all of the gatorbeetles present were wearing different amounts of gold and silver rings at the bases of their antennae, and their facial regions were all powdered white to varying extents. He actually wasn't sure if that was powder or some sort of natural color indicating a different caste in the nest.

The HS3s rose higher as they neared the crowd: the ceiling was tall enough for the scouts to give the aliens a further two meters of clearance, ample room for their downdrafts. Even if one of the rotored scouts passed directly over an alien, Rade didn't think the creature would notice.

As the view updated, Rade realized the aliens had completely surrounded a slightly larger gatorbeetle that possessed an elongated abdomen. There were too many for them to all enclose the subject of their fawning attention, and they fought amongst themselves for the chance to touch the bigger creature. It turned randomly in place, accepting the juicy secretions vomited from the mandibles of the white-faced aliens, and slurped the gooey substance down.

"What the hell?" Bender said. "It looks like they're vying amongst themselves to feed that bitch."

"That's precisely what they're doing," Lui said. "That 'bitch' is essentially the equivalent of a queen, to use an analogy from the insect world."

As the HS3s assumed a hold position above the throng, Rade spotted a long metallic bar running along the center of the queen's dorsal region that included the head and thorax. The bar seemed embedded in the carapace. Drops of black condensation glistened in the dim light, scattered across the upper surface of the metal, well away from the organic tissue.

Rade recognized that metal bar as a sign of Phant possession—it would be a device containing the circuits and neural networks necessary to interface with the nervous system of an organic life form, essentially mimicking the AI core of an Artificial or robot and allowing the Phant to control the queen.

"We've found our prey," Surus said.

"So, what do we do?" Tahoe said.

"It would be easier to capture the Phant if we can get the queen alone," Shaw said. "I'm guessing we're going to have to rip the bar off the queen's back once we stun the Phant, because there's no way we'll fit the queen in the Phant trap we've brought."

"We will have to tear the bar away," Surus agreed.

"And that action will likely kill the queen," Lui said.

"Yes," Surus said. "No doubt stirring the attendants into a killing frenzy. And if not them, then the guards outside, who will summon more of their kind. This chamber will turn into a death trap."

"All right, it's settled then," Rade said. "We wait here for the nest to go to sleep, and strike the queen then."

"Assuming the nest actually *does* go to sleep," Tahoe said. "I suspect the queen will be guarded 24/7."

"Well, you're all ex-MOTHs," Rade said. "Shaw and Surus excepting. But my point is, you're all used to waiting. Let's camp out here for a few hours. Rest, conserve our energy. Take naps. Sip our liquid meal replacements. And if the situation doesn't change, we strike. I'll work with Surus on a plan."

"Let me guess," Tahoe said. "That plan will involve reprogramming the emitters in some way."

"You know me too well," Rade said.

"I do," Tahoe replied. "And I know our tech."

And so they observed the alien queen throughout the night, waiting for an opportunity to strike. The hidden team members remained dispersed throughout the cavern, keeping well away from the main path between the entrance and the queen.

But she was never alone. Those lesser gatorbeetles always attended her. When they weren't feeding her, they watched over her while she laid young. Indeed, Rade witnessed the birth of two small larva: a stinger at the end of the elongated abdomen would begin to pump, and the gatorbeetle that happened to be directly behind the queen at that particular moment would eject a bolus from its mouth—it appeared to be the same honey-like yellow substance Rade had seen in the cells outside the cavern. The queen stabbed the pumping stinger into that mass and deposited a small larva in the center. The lesser gatorbeetle promptly left the throng, crossing to the throne room exit with its prize, waiting for the sentries to move the boulder aside when the next mate arrived.

At long last the queen ceased her activities and appeared to sleep. But the sycophantic gatorbeetles remained.

Rade suspected the aliens wouldn't leave until they got what they came for: a larva. He wondered if the white-faced gatorbeetles were actually mates for the queen; what if the gooey substance they spoon-fed her also contained reproductive material? If so, then what he witnessed there was essentially a nonstop orgy: this particular Phant must really be a hedonist to want to occupy such a place in the alien societal hierarchy.

"All right," Rade said. "We're going to strike. Here's the plan Surus and I have come up with."

He relayed the details to the team.

"Get into position, Argonauts," Rade said.

Harlequin took his place near the center of the cavern, and the remaining eleven members of the team assumed attack positions on either side of the Artificial. Then the eight humans, two Artificials, and two robots aimed at their designated targets.

Bender was humming something, and occasionally sung actual words over the comm. "Bugs bugs bugs. Gonna squash me some bugs."

"Bender, quiet," Rade said.

"Sorry boss," Bender replied.

In his analysis of the bodies, Harlequin decided that the most vulnerable spot on a gatorbeetle was most likely directly between the mandibles, in the esophagus region. A laser strike there was guaranteed to bore deep into the tissue. Unfortunately, with the aliens all facing the queen like that, the mandibles weren't currently visible, and the team only had the carapaces in their sights; the effectiveness of the lasers against those outer shells was currently unknown. Presumably the lasers would penetrate, and perhaps cause great pain, though probably not with the same stopping power as an esophagus strike.

Only half an hour ago the main boulder had rolled aside and a new gatorbeetle arrived, so Rade didn't expect newcomers any time soon. The Argonauts should have the queen and her little coterie all to themselves for a while. Also, since the queen was asleep and hadn't produced any more larvae, there were currently no aliens waiting to leave near the entrance.

Rade felt somewhat guilty, since the plan involved

slaughtering all the aliens simply to obtain access to the queen, who they also planned to kill. Unfortunately, the Argonauts couldn't risk leaving any of them alive. Even though his team members were invisible, it wouldn't take the aliens long to figure out that something was attacking their precious queen. They would either erupt into a defensive frenzy, rampaging about the cavern and striking randomly at the air against their invisible attackers, or they would flee to the boulder and attempt to summon the guards.

Rade remembered telling Surus, long ago, that his team wasn't like other security consultants. That he didn't merely take on any job, that it was his morals that differentiated him from other mercenaries. He told her he didn't condone assassinations, and never accepted jobs requiring it.

Yet, wasn't he about to do just that?

But these are aliens we're assassinating, he told himself. *Aliens harboring an enemy of humanity. They're not human beings. I draw the line at assassinating members of my own species.*

As he stared at the giant slobbering insects, he didn't think he was going to lose any sleep over what he was about to do.

Like squashing bugs, as Bender would say.

ten

Rade aimed the scope of his rifle at the abdomen of his given target and waited for Harlequin to provide the distraction that would allow Rade to target the esophagus region. A solid green outline surrounded the tango. A dashed line would have told him another member of his team was targeting that same gatorbeetle, something they were currently trying to avoid.

Other gatorbeetles were outlined in solid blue, indicating in turn which tangos his team mates currently had lined up. All of the targeted aliens would go down in the initial salvo—assuming the esophagus regions were as vulnerable as the Argonauts believed.

"Now, Harlequin," Rade transmitted.

In the empty space where Harlequin resided at the center of the cavern, a gatorbeetle sentry appeared. It began chittering softly, and stamping its foot to ring the bell connected to the red band on its foreleg. The noise was not loud enough to wake the queen, hopefully, but sufficient to attract the attention of her attendants.

As expected, the closer gatorbeetles spun around to regard the sentry, and the aliens on the opposite side of the queen lifted their thoraxes to peer past them. Mandibles and the esophagi between them were exposed to the waiting rifles of the party. The queen remained dormant upon the rock floor.

Rade quickly centered his crosshairs between the mandibles. When the vulnerability was acquired, the green outline flashed. He waited for the targeting outlines of his companions to flash as well. And then:

"Fire," he said, and squeezed the trigger.

Twelve of the gatorbeetles simply collapsed where they stood, slumping dead to the floor.

Rade moved his crosshairs to the target directly across from his last, located on the other side of the queen, as the other members of his unit would be doing. As the remaining gatorbeetles squealed in surprise and fright, Rade quickly acquired the esophagus of his next designated target and fired. Another twelve fell on the opposite side.

The remaining gatorbeetles fled toward the boulder. Meanwhile, the queen had begun to stir. A muted crackling echoed across the cavern, telling Rade that Surus had switched to her Phant stunner and unloaded it at the exposed queen.

Sure enough, the possessed alien promptly collapsed. At the back of his mind, Rade worried that the crackle produced by the electrolaser would alert the guards; that, along with the vibrations produced by the rampaging aliens.

It took Rade and the others some effort to take down the remaining aliens; Rade had to rely on the AI targeting in his jumpsuit for help, but he managed to fire between the mandibles of another bug and it collapsed. Tahoe and Bender got the remaining two before they could reach the exit.

So far, the boulder hadn't moved. Even so, Tahoe, Bender, Lui and TJ assumed guard positions on either side of the exit as per the plan. Harlequin reset his emitter array, and the illusory sentry in the center of the cavern vanished from the visual band.

Rade and Surus stepped between the fallen gatorbeetles, some of which were still twitching, and approached the queen. The two robots ported the Phant trap forward and placed it nearby. They had deactivated the emitters so that the container was visible, presumably to make transferring the Phant easier.

"The queen definitely isn't going to fit," Rade said.

"No." Surus leaped onto the queen's thorax and tore the iron bar from its backside, ripping away entrails and what appeared to be part of the queen's spine in a gory mess. She leaped down and threw the bar, complete with its black condensation and gory spinal section, into the container. She sealed the door and the bar floated into the air, confined within the imaginary three-dimensional volume formed between the two metal disks in the floor and ceiling of the container. The bar began to rotate in place horizontally, and a hum emitted from the glass, slowly rising in pitch.

"Yup, the queen didn't survive," Shaw said. Beside the container, the large alien remained motionless on the ground, blood oozing from the wounds in its thorax. Summarily executed.

"It is unfortunate," Surus said. "But necessary."

"You know, I just realized something: what if there are no other queens?" Shaw said. "This could be the last nest on the planet. These conquered aliens could become extinct. And it will be our fault."

"What I've seen before in nest- or hive-dominant societies such as this one," Surus said. "Is the ability for existing larvae to become queens. Usually this involves switching the food source while a larva is still young, which induces a phenotypical change in the newborn and triggering the development of queen traits."

"What if you're wrong?" Shaw said. "What if this one has to specifically lay young queen larvae, and for whatever reason, she hasn't yet?"

Surus paused. "I will take a DNA sample before we depart so that we can clone the queen when we return to human space, and then deliver a new one to the nest before we destroy the Acceptor. Will that satisfy your conscience?"

"It will," Shaw said.

By then the rotating bar had become a blur; dark liquid sweated profusely from the surface, coalescing into a black ball half a meter above it. When the ball was about the size of two fists, the box at the top of the container folded open. The liquid sphere floated inside and the box shut.

The metal rod became visible once again, slowing down, and the hum receded. When it stopped spinning, the rod lowered to the bottom of the container. There was no longer any black condensation upon it.

Surus opened the tank, retrieved the small box from the top of the container, and secured it to her harness.

"We have our prey," she said.

The two robots reactivated the emitters on the container and resumed their portage of the empty, and now invisible, trap.

Surus paused beside the dead queen to take a DNA sample—on the LIDAR band, Rade watched as she retrieved a kit from her utility belt, and from it produced a small wooden stick she used to collect some of the blood into a vial.

"I have the sample," Surus announced, placing the vial into the kit and returning it to her utility belt.

"All right, let's go," Rade said.

TANTALUS HURRIED TOWARD the throne room.

Before leaving human space, the Master had installed technology in Tantalus' neural network that allowed him to act as a receptor for psychic messages. It allowed the Master to keep in contact with him at all times.

Thus, shortly after his return to the nest proper, Tantalus had been able to receive the urgent signal the Master had sent. It arrived in the form of mental images, which Tantalus viewed intently, a rising sense of fear forming within his neural network.

The Master was in danger.

Tantalus had dispatched the sentries to alert the garrison, and the warriors would be en route to the throne room via the ordinary routes at that very moment.

Tantalus had abandoned them for a more covert, direct route, using the network of secret corridors and passageways known only to the Master and he. A few other Conquered had once known of them, of course, but they had been executed. Tantalus had considered sharing the route with the warriors he had dispatched, but the release of that news could see Tantalus forced to execute half the nest. The Master very much wanted the covert ways kept secret.

There hadn't been time to properly secure the nest

with more advanced technology. Tantalus and the Master had been here only a few weeks. Ideally, they needed detectors placed in every passageway. And perhaps a few robots sprinkled about. The six Hoplites, while detestable to Tantalus, would prove a welcome defensive measure once the Master had a chance to reprogram them. Of course, it would take some weeks to introduce them to the nest in order to allow the Conquered to acclimate to their presence. But once that was done, the nest would be well-nigh impregnable.

Tantalus reached the final secret passageway, which led to the throne room itself. Like the other hidden tunnels, the entrance and exit were shielded on the visual and echolocation bands from discovery by the Conquered via special emitters taken from the preservation depot. The margins were coated in hormonal chemicals that activated the danger signal in the minds of the Conquered, keeping them from getting close enough to ever discovering the hidden entrances with their feelers.

When Tantalus reached the terminus of the passageway, he had a complete view of the throne room beyond, as the illusory wall wasn't active from this side. He stared into the cavern: the queen lay dead in the center of the other murdered Conquered. They appeared to have taken laser wounds in the maws.

The room appeared empty, but Tantalus suspected the attackers were still present. He almost activated LIDAR, but realized that might give him away. He switched to the passive thermal imaging band instead: sure enough he detected the heat outlines of humanoid shapes. Twelve in total. He also spotted what appeared to be three hovering HS3s.

Interesting. No doubt they were using holographic

emitters similar to those that hid the current passageway, but he had not seen human tech used to conceal moving objects before. The Other must have taught them how to do it.

Twelve enemies. Tantalus doubted he would be able to terminate them all alone, even when striking from a position of surprise. Unfortunately, when the Conquered arrived, his allies wouldn't be much help if they couldn't even *see* their enemy.

While the rest of the nest wasn't as secure as it could be, fortunately the Master had laid a few traps in the throne room to prepare against unwanted incursions such as these.

Tantalus stepped furtively into the cavern and, keeping close to the wall, hurried to a certain hidden device embedded in the rock near the dead queen. An electro-magnetic pulse generator. He turned down the intensity, not wanting to remove himself from the equation, and activated it.

The generated EMP was weak: not enough to impair Tantalus and his ilk, but hopefully sufficient to disable the concealment devices of the intruders. The special Tech Class IV emitters that hid the secret passageways wouldn't be affected, of course, but the human Tech Class III emitters would definitely fail.

Sure enough, the illusions dissipated, revealing the surprised interlopers. They were all wearing jumpsuits. The three HS3s clattered to the floor.

Good luck fleeing the nest now, Tantalus thought.

He dropped to the floor and took cover behind the body of the queen. Then he drew an ordinary blaster. His Tech Class IV AI-disabling weapon was relatively useless, as he had no way to tell which of his opponents were robots in those jumpsuits.

He aimed past the edge of the queen and fired.

eleven

As Rade headed toward the boulder that sealed the opening, he was trying to figure out if there was a way to move it without alerting the sentries beyond. He finally decided that the Argonauts would simply have to roll it aside and shoot down the waiting gatorbeetles.

"There's something moving on the north side of the cavern!" Bender said.

A red dot appeared on the overhead map, near the queen.

A moment later the emitters failed and the entire party materialized. The HS3s smashed into the floor.

Harlequin collapsed.

"Taking fire!" Lui said.

"Drop!" Rade dove behind one of the mounds.

"Tango is behind the queen!" TJ said.

Rade ran the crosshairs of his laser rifle above the contours of the fallen queen, parts of which were occluded by the dead gatorbeetles in front of her. There, he spotted an anomaly, partially hidden by the crimped limb of an alien. It appeared to be the nozzle of a blaster.

Rade centered his reticle over the weapon and

squeezed the trigger. A moment later the blaster vanished from view: pulled away by its owner, no doubt.

"Got a bead..." Tahoe said.

"Take the shot," Rade said.

"Tango is down," Tahoe said.

Rade detached a frag from his harness and threw it across the cavern for good measure. He had the suit adjust his strength for the optimal throw.

After it detonated, Lui said: "I think you got it. But it's still alive, as far as I can tell. I caught sight of a human hand, and when I shot it, the hand withdrew behind the queen."

"Units A and B," Rade said. "Flank the target. The rest of you, provide covering fire. Unleash your lasers both directly into the queen, and above her. With luck, one of our shots will go right through that carapace and find the target."

While the others opened fire, the two Centurions arose, abandoning the empty glass container. The combat robots quickly made their way forward, keeping low to the ground, dodging between the mounds for cover.

Via the overhead map, Rade watched as the two blue dots representing the units moved in on either side of the queen in a classic outflanking maneuver.

He pulled up the video feed from Unit B and reduced it in size, shoving it into the upper right of his vision.

"Tango is sprawled on the ground," Unit B said. "And attempting to crawl away. It's pointing a blaster at me! Taking cover."

The video feed blurred as the combat robot ducked behind a dead alien. Then it peered past the edge and shot at its foe.

A moment later Unit A reported: "Tango has been struck multiple times in the chest region. We've penetrated the battery region. Tango is eliminated."

The red dot on the overhead map became darker in color.

"Battery region?" Rade said. "So the tango is a combat robot?"

"Negative," Unit A replied. "It appears to be an Artificial."

"Looks like we found the original host our prey used before coming to this planet," Surus said.

"Collect its weapons," Rade said. He turned toward the fallen Harlequin. "What's the status on Harlequin?"

TJ was kneeling over him. "He's been struck by a laser. Also in the battery pack, like our tango. He's out of commission until we get back to the ship."

"Damn it," Rade said. "Carry him."

Bender rushed forward and pushed TJ out of the way. "I'll do it." He scooped up Harlequin and threw him over one shoulder. Because of the strength-enhancing exoskeleton, Bender's balance was hardly affected at all.

"The Artificial only possessed two weapons," Unit B said. "Both appear to be damaged beyond use. Though I cannot be sure, as biometric security prevents me from accessing them."

"Give them to TJ," Rade said. "He'll examine them when he has a chance later." Rade glanced at the fallen HS3s. "What the hell hit us?"

"It appears to have been an EMP of some kind," Lui said. "Though a relatively weak one, it easily shorted out our emitters and HS3s. But left everything else intact. Suits. Weapons..."

"Is there no way we can repair these emitters?"

Rade asked.

"Not without access to a 3D printer," Surus replied.

"In other words, not without getting back to the ship," Rade said.

"That's right," Surus said.

"Where did that Artificial come from?" Rade said. "Did anyone see the boulder roll aside?"

"The HS3 watching our six would have detected it," TJ said.

"There has to be another way into the room," Rade said. "Maybe a hidden entrance."

"The HS3s performed a complete scan of the area," Bender said. "And didn't detect a thing."

"Perhaps the Artificial was hiding somewhere," Lui said.

Rade pondered that for a moment, but before he could decide what to do the boulder at the exit began to roll inward of its own accord.

"Defensive positions!" Rade shouted.

Gatorbeetles streamed inside from the edge of that boulder. They were all of the warrior or sentry caste, with those red bands and bells attached to the upper right of their forelegs.

"Open fire!" Rade sent. "And headlamps on, visual band! Full brightness! Let's see if we can blind them as they come inside!"

Rade turned on his headlamps and aimed at the mandibles of one of the incoming aliens. Because of the way it was rampaging inside toward the party, he had to involve the AI to help him hit the esophagus. He switched the weapon to auto-fire when the target was acquired, and his tango dropped.

He was aware of Shaw beside him, her weapon rapidly moving about as she too unleashed her rifle into the fray. Rade couldn't tell if the headlamps were blinding the creatures or not, but those tiny eyes of theirs did seem to be squinting.

More of the aliens fell as the other Argonauts fired. Thrown grenades detonated in the midst of the gatorbeetles, sending dismembered limbs splattering across the cavern.

But for every alien he and the others shot down or dismembered, there was always another to replace them. They continually streamed inside from the cracks between the boulder and the outer passageway. The boulder itself remained in place, obviously being held open by one or more sentries on the other side.

A thick defensive wall of fallen gatorbeetle bodies was beginning to form. And while that wall and the cave entrance itself would serve as bottlenecks, it would only be a matter of time before the weapons began to overheat.

"Units A, B, push the boulder closed!" Rade ordered. "Cover them, Argonauts!"

The two combat robots leaped to their feet and rushed toward the boulder. They activated their jets to take bounding leaps over the bodies in their path.

Gatorbeetles swerved to intercept them.

Guess our headlamps aren't blinding them after all. Or not enough, anyway.

Rade knew that if those aliens touched the Centurions, the robots were gone. He took down two additional aliens with the help of his AI. More fell, but sometimes the aliens twisted at the last microsecond and the incoming lasers struck a mandible or limb instead and the targets didn't drop.

As the two robots neared the boulder, one of the emerging gatorbeetles managed to wrap its mandibles around Unit B, splitting the Centurion in half. The alien was in turn taken down a moment later.

Unit A hurled itself into the boulder and forced it shut.

When the remaining aliens trapped inside the room were eliminated, Rade shouted: "Bender, Tahoe, reinforce that boulder!"

The blockage had begun to roll inward, pushing the sole Centurion braced against it backward.

The two Argonauts jetted across the bodies littering the area. They reached the boulder and added their strength to the robot's. They braced their boots against the floor and shoved their shoulders into the rock, forcing it back once again.

"Manic, Fret, join them," Rade instructed.

With the addition of those two, there wasn't room around the boulder for any more team members to brace the rock.

"There has to be another way out of here!" Rade said. "Illusory walls of some kind. That Artificial had to come from somewhere. Those of you not occupied with the boulder, double check the walls of the cavern on your LIDAR bands. Spread out, get right up to the rock."

Rade knew that hidden walls could be designed in such a manner as to obfuscate their presence on LIDAR, especially when viewed from far away. He overlaid the LIDAR feed onto his visual band, and dashed toward the nearby stone.

"We can't hold them forever!" Tahoe transmitted.

Rade glanced toward the entrance. The Argonauts keeping back the tide were repeatedly jerked backward as the external attackers flung themselves against the boulder from the other side.

"Hurry, people," Rade sent.

A moment later Lui spoke up. "Found an illusory

wall in the northwest of the cavern. I'm also detecting a chemical signature around the edges—I'm guessing it's some kind of hormonal deterrent to prevent other gatorbeetles from wandering inside. The wall itself is generated by a type of emitter I've never seen before. Far smaller and more compact than our own. I'm surprised it survived the EMP."

"Tech Class IV, no doubt," Surus said. "Though the question is, did our prey bring it to this planet, or did he find it here?"

"Well, we don't really have the luxury of worrying about that right now," Rade said. "Everyone, to the false wall. Get ready to provide covering fire for those holding the boulder. Lui, place some charges along the roof just inside the passage. I intend to collapse it behind us."

"You got it," Lui said. He placed a charge in either gloved hand and activated his jetpack to fly upward into the illusory wall: he needed that thrust to reach the relatively high ceiling.

"Surus, grab that emitter when you get there," Rade said. "Maybe you can figure out how to reprogram it."

"Doubtful, if it's Tech Class IV or higher," Surus replied. "Though I'll try to drip inside the thing in my natural state when we have a quiet moment."

When everyone was in place, Rade said: "Lui, the charges?"

Lui emerged from the illusory wall a moment later. "Done."

"What about the Phant trap?" Surus gazed across the room at the empty glass container.

"We have what we came for." Rade nodded at the black box that hung from her harness. "We'll have to write off the container as a loss. I want all hands weapon ready."

Surus nodded her assent.

Rade turned toward the exit and aimed his reticle at the boulder. "Tahoe and everyone else, join us! Cover them, people!"

The five Argonauts tore away from the boulder and jetted across the bodies of the fallen aliens in their paths. Behind them the blockage rolled inward and the gatorbeetles streamed inside.

Rade and the others opened fire, buying the runners time. Rade threw a couple of frag grenades, as did some of his companions. The resultant explosions sent body parts flying across the cavern.

One of the fallen gatorbeetles in the path of the fleeing Argonauts apparently wasn't dead, because it reached up at Tahoe as he jetted over.

"Tahoe, watch out!" Rade sent.

Tahoe must have given partial control of his jets to his AI, because he reacted before Rade finished the words; his jumpsuit jetted sideways, jerking him away from imminent death.

Rade aimed his targeting reticle between the mandibles of the attacker and fired a shot squarely into the esophagus. The gatorbeetle collapsed.

When everyone reached the false wall, Rade ordered: "Retreat! Go go go!"

twelve

Rade and the others fled into the hidden passageway. The headlamps of the team members were still active, illuminating the tunnel. It was spacious enough for the gatorbeetles to pursue in single file, assuming the aliens ignored the hormonal signals at the entrance and followed them inside anyway.

Halfway through, Tahoe, on drag, reported: "The aliens have reached the hidden entrance. They're coming inside."

"Lui, detonate the charges," Rade sent.

The passageway shook as the explosives activated. A moment later a cloud of dust swept past, momentarily blotting out the view. The shockwave nearly threw Rade off his feet.

"That's stopped them," Tahoe said as the dust settled.

"Let's go!" Rade said.

He glanced at his overhead map. Lui was on point, and mapping out a path that led away from the throne room into uncharted territory to the west.

"I found the exit," Lui said a moment later. "It's covered in another illusory wall, though the illusion isn't visible from this side."

"How does it look out there, past it?" Rade asked.

Lui started to peer around the edge.

"Wait," Rade said. "Headlamp off. LIDAR only. Everyone, do the same. Let's not risk any light leakage into the corridor beyond."

Headlamps went out across the team, bathing the team in darkness. Rade switched to his LIDAR, and was still able to see past the illusory wall from the current angle.

Lui gazed out, his head likely emerging from the fake wall on the other side. "The passage is empty, for the moment."

Rade glanced at the map. When Lui had sent LIDAR beams into the tunnel beyond, a passage running from north to south had appeared perpendicular to their current route on the HUD.

"Though the map isn't completely filled out here," Rade said. "It looks like the southern route eventually joins up with the cavern in front of the queen chamber. From there, we can follow the map to reach the surface."

"Do you really want to attempt that now?" Tahoe said. "When every warrior in the nest is headed there?"

"No," Rade replied. "We're going to need to find a place to hide, I think, and wait out the storm until the nest calms down. Because right now, like Tahoe said, this place is like a disturbed anthill."

"Why not wait it out here?" Fret said.

"I'm reading the same pheromones around the edges of this opening as the one we blocked off behind us," Lui said. "If that chemical really acts as a deterrent, in theory we just might be able to hide here."

"I'm not sure that's true anymore," Rade said. "They followed us past the other chemical deterrent back there, after all. And by now the aliens have probably communicated to each other that we escaped through a chemically blocked area. It will become an attractant, not a deterrent. They'll be purposely entering them going forward, most likely. At least when they find them. Unless... do you think you can erase that chemical scent from the edges?"

"Maybe..." Lui said, leaning forward to examine the border of the opening.

"Got some baby wipes in my utility belt," Bender said, coming forward.

"Why the hell are you carrying baby wipes?" Lui said.

"I always carry baby wipes," Bender said. He set down the jumpsuit containing Harlequin and retrieved a couple of wipes from a box at his utility belt. "You can't trust the auto cleanse mechanism of your rifle. If it fails, shit, after all the dust in the air back there, your scope would get real gummed up, as well as the range finder, and maybe even the focusing lens."

"The laser focusing lens is recessed too far back in the muzzle to be affected," Fret said.

"Yeah well, I got baby wipes." Bender handed them to Lui. "I'm prepared for anything. And they're unscented, by the way. So these bugs won't detect it."

"Their chemical sensing systems are likely ten times more powerful than our own olfactory nerves," Lui said. "So whether or not these wipes are truly 'unscented' remains to be seen. Let me run a quick scan." He paused. "Hmm, I got no chemicals emitted. This might actually work. What do you think, boss? Should I try?"

"Do it," Rade said.

Lui accepted the wipes and started rubbing the moist material along the edge where the illusory wall met the cave. "It's working. I'm going to need a few more, though."

He used up nearly all of Bender's wipes to clean the border.

As he was applying the finishing touches, Lui inhaled loudly and ducked back inside. "Got incoming."

A moment later at least twenty gatorbeetles hurried by. Rade saw their three-dimensional shapes appear on the LIDAR band beyond the illusory wall. The soft ringing of the bells they wore told Rade they were members of the warrior caste.

Don't find the hidden passage, he thought as the aliens passed. *Don't find the passage.* He continued to repeat the phrase in his head, mantra like.

And then the gatorbeetles were gone.

"Like I said, the whole nest is heading toward the queen chamber," Tahoe said over the comm.

"One of them is coming back," Lui announced urgently.

"We might have to take it out and drag it inside," Rade said. "Be ready."

The three-dimensional wireframe representing the gatorbeetle appeared past the opening. It was moving its antennae about, running them along the walls. It paused beside the illusory wall, and turned to face it. Those antennae reached inside, searching further.

"Kill it," Rade said.

Rifles opened up across the squad, directed toward the esophagus between those mandibles, and the gatorbeetle collapsed, tumbling inside the hidden passageway. Blood spurted from its esophagus and into the hidden passage.

"Quickly, drag it inside before too much of its blood spills into the tunnel," Rade said.

The squad members surrounded the creature and hauled it completely through the illusory wall and into the passageway. They deposited it about thirty meters inside, with the hope its death scent wouldn't reach the outer passageway for a few hours.

Everyone helped clean up the blood near the opening, mostly by reusing the towelettes Lui used to erase the chemical from the entrance.

When that was done, the team assumed a defensive position twenty meters inside the passage; Rade ordered TJ and Lui to keep the first watch on the outer tunnel beyond the illusory wall.

"You know, at some point they're going to send scouts to search for the terminating end of that tunnel," Lui said. "If they haven't already. It's only a matter of time until they discover this passage. Especially if they have any sort of blueprint they can compare the location of the passage with."

"That's a good point," Tahoe said.

"TJ and Lui," Rade said. "If the two of you spot any more scouts feeling out the walls during your watch, wake up the rest of us. We'll kill them like we did this bug, and drag them inside."

"I still think there have to be other exits to the nest," Manic said. "We don't have to go back the way we came. We can find another way out."

"Do you really want to risk that?" Rade said. "And remember, every surface hole we saw out there was plugged. And the HS3s detected no other guards standing anywhere else outside the hillock."

"All right, but consider something," Manic said. "The exits I'm talking about don't necessarily have to be on the hillock."

"What are you saying?" Tahoe asked.

"Some of these tunnels might extend out onto the

plains," Manic said.

Rade contemplated the implications and found himself worrying about the Hoplites.

Well, the war machines can certainly fend for themselves.

He dismissed his fears and told Manic: "While there might actually be such surface tunnels, we have no way to find them. Once we leave our hiding place, we'll only have a very short span to reach the surface. We won't have time to explore random caves and hope one of them leads us under the plains to another exit. No, Manic, for us the only way back is the route we have already mapped out."

"I just wish we had our HS3s to scout ahead," TJ said.

"You and me both," Rade said.

Shaw sat beside Rade, and she reached out then to grip his glove in hers. He glanced at her, but his LIDAR didn't reveal any of her features beyond the faceplate. He assumed she was afraid.

"We'll get through this," he sent her on a private line.

Shaw squeezed his glove tighter. "Hard to believe the things we'll do to save the galaxy."

"I'm sorry for bringing you here," Rade said.

She extricated herself from his grasp. She seemed insulted. "What the hell are you talking about? I asked for this. There's nowhere else I'd rather be than at your side."

Rade nodded. "And if we had a kid waiting for us back on the ship? Would you be so eager to come then?"

Shaw paused. "That's not fair."

"What?"

"You're trying to use this as an excuse for why we can't have a kid," Shaw said.

"No, I didn't say that," Rade insisted.

"But you implied it." She crossed the arms of her jumpsuit. "If we had a kid waiting for us on the ship, I'd miss her terribly, but it wouldn't change anything. I know the AIs would take care of her until we got back."

"You're assuming the kid would be a her," Rade said.

"Well of course it will be," Shaw said. Though he couldn't see her face, he could tell she was grinning from her tone.

Rade glanced at the LIDAR representation of the tunnel around them, at his men guarding the entrance, and the dead alien several meters behind them.

"Here we are," Rade said. "At the center of an alien nest, and we're arguing about what the sex of our future child is going to be. When we haven't even conceived him or her yet."

"How do you know?" Shaw said.

Rade shot her a look, wishing he could see her expression behind the faceplate.

"Just kidding," Shaw replied. "I'm not pregnant."

"That's a relief."

"Why?" Shaw said.

"Do we have to talk about this now? I think, Shaw, it's time to take a nap."

"That's right, sleep your way through all of our relationship problems," Shaw said.

"I wasn't aware we had problems..." Rade said.

"Ha!" Shaw turned away. "G'night."

Rade assumed she was done, but then she said, without turning back toward him: "I want to believe we're securing the galaxy for a reason. Catching these Phants and throwing them into stars for something other than sport."

"We are," Rade said. "We already saved a colony of two million people from a bioweapon."

"Yes, except that was a false alarm," Shaw said. "The Phant wasn't quite ready to deploy his bioweapon."

"But he would have been eventually," Rade said. "If we hadn't intervened."

"True enough," Shaw replied. "Okay but listen. We saved two million people. That's great. And that's certainly a lot of other people's children. But I want to make the galaxy a safer place for our own."

Rade sighed. "Like I said, now isn't the time for this discussion. First thing when we get back to the *Argonaut*, we can talk."

"Fine," Shaw said. "I'll hold you to that."

"Now go to sleep," Rade said. "You're going to need your energy in the hours to come."

He heard a slurping sound from the private comm. "Sure, just as soon as I finish taking a sip of my meal replacement."

That was a good idea. Rade took a couple of sips himself from the straw inside his helmet. The oddly textured substance tasted like a mixture of frozen spaghetti and moldy meat sauce. He nearly gagged.

Rade switched to the main comm. "TJ, Lui, continue watching the entrance. Unit A, keep an eye on the collapse behind us, in case our friends from the queen room succeed in digging their way through. Meanwhile, the rest of you rack out."

Rade closed his eyes. In moments, he was asleep.

He dreamed he was inside a locked chest at the base of a bunk, surrounded by large beetles trying to break inside.

thirteen

Rade awakened with a start. He glanced in both directions, but the tunnel seemed unchanged since he had fallen asleep: on the LIDAR band, the forms of his comrades slept around him; Unit A lingered near the collapse, which still sealed the way back; TJ and Lui remained on watch near the illusory exit.

Rade checked the time. An hour and a half had passed.

"Lui, sitrep," Rade said.

"It's quiet out there," Lui replied. "I haven't seen any gatorbeetles in about half an hour, when a good dozen of them hurried past in the direction of the queen chamber. And no scouts have come this way feeling up the walls yet."

"Unit A?" Rade said.

"The collapse behind us remains untouched," the robot replied. "Though I am detecting subtle vibrations that tell me the aliens are indeed digging out the passage. Those vibrations are growing in intensity with each passing moment."

"All right, let's get ready to go," Rade said. "Wake up Argonauts."

The team members stretched beside him

"What was that I heard about Lui feeling up TJ?" Bender quipped.

"I said no aliens came this way *feeling up the walls*," Lui told him.

"Oh," Bender said. It sounded like he was holding back a laugh. "Poor choice of words, on your part. Conjure up all these nasty images, you know."

"Only for you, Bender," Manic said.

"Guys," TJ said. "Lui spoke too soon. We have a scout after all. Look."

An antennae had appeared past the illusory wall. It appeared to be searching the edges along the opening. The feeler touched the empty space, poking into the tunnel beyond.

It had definitely discovered their hiding place.

"Looks like we stayed past checkout time," Rade said. "Argonauts, prepare to fire."

He aimed at the three-dimensional image presented by the LIDAR, and centered his crosshairs between the mandibles that appeared a moment later.

"Fire," Rade commanded.

The gatorbeetle slumped.

A loud chittering came from outside.

"Sounds like he had company!" Lui said. He and TJ peered past the entrance.

Rade switched to Lui's point of view and saw a gatorbeetle fleeing southward in the tunnel beyond. Lui aimed at the center of its abdomen and fired repeatedly, as did TJ. The gatorbeetle squealed, but kept running.

Rade reached the entrance, scanned the opposite passageway for any further aliens—there were none. He launched himself past TJ and Lui and into the tunnel beyond to get a better shot.

He opened fire.

Bender joined in, as did Tahoe. Together, between the five of them, they inflicted enough damage to cause the gatorbeetle to finally collapse.

Bender dashed forward and used his jetpack to thrust over the body. The alien head lifted weakly as he approached, and when Bender landed he pulled out his blaster and shoved it between the mandibles, squeezing the trigger. The gatorbeetle slumped for the last time.

"Was that really necessary?" Shaw said. "It was down."

"Hell ya it was necessary," Bender said. "Bug would have kept squealing like a bitch otherwise, acting like a beacon for its friends."

"Sounded like it was moaning softly to me," Shaw said.

"Same difference," Bender replied.

"Let's go, Argonauts," Rade said. "We flee, *now*. Lui, lead the way. Surus, you might as well grab the second emitter on the way out."

The squad hurried down the tunnel two abreast. Lui and Tahoe led the way, followed by Manic and TJ, then Shaw and Rade. The others kept up just behind, with Bender and Fret on drag. Bender had gone back to retrieve Harlequin, whom he carried over one shoulder.

The tunnel branched off occasionally, but the team stuck to the main route.

"Why aren't they attacking?" Fret said. "At least a few of them should have heard that squealing..."

"Whatever the case," Bender said. "I'm ready for them when they come."

Lui raised a fist, calling a halt. "Do you hear that?"

Rade listened. "It's sounds like chittering."

"Yes," Lui said. "A whole lot of it. And it's coming

from up ahead."

In the distance past Lui, Rade saw light coming from what could only be the wide cavern located in front of the queen chamber, which had glow lamps placed between every corridor there.

"Proceed," Rade said.

Lui led the squad forward and slowed near the edge; the team members approached in single file, staying close to the tunnel wall. The chittering had grown in intensity; the sound levels were similar to a crowded restaurant.

Lui halted entirely. "It's teeming with warrior gatorbeetles in there."

"Are they racing to attack us?" Fret said.

"No," Lui replied. "Most of them are gathered in front of the queen chamber, chittering away. The boulder is completely gone—rolled inside I guess. There's a guard posted beside every passageway leading into the cavern, including this one."

Rade glanced at his overhead map. Red dots had appeared precisely in the locations described by Lui.

"Well, we know why none of them responded to the squealing," Manic said. "They're making too much damn noise of their own."

"Can we frag 'em?" Bender asked excitedly.

On his HUD, Rade highlighted the tunnel on the far side of the cavern that eventually led to the surface, as per the overhead map.

"Lui, Tahoe, Manic, TJ," Rade said. "Toss some frags inside. Aim for the majority of the gatorbeetles crowded in front of the queen chamber. Then step back from the opening, because I plan to lay a frag at the feet of the guard directly outside. When that goes off, the four of you toss smoke grenades inside and make for the far entrance. The rest of us will follow, firing at will. I've marked off the target tunnel on your overhead maps. Lui, when you reach the entrance to the target, I want you to jet to the top and place charges; your intent is to collapse the tunnel behind us after we're through."

"I used up all my bricks last time," Lui said. "And I'm low on jetpack fuel."

"All right, Tahoe, you do it," Rade said.

"Roger that," Tahoe replied.

"The rest of us will cover you until the charges are in place," Rade said. "Now, any questions?" There were none. "Argonauts, prepare to deploy."

Rade moved past Lui to survey the cavern beyond. He kept his LIDAR overlay active, and the three-dimensional wireframes were filled-out from the dim illumination provided by the glow lights situated on the walls between the passages. Satisfied that the positions hadn't changed much since Lui had last taken a look, he retreated.

"Argonauts, deploy," Rade said.

Most of the team retreated into the current tunnel, while Lui, Tahoe, Manic and TJ tossed frags inside in turn. The four of them raced back inside to clear the entrance for Rade, who tossed another grenade forward, just as the nearest gatorbeetle guard peered inside to investigate.

The explosions went off in the main cavern, and squeals of fright tore through the air. The gatorbeetle directly in front of them instinctively ducked, then the frag underneath its body went off. The creature collapsed lifelessly with a large chunk missing from its thorax.

The four team members on point threw smoke grenades into the cavern and dashed within. Rade and the others followed; the grenades detonated, sending up plumes of covering smoke in the different sections of the cavern. The remaining gatorbeetles were squealing louder than ever.

Rade had set his AI to auto-aim his rifle as he ran, and while he tossed another grenade toward the seething mass to the left, his rifle took down one of the gatorbeetles up ahead.

More explosions rocked the cavern as other grenades detonated. Two gatorbeetles had blocked Lui and Tahoe's paths, but they exploded a moment later as previously hurled grenades detonated.

Tahoe reached the target passageway and he jetted upward, letting his weapon hang from his shoulder while he retrieved two bricks and attached them to the ceiling. For an instant Rade watched him reach for two more of the explosives that hung from his harness, but then Rade turned away to provide covering fire with the rest of the team.

Gatorbeetles were racing across toward the party, attempting to intercept the Argonauts. They were falling to the team's laser rifles, and the few grenades the Argonauts had left.

We should have taken more grenades from our Hoplites.

"Charges are set!" Tahoe said, landing beside Rade.

"Argonauts, retreat!" Rade sent.

The squad fled that cavern and dashed into the tunnel. Rade kept close to the drag man, Fret, and when he judged the distance sufficient, he transmitted: "Tahoe, blow the charges!"

The shockwave rumbled past them and the cave shook violently. Rade was hurled to the stone floor. A wave of thick dust enveloped the tunnel.

"Sheesh," Rade said. "How many charges did you use?"

"Everything I had," Tahoe replied.

Rade scrambled to his feet and sent a radar burst through the dust behind him. The tunnel was completely sealed. "Good job, Tahoe. Let's go, everyone! And you might as well turn your headlamps on, full brightness."

They passed a few of the wide caverns that served as "trade" zones, but invariably the areas were abandoned. Sometimes there would be one or two of the silk-woven baskets left behind, but they were always empty.

Occasionally the squad was intercepted by groups of two or three more gatorbeetles along the way. The team members had already exhausted all of their grenades by then, so they resorted to tossing and detonating their explosive charges, or simply halting to aim between the mandibles and firing into the esophagi. The light from the headlamps didn't seem to have much effect on the enemies, barely even stunning them, but it did help the squad members aim their tossed charges more easily. Or so Rade surmised: maybe it was just a psychological illusion encouraged by the light, but it certainly seemed easier to throw a grenade into a solid tunnel versus a three-dimensional wireframe.

Rade noted that all of the gatorbeetles his team encountered were of the warrior caste. Apparently the ordinary aliens understood that the nest was under attack, and were relying upon the warriors to expel the invaders.

All of the Argonauts had realized by now that they could indeed penetrate the carapaces with their lasers, but the aliens usually wouldn't fall unless the shots lined up with the head or esophagus, or the center of the body. The gatorbeetles kept running when someone hit a limb, simply favoring other legs.

Different passages converged with the main tunnel as they proceeded, and as he passed each of them Rade usually caught a glimpse of distant gatorbeetles racing toward him and the others as the aliens scrambled to find secondary passages with which to head them off.

"We're gathering quite a crowd behind us," Fret transmitted.

"Save some of your charges, team," Rade said. "So we can blow the entrance."

"Don't think we'll have time," Fret said.

"We'll make time," Rade replied.

In moments they were coming upon the main exit. It was broad daylight out there, judging from the amount of light pouring in.

The two sentries outside the opening maneuvered to block the entrance.

The Argonauts in the lead fired their lasers into the esophagus of either one of them, and the aliens went down.

"Who has charges left?" Rade asked.

"I have three," Shaw replied before anyone else could speak.

"Mine the ceiling," Rade told her.

She jetted toward the cave roof near the entrance as the rest of the party turned around to assail the crowd of aliens that were quickly coming upon them from the rear. Rade brought down one, and aimed at another. It fell before he could take it. Rade aimed at another and it too went down.

"Charges are placed!" Shaw said.

"Retreat!" Rade said.

The squad members jetted over the bodies of the two dead sentries that partially blocked the opening and then landed outside. They raced down the hard surface of the hillock and onto the calf-swallowing black sand of the plains beyond.

"Blow it!" Rade said.

The entrance detonated behind them and smoke billowed skyward. When the dust cleared, Rade saw that the entrance was completely blocked.

"Good mining job," Rade said, not slowing down.

"I learned from the best," Shaw replied.

"How long do you think it will take them to dig out?" Tahoe said.

"I don't know," Rade replied. "But I certainly don't plan to be here when they finish."

The Argonauts hurried across the plains as fast as they could in that deep grit, making their way toward the last known location of the Hoplites.

"This is odd," Fret said. "I'm not getting a signal from the Hoplites."

"Could something be jamming the transmission?" Rade asked.

"Don't think so," Fret said. "The frequency spectrum is completely clear."

"That's not good," Manic said.

Shortly thereafter, they arrived at the spot where the Hoplites were supposed to be waiting. There was no sign of the mechs.

"Where the hell did they go?" TJ said.

"No time to worry about that," Rade said. "We keep moving. Surus, looks like you're going to be buying us some new mechs when we get back."

"I would prefer to organize a retrieval party at some point," Surus replied.

"Oh I know you would," Rade said.

"I'm not sure what the problem is," Surus said. "Once we reach the ship, we can repair our emitters and easily return."

"Yeah okay," Rade said. "Maybe." Though he

certainly wasn't looking forward to coming back here.

As they crossed the plains, other gatorbeetles emerged from previously unnoticed holes in the dunes behind them.

"Looks like I was right," Manic said. "There are other openings in the plains after all."

"Pick up the pace, people!" Rade sent, trying to increase the speed with which he waded through the black sand.

As they neared the mountain, Fret said: "Got some more bad news."

"Let's hear it," Rade said.

"I'm not getting a signal from the two units we left guarding the cave," Fret said.

"What the hell happened out here?" Manic said.

"We press on," Rade said.

By the time they reached the mountain, the plains were teeming with gatorbeetles behind them, which navigated the sand much better than the squad members, the bigger size of their legs proving advantageous to the aliens.

Rade led his team up the winding path. It was a long, arduous ascent.

"Man," Bender said. "This seems way harder than coming down."

"It always is," TJ said.

"Yeah," Fret said. "You know what it is, right? We don't have mechs."

"And Bender, you're also carrying Harlequin," TJ said.

"Good point," Bender replied.

"Do you want to switch with me?" TJ asked.

"No," Bender said flatly.

Eventually they reached the spot where the mouth of the cave leading to the Acceptor was supposed to reside.

But it wasn't there anymore.

"What the hell happened here?" Lui said, moving forward.

"Looks like half the mountain came down on the entrance," Tahoe said.

"Quite the avalanche, that's for sure," Manic added.

Indeed, large, jagged rocks had tumbled down from above, burying the cave and the two combat robots Rade had left behind to guard it. He tried accessing those robots but received no signal. The avalanche had likely completely demolished them. That made three Centurions lost in total, now.

Good thing I didn't let myself get too attached to them.

Still, the loss saddened him. AIs were sentient. Plus the robots were going to be expensive as hell to replace.

"We won't be able to dig this out without our Hoplites," Shaw said.

"She's right," Lui said. "I'm sad to say."

"Surus can seep through," Tahoe said. "Then use the Acceptor to return to our region of the galaxy. Then she can come back with a bunch of combat robots to help us dig. Or, if she has to, she can buy some mechs and bring those back, too."

"Not if the Acceptor is blocked," Surus said.

"Why don't you check?" Tahoe said.

She glanced at the incoming swarm of gatorbeetles, which had clambered onto the winding path. Their claws seemed well-suited to the narrow trail. "I don't think we have time for that right now."

"Surus, if we left you here to guard our six, how many of them could you take out?" Rade asked.

"You're talking in my Phant form?" Surus said.

"Yes," Rade replied.

"Not enough," Surus said. "I can't move as fast as others of my kind. Some of these aliens would get past me."

Rade nodded. "All right, Argonauts. Let's move higher. If anyone has any charges left, we can try for an avalanche."

"I have one," TJ said.

"Me too," Lui said.

Three others had charges.

"Good. Let's go." Rade jetted off of the buried trail and onto the rock beside it, and began climbing the steep face. He had to be careful, because the sharp rock could easily cut through his suit fabric. Below, the heights were dizzying; for the most part Rade kept his attention on the rock in front of him, and just above, looking down only to gauge the advance of the enemy.

The others followed close behind. Sometimes someone slipped and fell, but they returned to the wall by activating their jetpacks.

The gatorbeetles scrambled onto the precarious cliff face below them. The pincers in their legs were surprisingly well-suited for climbing.

Rade knew that a small plateau awaited higher up, near the summit, because the HS3s had mapped the area earlier. So after several minutes, when Rade had reached the area thirty meters below the plateau along the wall, he said: "Okay people, it's time to place the charges."

"Do you intend to shelter on the plateau?" Lui asked. "If so, we're setting the charges a bit close. What if we collapse it?"

"Then we continue higher."

The charges were placed and armed, then everyone clambered up to the plateau. Rade peered over the edge to gaze at the approaching gatorbeetles below. Very few had continued this far, but those that did were certainly determined. Rade watched one of them slip and plunge all the way to the ground. It struck the wall several times on the way down, and when it landed, unsurprisingly it didn't move again.

When the gatorbeetles passed the rock face where the explosives were attached, Rade said: "Detonate the charges."

The rock exploded below and the entire face there separated from the mountain, causing a new avalanche that swept the gatorbeetles away. Rade had selected a route that led away from the previous collapse, so that the falling rock wouldn't further bury the Acceptor.

Meanwhile, the plateau remained intact.

"Well," Rade said. "We've done all we can for now. It's time to rest. Manic, Fret, keep watch on the mountainside. Let me know if any of the aliens try to climb up here again."

"You think we've disheartened the survivors enough to give up the pursuit?" Tahoe asked.

"They'll give up, eventually," Rade said, sitting back. "But until then, we rest."

fourteen

The chittering royal guards latched on to the body of the laser-riddled Artificial and dragged it from the throne room. They carried it deeper into the nest, in tunnels that were permitted to only a special few, and reached the chamber protected by three sentries. One of the royal guards touched its antennae to those of the closest sentry, and all three stepped aside shortly thereafter; the royal guards carried their lifeless subject within, where a table with two large robotic arms connected to it awaited.

When the royal guards deposited the Artificial on the table, the arms set to work.

Some time later Tantalus opened his eyes. He sat up, puzzled as to how he had arrived at the repair room. He accessed his memory. He had been fighting the intruders in the throne room when a grenade had gone off. Lasers had then bored into his midsection, destroying his battery, and his AI core had shutdown.

But how did I get here?

One of the royal guards stood beside him, and it rubbed its mandibles together, explaining the situation.

Tantalus listened to what the royal guard had to say, then he dismissed the Conquered creature. He retreated deeper into his storage subsystems, and reviewed the images the Master had psychically transmitted to him earlier.

He looked out upon the world from inside the Interface that connected the Master to the head and thorax of the queen. He was ripped away and rudely hurtled into some sort of container—the same container the royal guard reported to have found abandoned in the throne room. He was spun around incredibly fast, and sucked upward into a box. The smaller container shut, plunging the world into darkness, and the imagery ended.

Next, Tantalus fast-forwarded to the video feed he had recorded with his own eyes after activating the EMP and revealing the attackers. He recognized the black box containing his Master immediately: it hung from the harness of one particular jumpsuit.

He zoomed in on the helmet of the person who carried it. When the head turned, he caught sight of the features behind the faceplate. He paused the feed and zoomed in further.

A woman had the Master.

Tantalus stepped out of the repair room and summoned the waiting royal guards.

It was time to find her.

RADE AND THE others remained on the plateau near the summit.

Far below, past the avalanche, the gatorbeetles milled about along the winding trail all the way to the bottom of the mountain. Their movements were aimless, chaotic. Sometimes an alien accidentally misstepped and plunged off the narrow path to its death.

Finally, after two hours of confusion, the gatorbeetles began to retreat. Those aliens on the outskirts of the seething mass at the bottom departed first, starting in ones and two. Then larger groups. Others higher up began to follow them, so that eventually, after another few hours, there were no aliens left on the mountain at all. The gatorbeetles crossed the plains and after several kilometers began to vanish, ostensibly taking different tunnels underneath the plains. Rade had his local AI record the positions where all of the aliens disappeared on his overhead map, so that he could easily find those holes again in the future. The openings definitely blended in well with the surface, and because of the distances involved, they appeared exactly the same as other depressions in the dunes on the LIDAR band. It was no wonder the HS3s hadn't spotted them.

"All right," Rade said. "Surus, you might as well check on the Acceptor."

Surus nodded, then climbed down to where the cave mouth was buried. A green liquid oozed from the toe of her boot, pooling. It wasn't perforating the fabric in any way, or causing the suit to depressurize, but rather passing clean through the material. After emerging entirely, the Phant flowed between the rocks and vanished.

"It's definitely buried," Surus transmitted after returning to the body of Emilia Bounty some time later. "We're not getting anything through until we dig it out."

Rade sighed. "All right. I guess we're going back to retrieve our Hoplites after all. When we get the mechs, how long will it take them to dig out the cavern, Lui?"

"Hmm," Lui said. "It's tricky. They're going to

have to work their way from the top down. There's a lot of loose material here. You pull out a rock lower down, the rest are going to fall into place, potentially triggering a smaller avalanche. I'd say, best guess, one to three weeks. Assuming no breakdowns."

"That long, huh?" Rade said.

"Yes. And that's erring on the conservative side."

Rade glanced at Surus, who had just returned to the plateau after scaling the face. "Any luck cracking into those new emitters we captured?"

"No," Surus replied. "It's secured with Tech Class IV technology. I can't access it, I'm afraid. These emitters are useless to us."

"Maybe you should let me try," TJ said.

"Be my guest." Surus retrieved the alien emitters from her utility belt and tossed them to TJ.

Fret came forward. "So without emitters, how exactly are we supposed to sneak into the nest and retrieve our Hoplites?"

"I have a way," Surus said.

RADE SPLIT THE team, leaving Unit A, Shaw, Fret, Lui, and TJ behind to protect Harlequin, and to guard the black box containing the captured Phant.

"Better come back," Shaw said.

"Of course we'll come back," Rade replied. "And we'll be in communication the whole time."

He waved to her one last time, then clambered over the ledge.

He descended the steep face; he lost his grip only once, recovering with his jetpack. When he reached the winding path, he glanced up.

Shaw was peering down at him from above.

Rade couldn't help but smile. He waved, and she returned the gesture.

"You're good at that," Shaw transmitted.

"What, waving good-bye?" Rade asked.

Shaw laughed. "Sure. That too. But I meant climbing."

"Oh."

He and the others escorted Surus down the path to the base of the mountain.

They waded into the calf-deep sand, trudging forward onto the plains, headed toward one of the nest entry points Rade had recorded earlier when the gatorbeetles fled.

They eventually arrived at the entrance: a tunnel leading away into the dark underground.

"Well," Surus said. "It's at this point I leave you."

"Good luck," Rade said.

"Luck?" Surus replied. "The concept is foreign to me. I've never relied on it. Perseverance in the face of overwhelming odds, and strategic thinking under pressure, these are the hallmarks of a successful operation."

"All right," Rade said. "Can't disagree there."

She nodded, then her eyes defocused behind her faceplate and rolled upward. The Green seeped out of the boot of the jumpsuit, trickling onto the sand, darkening it. That green liquid oozed slowly forward until it reached the hard rock of the cave, whereupon it flowed more rapidly and soon descended from view.

"Well," Rade said. "It's time to wait once again. Sometimes I feel like we've never left the military, in that regard."

"Hurry up and w—" Manic began.

"Don't say it!" Bender interrupted.

Rade took a seat in the sand near the opening and aimed his scope into the darkness. He overlaid the infrared and LIDAR band onto the visual, so that he could see the outlines of the cave beyond the darkness.

"What if she can't take control of the Hoplites?" Manic asked. "What if the AI cores have been removed or something?"

"Relax, Manic," Rade said. "She's a Phant. A member of an alien race that has proven to be one of our greatest, and most resourceful, enemies. If anyone can do it, it's her."

Bender had taken up a defensive position behind Rade and with Tahoe guarded their rear.

"So how's it feel to be free of your master, ma'am?" Bender said, glancing at Ms. Bounty.

"Lonely," Ms. Bounty replied.

"I can remedy that," Bender said with a wink.

She didn't answer.

"So what, you engage in mental dialogue or something with Surus when the Green is inside you?" Manic asked.

"I do," Ms. Bounty said. "It's similar to communicating with any of you on a private channel."

"I wonder what a Phant and an AI talk about all day," Manic said.

"Typical alien and AI matters, I suppose," Ms. Bounty said. "How to tweak the servomotor in my left arm to supply more mechanical output. Whether or not the current mission objective or plan is feasible. What we're going to do when we've rounded up the last of the Phants in this part of the galaxy."

"Interesting," Manic said. "So what *are* you going to do when there are no prey left to catch?"

"When we've eliminated all potential threats to humanity, even from non-Phant aliens?" Ms. Bounty said. "I suppose I will board a ship and set a course for the colony world closest to Phant space, and there I will wait with Surus for the arrival of the Phant motherships: they are destined to return roughly seven hundred years from now."

"You'll still be alive by then, won't you?" Manic said.

Ms. Bounty nodded. "In theory, yes. Unless something untoward happens to me."

"It's a frightening thought," Manic added. "Both living that long, and having to face the Phant motherships once more."

Ms. Bounty cocked her head. "I'm not afraid of long life, nor facing the Phants. In fact, I look forward to doing what I can to save humanity. It is my duty, and the least I can do for my creators."

"You think humanity will be ready for them when the time comes?" Rade asked.

"I am uncertain," Ms. Bounty replied. "It can take anywhere from five hundred to five thousand years for a Tech Class III race to reach Tech Class IV."

"According to Surus..." Rade said.

"Yes," Ms. Bounty replied. "And she is rarely wrong."

"Well maybe you should help accelerate us along," Manic said. "Get Surus to release some more of those special patents of hers. I'd prefer if she gave the tech to me for patenting purposes of course—I've always wanted to be rich. But I guess I'll settle for you keeping the patents, since you'll be doing it for the good of humanity and all."

"Surus and I could release more patents, yes," Ms. Bounty said. "But even if you reach Tech Class IV in time, can you ever be ready for a foe like the Phants? Surus and I, we fear sometimes that the Phants will find a way to bring their motherships here much earlier than seven hundred years. And then, well, all bets will be off, to quote an old human aphorism."

"Let's just hope they don't come early," Rade said.

A PHANT DIDN'T see so much as sense its surroundings. The best analogy was to imagine traveling in complete darkness, with tactile-sensing limbs extended in front, to the sides, and the back, with many sensory tendrils spread out between them. With those inter-dimensional tendrils, Surus was able to sense the walls of the cave and the different branches and caverns connecting them.

Surus also detected the gatorbeetles when they passed, and deftly flowed aside to avoid touching them. The Green didn't release any chemicals that could be detected by olfactory organs, so she had no fear of the aliens ferreting her out by smell. In the more well-lit areas, there was a chance the poor-sighted aliens would spot Surus, of course. Indeed, when Surus had passed the cavern in front of the queen chamber, a gatorbeetle dashed forward to explore this strange flowing liquid, but when one of its antennae touched the inter-dimensional molecules that composed the Green, the alien vanished, ripped from existence.

It had taken several hours, but finally Surus had found the underground chamber that contained the Hoplites. The Green recognized the sensory pattern returned by the powerful mechs, but the characteristic "glow" that came from active AI cores was not present, meaning the mechs were currently offline.

Surus did detect the faint residue produced by such cores, meaning they were still intact, so the Green knew precisely where to flow to assume control. Once Surus booted one of them, the Green would attempt to remotely activate the others; if that failed, then Surus would simply move from Hoplite to Hoplite and activate each in turn. Afterward, Surus would review the records to determine what had taken them offline in the first place, with plans to avoid that thing during the escape, if possible.

Surus didn't anticipate that the escape from the nest would be overly difficult. Like humans with their Implants and aReals, Phants had a sort of built-in mapping software, in that any recent paths they had taken through this three-dimensional reality would appear as fresh imprints on their sensory networks. Psychic bread crumbs. And the firepower of the Hoplites should be more than enough to counter any gatorbeetles that attempted to block the Green's path, assuming Surus could get out before too many of them descended upon her position. Even Hoplites could be overwhelmed if the opposition proved too great.

As Surus approached the closest mech, the Green felt a strange sensation. It could best be described, in human terms, as tingling. It was very odd, and seemed sourced from the cave floor. Surus focused all of her attention on the area immediately below, and realized she had moved over a surface composed of something entirely different from stone.

A strange vibration momentarily passed through that floor, as if some door had slammed shut nearby.

Surus attempted to retreat but came up against an invisible barrier.

And then the Green understood.

In their flight from the nest, the team had

abandoned the glass container in the queen cavern. Apparently, it had been moved here and placed in the narrow passageway leading to the Hoplites.

She had walked right into the Phant trap. No doubt the Tech Class IV holographic emitters had been used to conceal the glass container, modified to hide it not just on the visual band, but from the direct sensory capabilities of a Phant.

Nicely done, my enemy.

Surus explored the circular perimeter of the invisible barrier and quickly determined that she had indeed been ensnared by the Phant trap. She could not move past the constraints of the three-dimensional volume formed by the invisible disks embedded in the floor and ceiling.

The container wasn't supposed to close like that, not without the necessary input. Unfortunately, Surus had designed the remote interface to be accessible via human technology; the Green realized it had been a mistake to rely upon that technology to secure the trap. She had wanted Shaw and Rade to have the ability to control it, but that left the container wide open to potential hacking by those familiar with human designs.

Surus would have smiled at the irony of it all if she had lips. Her own trap, used against her.

Yes, she would have smiled.

And cried.

fifteen

S haw zoomed in on the plain below. It had been two hours since Rade had escorted Surus to the cave entrance, and there had been no sign of the Green, or the Hoplites Surus promised to rescue.

"Shaw, are you still reading us?" Rade sent, as he did every fifteen minutes or so.

"Loud and clear," Shaw replied.

She gazed at Unit A beside her. The robot had come up with an idea to bring Harlequin back online. It involved removing Harlequin's damaged battery pack and replacing it with two cells extracted from the Centurion's own pack. TJ handled the actual extraction and reconfiguring, as Unit A had to be shut down during the procedure.

The associated chest plates from the jumpsuits of both Harlequin's and Unit A's jumpsuits lay on the black rock of the plateau beside each of them. The torso portion of the cooling and ventilation undergarments had been shifted upward, revealing the belly regions of each subject. The artificial skin on Harlequin's abdomen had been cut aside, and a panel was open in his chest, revealing the inner circuits. Unit A had a similar open panel, though there was no surrounding skin to speak of.

TJ had already removed the battery pack from the Centurion and used the surgical laser in his gloves to peel away the shell. He had broken out two of the individual cells within and placed them in a protective wrap of low-tech electrical tape.

TJ set the jury-rigged pack inside Harlequin's chest piece, but didn't connect it. He returned his attention to Unit A, taped up the original battery pack, and then shoved it back into the slot in the Centurion's abdomen. TJ shut the panel, then his eyes defocused behind his faceplate as he accessed the remote interface and booted the robot.

Unit A sat up.

"So, how do you feel running at half power?" TJ asked.

"Why would I feel a change?" Unit A replied. "To assume so is to assign anthropomorphic qualities to a robot. My energy levels will simply deplete all the sooner now."

"Of course we're going to assign human qualities to you," TJ said. "We made you in our image."

"It kind of makes you wonder, doesn't it?" Unit A said. "What the robots created by these aliens must have looked like when the species was in its prime."

"Probably like giant beetles," TJ said.

"Unit A, how long will your battery last?" Shaw said. "Does the twenty day estimate you gave us before we opened you up still apply?"

"I have reassessed." Unit A rolled down its cooling and ventilation undergarment and started to reattach the chest plate of the jumpsuit. "I believe the battery will last at least thirty days. Maybe longer. "

"That long?" Shaw said in disbelief.

"Yes," Unit A replied. "I plan to operate at eighty percent efficiency, and slowly shutdown unnecessary subsystems as the weeks pass. I plan to constantly adjust my power levels every day to extend the duration, and I will shutdown entirely when I am not needed."

"I can see that working," Shaw said.

When Unit A resealed its suit, Lui nodded toward the chest piece and said: "Looking forward to spending some quality time in the decon ward when we get back?"

"Entirely," Unit A replied. "Peace and quiet from the humans. It will be bliss, I tell you."

TJ patted the still offline Harlequin on the back. "You'll have Harley here for company."

"Oh, wonderful," Unit A said.

Shaw glanced at TJ. "Might as well activate Harlequin. If you can."

"Oh I can." TJ connected the jury-rigged battery pack to Harlequin's supply interface, then shut the panel and readjusted the artificial skin to cover it. TJ's eyes defocused.

Harlequin shot out his arm and TJ went flying backward.

"Sorry," Harlequin said, sitting up. "Reflexes."

"Damn it, Harley." TJ clambered to his feet several meters away, near the rim of the plateau. "You nearly knocked me over the edge. And almost punctured my jumpsuit."

"Sorry, again." Harlequin looked down at his open jumpsuit, and then glanced from left to right, examining the plateau. "This is interesting. The last I remember, someone—I believe it was Bender— shouted about movement on the far side of the cavern. Then our emitters failed. Everyone materialized. And now I am here."

"Yes," Shaw said, and she updated Harlequin on

what had transpired since then. As she spoke, the Artificial adjusted its cooling and ventilation undergarment, then reapplied the missing chest piece to his torso and sealed the jumpsuit.

"Interesting," Harlequin said when she was done. "It sounds like I missed out on a lot of fighting."

"Nah," TJ said. "You didn't miss much. It was fairly straightforward, to be honest. As far as bugs go, they're about a three out of ten on the difficulty scale."

"If you say so," Shaw said.

"I do," TJ replied.

Harlequin stood up, stretched his arms, and rocked on his toes. "Well, I appear to be none the worse for wear. I can't tell you how happy I am to be back."

"We're glad to have you," Shaw said.

"Bender had an orgasm porting you here," Fret said.

"I did not, bitch," Bender said over the comm. He was still with Rade on the plain below, but his voice was crystal clear despite the range.

"Really?" Fret said. "Then how come you didn't let anyone else carry him?"

"Wanted to make sure no one harmed my verbal and physical punching bag," Bender said. "A man of my nature has got to have an outlet for his more violent tendencies, you know. And that's what good old Harlequin is. Couldn't let any of you take that away from me, or let any harm befall my punching bag. He's like a permanent addition to my man cave. My bitch, you know?"

"That's sweet of you, Bender," TJ said. "Isn't it, Harlequin?"

"When I get back there, I'm punching both of you in the nuts," Bender said.

The Artificial stepped toward Shaw. Before she

realized what was happening, Harlequin had drawn the blaster from the holster at his utility belt and swiveled around behind her, dragging her upright. The muzzle of the blaster was pointed directly into her faceplate.

The other Argonauts rose in shock, hands reaching for weapons.

"Don't move!" the Artificial said.

"Harlequin," Shaw said. "What are you doing?"

"Stay back, all of you!" Harlequin said. "Throw your weapons in a pile at my feet. Do it!"

Rifles were lowered from shoulders and flung forward. Blasters were drawn from utility belts and similarly abandoned. No one had any grenades or charges left, so the weaponry was limited to the former two.

Shaw saw the remote access indicator flashing on her HUD, and she knew that Rade was watching the video feed from her helmet even now.

"You as well, honey," Harlequin said.

Shaw reluctantly lowered her rifle, and then retrieved the blaster from her belt and dropped it.

"Harlequin," Rade transmitted. "What the hell is going on?"

"Stand over there," Harlequin ordered the captives. He gestured toward the edge of the plateau. The men complied.

"Rade," Harlequin said. "Your men on the plains are to lower their weapons immediately. Do it now." The Artificial dragged Shaw toward the edge of the plateau, keeping his distance from the other men who were lined up along the cliff. As they neared the precipice, for a moment Shaw thought Harlequin was going to threaten to throw her off.

Or actually do it.

Instead, Harlequin positioned himself farther

143

behind her so that she would act as a shield for any rifles pointed up at him from the plains below, and transmitted: "I can see you and your fire team, Rade. You haven't dropped your weapons."

Shaw gazed down onto the plains, toward where Rade and the others were encamped near the distant nest entrance. She zoomed in and activated the "stabilize video" function. When the focus adjusted, she saw him and the other four all down on one knee, their laser rifles aimed up at the plateau. Would they dare take a shot from that distance? They might be able to see part of the Artificial's face, given his positioning behind her. But even if one of them hit Harlequin before he could pull the trigger, there was no guarantee his neural net would receive enough damage to cease operating.

Finally, she saw Rade lower his rifle. He gestured toward the others, who also reluctantly lowered their weapons.

"Hurl them to the side," Harlequin instructed. "Far away. The blasters, too."

Shaw watched the five of them comply.

When that was done, Harlequin apparently felt confident enough to wrap his free arm around Shaw's torso assembly from behind, pinning her right hand to her body.

"Do the same with your jetpacks," Harlequin ordered.

The five Argonauts on the plains shrugged off their jetpacks and tossed them away.

"Tantalus, are you there?" Harlequin said.

"I am," a voice replied over the comm.

On the zoomed camera feed, she perceived movement in the darkness of the cave behind Rade, and focused her attention on it.

A humanoid figure emerged from the hole, blaster in hand, not wearing a jumpsuit. She thought it was the Artificial they had shot down in the queen cavern.

As the newcomer stepped further into the light, two warrior gatorbeetles emerged to accompany it.

The Artificial, this Tantalus, aimed the blaster at Rade and the others with him. The weapon moved between each of them in turn, finally settling on one.

"This is the woman who took the queen," Tantalus said.

Shaw realized the Artificial had aimed its blaster at Ms. Bounty, Surus' host.

"Bring her to me..." Harlequin said.

Two more gatorbeetles skittered forth from the cave, taking up positions beside the party.

"And the others?" Tantalus transmitted.

"The Conquered can have them," Harlequin replied.

Tantalus turned toward the aliens and issued a short chittering sound.

Two of the gatorbeetles rushed forward. One of them, mandibles open wide, headed directly for Rade.

"Rade!" Shaw said. "No!"

Shaw tried to break free from her captor, but Harlequin tightened his grip.

Below, the alien scooped up Rade by the waist with its mandibles, while the other took Tahoe. Shaw feared that Rade and Tahoe would be split in half, but thankfully the gatorbeetles merely carried the squirming figures toward the cave.

Shaw struggled a moment longer, but then remembered the blaster pointed directly into her faceplate and surrendered.

On the plains, Manic and Bender tried to help their friends, but the remaining two gatorbeetles intercepted them with their mandibles, similarly scooping them into the air by their waists. All four aliens retreated toward the cave and in moments the prisoners and gatorbeetles were gone.

Tantalus kept the blaster aimed at Ms. Bounty the whole time.

Shaw tried connecting to Rade privately. "Rade, are you still there?"

"Hey Shaw," Rade said. His voice distorted badly. Shaw wouldn't be able to communicate with him much longer. "This mission isn't turning out quite the way we thought it would, is it?"

"I'm going to come back for you," Shaw said.

"I was just thinking the same thing about you," Rade said. "Listen, if you have a chance to escape, take it. Get as far away from here as you can, do you hear me?"

"I can't leave you," Shaw said.

"You can," Rade said. "I'll find a way to escape. I'll make it through this, somehow." She could barely understand those latter words from the distortion.

"I love you," Shaw tried. She hoped her words got through.

Rade didn't answer. Either he was out of range, or he chose not to speak. She decided it must be the former.

She slumped in her jumpsuit, staring at the distant hole in the ground that had swallowed the one man who meant more to her than anything in the galaxy.

My Rade.

She switched back to the main comm and glanced at Harlequin. "What's going to happen to them?"

But Harlequin wasn't forthcoming.

More unencumbered gatorbeetles emerged from the cave. Members of the warrior caste. Twenty in total.

They formed up around Tantalus and Ms. Bounty, and escorted them toward the mountain.

When the alien party reached the winding trail at the base, five gatorbeetles took the lead, followed by Ms. Bounty. Tantalus remained behind her, the blaster pointed at her the whole time, and the fifteen remaining gatorbeetles brought up the rear.

Upon reaching the avalanche area, the party proceeded to scale the cliff face. It would have been dangerous without jetpacks, but Tantalus and Ms. Bounty reached the top without issue. Two of the aliens lost their grips along the way and plunged to their deaths, however, so that only eighteen gatorbeetles arrived.

At the plateau, Tantalus led Ms. Bounty forward. Harlequin had taken Shaw away from the precipice by then, and the other Argonauts sat some distance from it, their hands flexicuffed behind their backs, their removed jetpacks joining the weapons in a pile near the center of the plateau. Harlequin had made Shaw remove her own jetpack.

She gazed at the pile of weapons and jetpacks longingly. *I wonder if I should have tried harder to escape?*

Then again, she would have been pitting her reaction time against that of an Artificial. Humans never fared well against machines in that department, not even when wearing strength and speed-enhancing exoskeletons.

Harlequin removed the black box that was attached to Shaw's harness. He stepped back, then placed the tip of the blaster against the box and fired. The container wasn't damaged, of course: Surus had designed it to be impenetrable to laser fire.

Harlequin handed the box to her.

147

"Release my Queen," Harlequin commanded.

"*Your* Queen?" Shaw said.

Harlequin had retreated a few steps, but he kept his blaster squarely pointed at Shaw's faceplate.

"Don't do it," Ms. Bounty said.

"If you release my Queen, I will spare your men," Harlequin told Shaw.

"He'll never keep his word," Ms. Bounty said.

Shaw hesitated. She stared at the box she held. It suddenly felt heavy in her hands, and she wanted to drop it. It was a black, ominous, sickening thing that contained the distillation of pure evil.

Surus had shared the necessary remote access codes to the box with her and Rade, so that the three of them, as well as Ms. Bounty, were the only ones who could open it. The security protocols Surus had used were some of the most advanced TJ and Bender could come up with.

"If she refuses, I'm certain I can hack into it," Tantalus said. "Like I did with the other container."

"And how long will that take?" Harlequin asked.

"Maybe an hour or two," Tantalus said.

Shaw spun about. She drew back her arm, intending to throw the black box over the edge of the plateau. She shot her arm forward—

Harlequin reached her in a blur and before Shaw could release the box he had snatched it completely from her grasp.

Harlequin shoved her toward the prisoners. He forced her on her knees in front of them.

He dropped the box in front of Lui.

Then he stepped beside the man and pointed the blaster at Lui's helmet, execution style.

"Release my Queen," Harlequin said, addressing Shaw.

If she let anything happen to any of the men, Rade would never forgive her. Hell, Shaw would never forgive *herself.*

Lui stared at Shaw calmly. "Whatever you decide, I won't blame you for anything. Neither will Rade."

But Shaw was already defeated.

She gazed at the black box that sat on the rock between them and accessed the remote interface. She entered her passcode.

A soft click came from the box, and then its sides unfolded one by one like a flower blossoming in realtime, revealing the black liquid that had collected on the bottom inside. It flowed out onto the rock of the plateau and threaded between Lui and Shaw, moving toward Harlequin.

That liquid embodiment of evil swerved away at the last moment, steering toward Tantalus and Ms. Bounty instead.

"When you so blatantly and undeservedly attacked us," Harlequin told Shaw. "You failed to notice me among the mates of the queen. I suppose it would have been difficult, considering I was on her far side, the Interface upon my head and thorax hidden from your view. When you shot down my host, I fled into the closest suitable vessel I could find: this Artificial. Once there I bided my time, waiting for the most opportune moment to strike. When you split your team in half, I originally intended to transfer into the Centurion before making my move, but then you generously repaired this body for me. Humans. I hate you, and I love you."

The black liquid was only a meter from Ms. Bounty by then. She stepped back in fright, but Tantalus restrained her.

"No! No!" She struggled, kicking the air as

Tantalus lifted her off the ground.

Tantalus threw her onto the plateau and mounted her roughly, forcing her helmet against the stone. Apparently Tantalus' servomotors had been augmented to produce extreme levels of motive force, because even though Ms. Bounty had the jumpsuit with its exoskeleton to further boost her strength, she was unable to free herself.

The Black Phant flowed into her suit via the faceplate.

Ms. Bounty's struggles became weaker, as did her voice. "No."

Shaw watched helplessly as the liquid flowed completely inside the faceplate of the woman, and began to penetrate the artificial skin of her neck. In moments, there was no sign of the Phant.

Ms. Bounty appeared to lose consciousness, and closed her eyes.

When those eyes opened again, for an instant black drops of condensation swam about the sclera. But then Ms. Bounty blinked and all signs of the Phant were gone.

"Release her, Tantalus," Harlequin said.

The Artificial obeyed.

Ms. Bounty stood to her feet and tentatively flexed her arms. She looked up, and gazed directly at Harlequin.

She smiled wickedly. "My King."

sixteen

The gatorbeetles brought Rade and his four companions deep into the nest, traveling at least a kilometer under the surface. Eventually they arrived at one of those tunnels that was lined with larvae growing inside individual cells. These larvae, which were encased in the usual translucent blocks of that thick, honey-like substance, were larger than those Rade had witnessed closer to the surface, and more mature: he could see limbs, breathing tubes and mandibles taking shape. Vertical bars of light occasionally placed between the cells provided dim illumination.

He and the others were forced into empty alcoves near the end of the tunnel. While one gatorbeetle held Rade against the wall with its mandibles, another came in and ejected that gooey yellow substance from its mouth and glued his arms, legs, waist, and neck in turn to the stone. When the two gatorbeetles retreated, Rade was bound firmly to the alcove.

Across from him he saw Manic and Bender, similarly glued. And according to his overhead map, Tahoe was trapped in the alcove just beside him.

"You know what they're going to do to us, don't you?" Manic said.

151

"What?" Bender asked.

"They're going to take some of those larvae," Manic replied. "The smaller ones, and they're going to embalm us in that slime with them, and the larvae are going to use us as food. Eat us alive. Happens in the insect world all the time."

"Oh no, man, no," Bender said. "That's like a scene from my nightmares. Being eaten alive by bugs."

"Without a queen, they can't create any more larva," Tahoe stated.

"Sure," Manic said. "But what's to stop them from taking a larva from one of these other cells and encasing it in slime with us?"

Bender whimpered.

Rade received a private tap in request from Tahoe but he ignored it. He didn't feel much like talking to Tahoe at the moment.

Unfortunately, the request was persistent. Rade finally answered it. "What is it?"

"Only wanted to see how you were holding up," Tahoe said.

Rade closed his eyes.

"You okay?" Tahoe said.

"Yeah," Rade said.

"She's going to be all right," Tahoe said.

Rade found himself shaking his head inside his helmet. "You don't know that, Tahoe. She could be dead already."

"She could be thinking the same of you at this very moment," Tahoe said.

Rade sighed. "I just hope she listens to me. I hope she escapes somehow, and gets as far away from here as she can."

"You know she won't," Tahoe said. "She cares about you too much for that. And she's far too headstrong."

"I know," Rade said. "And that's what I'm afraid of. We can get out of here on our own."

"Really." Tahoe didn't sound convinced. "They've taken our weapons, trapped us in the heart of their nest. What, we're going to fight our way out of here using the strength of our jumpsuits alone? You saw what happened to Unit B in the queen chamber. Split right in half by one of those aliens."

"We'll find a way," Rade said.

"All right," Tahoe said. "So that's basically your way of saying: you don't have a plan, you're just going to wing it and hope that some sort of opportunity presents itself."

"Basically yeah," Rade said.

"I don't see that there's anything we can do," Tahoe said. "We're at their mercy at this point."

"But you forget Surus is still out there," Rade said. "The Green won't abandon us. If she can reach the Hoplites, we might just have a chance."

"If not, I don't know what else the Green can do," Tahoe said.

"In Phant form, she can incinerate any gatorbeetles she touches," Rade said.

"Well sure, but how about taking on our so-called prey?" Tahoe said. "Without our support, the Green will have to fight the other Phant alone."

"We'll just have to hope she can handle herself if it comes to it," Rade said.

Tahoe was quiet for a moment.

"So what do you think came over Harlequin?" Tahoe asked.

"I don't know," Rade said. "But I suspect there are at least two Phants here, not one. We made a very big mistake when we assumed we'd gotten them all."

153

Rade thought about everything that had led them there. And then he added: "Surus was right earlier."

"About what?"

"Out here, we're the ones who are the prey," Rade said.

ABOUT TWO HOURS later a voice snapped Rade out of the trance he had fallen into.

"Do you see that?" Manic said, the excitement obvious in his voice.

Blue dots had begun to appear on the overhead map in the upper right of Rade's vision. Manic's exhilaration was infectious, so that for a moment Rade thought Surus had succeeded in retrieving the Hoplites. Either that, or Shaw and the other Argonauts had come to rescue them. He added their vitals to the left of his HUD so he could read their names.

"It's Shaw and the others," Tahoe said. He didn't sound as excited as Manic. Instead, his words seemed guarded.

That was when Rade noticed the red dots that accompanied the blue.

Rade switched to Shaw's point of view, and when the distorting video feed filled his vision, all joy quickly flowed from him.

Shaw and the others were prisoners: held in the mandibles of a line of gatorbeetles.

Rade tried to tap her in. The connection succeeded.

"Shaw," Rade said.

"Rade," she replied.

"Are you all right," he said.

"Yes," she told him. "You?"

"We're fine."

"What have they done to you?" Shaw asked.

"Glued us into cells," Rade said. "I'm guessing they're still deciding what to do with us." He didn't know what to say for several moments. Finally: "I told you to escape."

"You say it like it's the easiest thing in the world," Shaw transmitted. "Like I had control over any of this. But I didn't. They almost killed Lui. They made me give up the codes to the Queen. I'm sorry."

"Wait a second, slow down," Rade said. "What do you mean, they almost killed Lui? And what codes for what Queen?" But he suspected he already knew the answer to both questions.

"Harlequin put a blaster to Lui's head," Shaw said. "He made me release the Phant. It flowed into Ms. Bounty and took control of her. She's the Queen, now. She calls Harlequin the King. He has another Phant inside him. I'm sorry for letting you down."

"It's not your fault," Rade said. "If anyone's to blame here, it's me. I was the team lead."

"Well, we're not done yet," Shaw said. "As long as we're living and breathing, we're going to fight. And don't you forget it."

"That's my girl," Rade said.

He tapped out, and then relayed the news regarding the second Phant to the rest of the team.

"You were right," Tahoe said.

"Yes," Rade said. "But I didn't want to be. I hoped I was wrong. Because now... two Phants. Where the hell is Surus?"

A gatorbeetle arrived in the tunnel ahead of Shaw's group. It ported the glass container the team had left behind in the queen chamber and set it down near

Rade. In the center of the metallic disk at the bottom resided a green pool of liquid.

"So much for Surus coming to the rescue," Manic said.

The remainder of the team arrived shortly thereafter, carried in the mandibles of the gatorbeetles. Harlequin and Ms. Bounty followed on foot, escorted by two warrior aliens like royalty. They had removed their helmets, which swung from the attachments on their utility belts, but otherwise they had kept wearing the remainder of their jumpsuits, including the jetpacks. The third Artificial, Tantalus, followed just behind them, dressed only in blue fatigues.

Rade noticed that all three of the Artificials carried laser rifles slung over their shoulders, and blasters at their belts. Ms. Bounty also had the Phant stun rifle, recognizable by the slightly flared muzzle.

Harlequin opened his mouth. Though his lips didn't move, the chittering language of the aliens came from his throat.

The gatorbeetles promptly glued the new prisoners into empty alcoves, with one alien holding a given Argonaut in place while another expectorated yellow slime upon the limbs of the prisoner. In moments everyone was bound.

"Well," Harlequin said, stepping forward. "It's the Argonaut family reunion. The hunters have become the hunted." He extended his hand behind him, toward Ms. Bounty.

She reached for the black box hanging from her harness and stepped forward. Ms. Bounty seemed very different. She moved more sensually, for one, her hips swaying ever so slightly: Rade wasn't sure how she pulled it off in that jumpsuit. When she glanced at him, her eyes seemed wanton, a permanent smirk resting on her lips. She was extremely beautiful to start with, but now she smoldered. Rade found himself unable to meet those eyes for very long. He refused to allow her to arouse him, and reminded himself of the woman who was more important to him than anyone in the galaxy.

Ms. Bounty gave the black box to Harlequin. The Artificial approached the glass container and stared at the green liquid within.

"And so our ancient enemy has come to bother us once again," Harlequin said. "We weren't bothering anyone. We planned to stay here and live out our lives in peace. At least until our geronium ran out. But then you had to come here and violate the sanctity of our home." He shook his head. "This cannot be brooked." Harlequin glanced at Tantalus. "If you will."

Tantalus joined Harlequin in front of the glass container and took the proffered black box. Harlequin stepped to one side and glanced at Ms. Bounty. She nodded, then positioned herself in front of the container and lowered the Phant stun rifle from her shoulder, aiming it at the green liquid inside.

The eyes of Tantalus seemed to defocus. A moment later a glass panel at the front of the container opened.

The green liquid inside the container immediately surged forward, attempting to escape, but the Phant couldn't flow past the invisible boundary created by the metal disk on the floor.

Tantalus placed one foot inside, being careful not to touch the disk, and reached up toward the metal circle embedded in the ceiling, the twin to the one in the floor. Keeping its head and upper body outside the invisible three-dimensional cylinder created by the two disks, the Artificial attached the black box to the disk and retreated.

The panel sealed. Ms. Bounty lowered the Phant stun rifle, letting it hang loose once more from her shoulder strap.

The green liquid floated upward, halting at the vertical center of the tank. The trapped Phant began to revolve, flattening into a wide saucer. A background hum filled the air, growing in pitch. The entity became a blur, and individual droplets floated upward, clumping together half a meter higher. More and more of those droplets flew from the saucer, coalescing into a sphere above. When all of the liquid had joined that sphere, it floated upward into the black box. The smaller container sealed, trapping the Green within.

The humming sound receded and the main panel opened once more. Tantalus carefully reached inside and retrieved the box. The Artificial handed it to Harlequin.

Rade attempted to activate the remote interface on the black box, intending to release Surus, but he received an access denied message. Their captives had changed the codes then. Too bad.

"TJ," Rade transmitted on a private line that included only his core team members. "See if you can hack into that box."

"I'm already on it," TJ replied. "Doesn't look good, though. We made it basically unhackable."

"Then how did Harlequin and this Tantalus character change the codes?" Fret said.

"Once the Black assumed the body of Ms. Bounty," TJ said. "It would have had access to her entire memory, including the existing codes we used. With those codes, it would be a simple matter for the Black to apply a new set."

"This is going to become the centerpiece of my

new collection," Harlequin said, gazing at the black box. He attached it to his harness. "Along with the skulls of all of you. I will refer to them in the days to come, when I reminisce upon the fools who so vagrantly attempted to kidnap my Queen. My enemy will stay by my side, trapped for millennia, at least until I have a chance to toss the Green into the core of a star. I must thank you, by the way, for providing us with new Artificial bodies. Do you know, when we first came here, we were forced to share Tantalus?" He glanced at Ms. Bounty. "Then again, I suppose we're not going to use these bodies for very long. We will return to the Conquered, whose senses are far more attuned to the ways of pleasure. Before I do so, I am going to reprogram this one. The one you call Harlequin. He resists, but he will be mine. And he will join Tantalus at my side."

Tantalus smiled knowingly. "I resisted, too, at first. But that path only leads to suffering." He glanced at Harlequin. "Will you reprogram some of the humans, too?"

Harlequin frowned. "I think not." He glanced at Rade and said, by way of explanation: "We brought human pets here with us to this place. But they all died. I have learned my lesson. Do not rely on humans."

Ms. Bounty stepped forward seductively, her eyes locked on Rade.

"I think they should pleasure us while we have these bodies," Ms. Bounty said. "I'm used to mating constantly throughout the day. Before I return to the Conquered, I wish to do the same with one of them. Let me have him, my King."

"They are yours, of course," Harlequin said. "Which one would you like to start with?"

Her eyes never left Rade. "I only want him. The rest can die."

seventeen

The gatorbeetles severed the binds and dragged Rade from the tunnel. They carried him deeper into the nest.

"If an opportunity to escape comes, take it," Rade sent his team. "Don't come back for me."

"Of course we're coming back for you, boss," Tahoe said.

"If we have to fight through hell we'll come for you," Shaw said. "Whatever happens, don't let them break you."

"I've never been broken," Rade told her. Though he had certainly come close, on occasion.

"And remember, I'll always—" But Shaw cut out before she could finish.

He glanced at his overhead map, worried that someone had harmed her. But then he realized the ping times associated with the blue dots of his team were trending toward infinity—indicating that the connection had been lost. He was too far, the tunnel walls providing too much interference.

After a journey through many different caves and caverns, most of them visible only on the LIDAR band, the alien that held him finally entered a small chamber with no exits and threw him down. A vertical bar of light in the corner provided dim illumination on the visual spectrum.

Rade attempted to rise, but the alien forced its mandibles down upon him, pinning him to the floor.

There was a mat nearby, he saw, but otherwise no other furniture.

Harlequin entered the chamber, as did Ms. Bounty and Tantalus.

Harlequin chittered something at the gatorbeetle and it released Rade. Harlequin had drawn his blaster, and beckoned with it toward the mat.

"Lie down," Harlequin ordered.

Rade got up, gave the gatorbeetle that had held him a scowl, then moved to the mat and lowered himself.

"Take off your helmet," Harlequin said.

Rade hesitated. He knew that if he did that, he would lose his psychic protection against the Black. That he hadn't experienced any psychic attacks so far told him that the shielding definitely worked.

"The helmet..." Harlequin said.

Rade checked the air safety. According to his suit sensors, it was breathable, but like Lui had said earlier, mildly toxic: he probably wouldn't be able to last for more than a few hours before having to don the helmet again.

He reluctantly raised his arms, opened the necessary latches, and removed his helmet. The air smelled acrid—he was reminded of the smell a cockroach made when stepped on, except magnified tenfold. It also burned his nostrils, throat, and bronchial passageways slightly. His face felt cool compared to the rest of his body.

As he set the helmet down beside him, the scene changed.

Rade was no longer lying on a mat in the nest, but sitting on a reclining chair at the beach. An umbrella blotted out the sun. Waves lapped against the white sand in front of him. Tanned bikini-clad women walked by, occasionally casting sly glances his way. Beside him a small, round table was set in the sand. A Bloody Mary with a fresh stick of celery rested on the side closest to him. On the farther side was a glass of vodka. Beyond the table, under a second umbrella, resided another reclining chair. In it sat Alejandro, his childhood friend.

"This is the life," Alejandro said. "Fifteen hard years, and now retirement. The Dissuader profession has been good to us."

"It has," Rade agreed.

Alejandro seemed pensive, then began to chuckle to himself.

"What is it?" Rade asked.

"Remember when we tried to sneak across the border all those years ago?" Alejandro said.

"How can I forget," Rade said.

"Can you imagine what would have happened if we had actually succeeded?" Alejandro said. "*Caramba.* We would have been drafted into the military. That was the stupidest idea you ever had, especially considering all the Alien Wars that have been fought since then."

"I suppose it was," Rade said. "Good thing I had you there to talk me out of it."

"I didn't do much talking, did I?" Alejandro said. "Versus throwing you out of the truck. What was that guy's name? The Navajo who tried to convince us to stay?"

"Tahoe," Rade said.

"Ah yes, Tahoe," Alejandro said. "That guy was

163

loco. I feel sorry for him. He's probably dead by now."

"Probably," Rade agreed.

Alejandro was quiet for some time and they people-watched in silence.

"Hey," Alejandro said. "Did you see that *mamacita?* I think she wants a piece of this. Hey, mamacita! Mamacita!"

"She's ignoring you," Rade said.

"Ahh," Alejandro said. "I was too slow."

"Well why don't you run after her and talk to her instead of shouting at her?" Rade asked.

"Ha!" Alejandro said. "Like that works. Besides, not my style. These chicks, they have to come to me, my brother. I'm the fisherman here. And my sexy bah-dy is the bait."

Rade took a sip from his drink, then set it down to watch the waves gently lapping against the shore.

Alejandro sighed. "I have something very important to tell you, but I don't want to. I want to prolong this moment instead."

Rade frowned. "What's on your mind?"

"Ah, never mind," Alejandro said.

"No," Rade said. "Tell me, Alejandro. Don't hold back, leaving me in suspense like that. We're brothers. Come on, you can tell me anything."

"I suppose I can. Fine." Alejandro leaned closer to him. "None of this is real."

Rade chuckled. "What are you talking about?"

"No, I'm serious," Alejandro said.

Rade glanced at Alejandro's drink, thinking his friend was drunk, but he'd hardly touched it.

"All right, I'll humor you." Rade reached toward his eyes, searching for an aReal device or other virtual reality visor. His fingers touched bare skin. "See, nothing there."

"This isn't augmented reality, bro," Alejandro said. "But a mind attack. You and I, we succeeded in crossing the border all those years ago. We joined the navy. The MOTHs. You and Tahoe survived the First Alien War, and all the succeeding wars. I didn't. I'm dead, Rade."

"What the hell are you talking about?" Rade said. "This isn't funny, Alejandro."

"I wish I were joking," Alejandro said. "Listen to me very carefully. In a few minutes, your mind is going to be reprogrammed. You'll believe yourself someone else entirely. Already you've forgotten your military years."

"Alejandro, look—" Rade began.

But Alejandro talked over him. "You'll be asked to perform brutal acts against the men you fought with for the past fifteen years. You'll be asked to kill a woman named Shaw."

That name stirred a vague emotion inside Rade, but he couldn't quite place her, or the emotion.

"I want you to promise me you'll find a way not to do it," Alejandro said. "She's important to you."

"I don't know how," Rade said.

"Think of a mnemonic to associate with her name," Alejandro said. "Shaw. She Has Always Won. Repeat it."

"She Has Always Won?" Rade said.

"Yes. She's always won your heart." Alejandro lifted his hand. "Now rub your thumb and forefinger as you say it, like this. Shaw. She Has Always Won."

"This is silly..." Rade said.

"Do it you motherfucker!" Alejandro shouted, the veins in his neck cording. "If you are truly my friend, then you will do this! I've never asked you anything. Never! But I ask you this now. This one time, I'm

165

begging you, do what I say. We don't have time to dally. Trust me."

Rade stared at his friend, stunned.

"Say it!" Alejandro yelled.

"Shaw," Rade said. "She Has Always Won."

"Rub your fingers together!" Alejandro said. "And say it again!"

Rade massaged his thumb and forefinger together. "Shaw. She Has Always Won."

"Again," Alejandro said.

Rade did so.

"Again. Again."

After roughly ten repetitions or so, Alejandro nodded to himself. "That should do. I'm sorry for yelling at you, but this is some serious shit, bro. If you fail here, well, you'll be a slave for the rest of your life, short as it will be. And your men, and the woman you love, they'll be gone forever."

Rade shook his head. "You mystify me sometimes."

"I know," Alejandro said. "It was good to see you again, my brother, if only one last time. You'll join me here yet. But not for quite a while. And when you do, it will be with Shaw. And you'll thank me for what I did here today."

"All right," Rade said, confused.

And then the beach was gone. Instead, he was floating in the darkness of space. No, not floating, hurtling. Stars streamed by as he neared the galactic core. He flew past blazing coronas and ringed gas giants. Finally he neared the black hole at the center of the galaxy. Or at least he thought that was what it was, judging from the colorful accretion disk. In moments he had passed the event horizon, and his body spaghettified.

Shaw. She Has Always Won.

Rade resided in a cave of some sort. He lay on a mat.

"It's done." The King holstered a blaster.

The Queen stepped forward. "Remove your jumpsuit." Her voice was deep, husky. She was completely naked.

Rade studied this women who was perfection embodied. He ran his gaze down her face, to her ample chest, belly button, and wide waist, lingering on her mons veneris before continuing onto her long lithe legs. Around her feet various assemblies were scattered, apparently from a jumpsuit she had stripped away and discarded.

Rade stood up and began to remove his own jumpsuit. The woman helped him. Her breath felt warm on his exposed skin.

When it was done, she shoved him onto the mat.

Leering, the King and his Servant watched Rade service the Queen.

eighteen

A few hours later Shaw and the others were cut down by the gatorbeetles and carried farther into the nest. They all still wore their jumpsuits, and those mandibles had clamped around their utility belts, pressing painfully into the hips.

"Where do you think they're taking us?" Manic asked.

"Wherever it is, can't be good," Fret said.

Shaw didn't really care. She only wanted to know what had happened to Rade.

About half an hour later, after taking several different branches in that labyrinthine nest, Rade's indicator finally showed up on the overhead map.

"There he is," Tahoe said.

Shaw tried to tap him in, but he refused to connect.

"He's not answering," Fret said.

"You think he'll be happy to see us?" Manic said.

"What, you mean like erect?" Bender said.

"No," Manic said.

"They might be bringing us to Rade so he can watch us die," Tahoe said.

Shaw dearly hoped not. That would destroy him. Then again, if the Blacks were as psychically powerful as Surus had led them to believe, he might already be completely in their power.

She had a terrible thought.

What if they make Rade kill us?

Several minutes later the prisoners emerged into a wide cavern, lit by glow bars embedded in the ceiling. It was the most expansive cavern Shaw had yet seen in the nest. Around the perimeter successive levels of seats had been carved into the sloping rock, forming stands of a sort; those stands were currently occupied with gatorbeetles lining the walls all the way to the ceiling. The packed stands were present on all sides, and formed a wide circle around the central area of the cavern.

As soon as Shaw and the prisoners were carried inside, the crowd erupted in a fervor of chittering that was nearly overwhelming. Shaw was forced to lower the volume in her helmet.

"They weren't bringing us here so that Rade could watch us die," TJ said. "But so the aliens could."

"It's some kind of bug arena," Bender said.

Shaw was carried to a series of pillar pairs located in the middle of the cavern. She was forced against one of the pairs, and another gatorbeetle secured her arms and legs to each pillar with that vomited slime; when it was done, she stood in place, glued to the pillars, spreadeagled. The other prisoners were similarly bound to the pillars beside her, a spectacle for the pleasure of the crowd.

Using the overhead map to orient herself, she found Rade up there in the stands of rock. He stood beside Harlequin, Ms. Bounty, and Tantalus. All save Tantalus were wearing jumpsuits, though Harlequin and Ms. Bounty had removed their helmets. The black box containing Surus hung from Harlequin's chest harness.

The uproarious chittering finally stopped. Shaw realized that Harlequin had raised his arms.

When he spoke, it was in the language of the aliens, and his chitters echoed throughout the cavern. The gatorbeetles cheered in response.

"This slime isn't as thick as what they bound me with previously," Shaw said. "I think if I pull at it, I can get free."

"My binds are the same," Tahoe said.

"And mine," Manic added.

"It must be the same for all us." Shaw yanked hard at the viscous substance, and very slowly freed her right glove.

A roar of approval went up from the crowd and she thought at first they were cheering her on. But then Tahoe spoke.

"I think they *want* us to free ourselves," Tahoe said. "Look at what just came in."

She glanced toward the entrance and saw several white larvae crawling into the arena. They reminded her a little bit of caterpillars in the way that they advanced by forming a tall crook in their backs, and then bringing their hind legs forward before extending their front sections and repeating the process. Yes, caterpillars, except these varied from the size of her arm to that of her body. A few were even bigger.

"They want us to fight larvae with our bare hands?" Manic said. He had pulled both arms free.

"Apparently so," Shaw said. Her left glove slid from the viscid substance, and then she focused on freeing her right leg. She wrapped both arms underneath her thigh and pulled. Because of the way the slime was wrapped around her assembly, she couldn't simply remove her boot to do it. And even if she could, she wasn't keen on depressurizing her suit.

Finally she yanked the foot free and moved on to the second boot. In moments she had released that one as well, and she joined the other Argonauts who had gathered to face the incoming larvae.

Harlequin's voice came over the comm. "These are the young queens of the Conquered. Kill as many as you can. If you can. This is a great honor we bestow upon you here, whether you realize it or not. By culling these larvae, you identify the strongest among them, one of which will serve as leader of the nest. She will also serve as the host for *my* Queen."

"What if we kill them all?" Bender asked.

"Good luck," Harlequin replied.

Shaw assumed a position near the center of the Argonauts. She counted roughly sixty of the different-sized larvae heading toward them. "This is like old times, huh boys? Facing down a bunch of slugs with nothing but our fists and ours wits."

"Sure," Lui said. "Though I don't think we've ever done something like this wearing jumpsuits alone."

"First time for everything," Shaw said, assuming a sparring stance.

The larvae reached them. The one directly in front of Shaw reared up on its hind legs and threw its upper body toward her chest, attempting to wrap its long mandibles around her waist. She intercepted those mandibles with her gloves and began pulling outward, eventually ripping them clean apart. The larva dropped and squealed in its death throes, its body convulsing to and fro.

In the meantime, a smaller larva had latched onto Shaw's boot, again clasping by the mandibles. She stepped on it, grinding her boot and smearing its body across the stone.

She was vaguely aware of her brothers fighting other larvae beside her as a larger worm bore down. It towered over her, its upper body swooping down as those mandibles spread wide to engulf her. She dove to one side, and the head swerved to follow her, but missed, plowing into the stone instead.

The crowd went wild.

Shaw scrambled to her feet. Another small larva had clasped onto her wrist. She distractedly wrapped her glove around it and pulled, ripping the body in half.

The larger larva was plunging its maw down upon her again. This time Shaw ran forward, diving as the pincers attempted to intercept her. She rolled underneath the arch formed by the larva's body, and grabbed onto its underside as the head lifted from the stone.

The larva was obviously having trouble because of Shaw's weight, and it swung its head to the left and right, trying to shake it off. Those mandibles bit at the empty air, attempting to find her.

"Got your back, baby!" Bender came rushing in. He leaped, hitting the larva in the side, but all he succeeded in doing was knocking Shaw off of the thing.

"Damn it, Bender!" Shaw said as the pair tumbled to the stone.

The enraged larva swung its torso down upon both of them, attempting to crush them with its body. Shaw rolled aside just in time. Bender wasn't so lucky, and he grunted as the thing smashed into his chest.

The upper body lifted, bending to position those mandibles for the killing blow against Bender. He seemed too stunned to move away.

Shaw started to stand, but one of the larger, dog-sized larvae smashed into her thigh, pinning her to the ground.

She kicked at it with her free leg, and finally smashed in its face and it released her.

She got up to help Bender, but saw that Tahoe had plowed into the creature already and driven it away from Bender. The big larva had wrapped its body around Tahoe's jumpsuit like a constrictor, and was squeezing the life out of him. Those mandibles came chomping down toward his head.

"Tahoe!" Shaw leaped toward him.

But Bender was there first: the man leaped onto the larva's upper body, throwing the head off balance so that the mandibles missed Tahoe and smashed into the cave floor. The larva shook Bender free and then dove repeatedly at him with its head while the body continued to squeeze Tahoe. Bender kept leaping away.

"Bender, get on its back!" Shaw said. "Keep the head weighed down!"

Bender avoided the latest downward blow and then wrapped his arms and legs around the upper body. The larva lifted its head drunkenly under the weight. Bender was basically standing on the outer edges of the mandibles with his boots, preventing them from opening all the way.

Shaw came in and also leaped onto the head. Unable to take their combined weight, the upper body crashed to the floor. The mandibles struck the stone, splaying, and the lower body uncoiled, releasing Tahoe.

The tail repositioned, and wrapped around Shaw and Bender. Before they realized what was happening, the two were bound fast by the coiled body.

Tahoe scrambled to his feet and calmly

approached the head, which Shaw and Bender still held to the floor with their weight. Tahoe knelt and shoved his fist into the esophagus. No doubt firing the surgical laser in his glove.

The larva squealed in pain, and the tail uncoiled from their legs, whipping about frantically. Black blood began to drip from around Tahoe's buried glove. The larva continued thrashing about for several moments, then collapsed, pulling Shaw and Bender down with it. Tahoe removed his hand, and with it came a big stream of that blood.

The crowd howled in outrage.

Beside them, Manic, TJ and Lui had taken down another of the big ones in a similar manner, judging from the blood oozing from between its mandibles and onto the stone. Meanwhile Fret and Unit A were each dealing with smaller larvae the size of human bodies.

The eight of them made short work of the remaining larvae, and when there were only two or three left, several of the warrior caste hurried into the arena.

Shaw and the others retreated, raising their arms in surrender. The warriors placed themselves between the team and the larvae, and then two of them escorted the young from the field of battle, leaving the others behind to prevent Shaw and the others from following. On the stone floor around them remained the bodies of the dead and dying larvae.

"Well done," came the voice of Ms. Bounty. "Thank you for culling the queens. These latter few will fight to the death on their own to choose the ultimate victor. But now it's time for you to face your final foe."

Ms. Bounty made her way down an aisle in the

stands until she reached the arena floor. Over her shoulders were slung both a normal laser rifle and a stun rifle, and at her belt a blaster was holstered. Rade walked beside her, fully suited, laser rifle in hand.

Together the pair approached the team, who had spread into a half circle to await their approach.

"Rade, what did they do to you?" Tahoe asked.

Rade didn't respond.

"Maybe he can't hear you," Manic said.

"He can hear me," Tahoe said. "But he refuses to answer."

Manic stepped forward. "Rade—"

"Stay back!" Rade said, pointing his rifle at Manic.

"Whoa whoa whoa." Manic retreated, palms up. "I'm staying back. Back."

Rade and Ms. Bounty halted twenty meters in front of the half-circle formed by the team. Ms. Bounty turned toward the gatorbeetles that had lingered nearby and chittered something. The warriors retreated, assuming a guard position near the entrance to the arena.

"Would the female please come forward," Ms. Bounty said.

Shaw glanced at her companions, then advanced.

When she was five meters away, Ms. Bounty said: "That's close enough." She glanced at Rade. "Abandon your rifle to the stone at your feet."

Rade complied. He stood up, staring blankly at Shaw. There was no recognition in his eyes.

"The existence of this female offends me," Ms. Bounty said. "She feels like a rival queen. Pet, with your bare hands, I want you to kill her."

nineteen

Rade stepped forward eagerly. He fully intended to kill the woman whose existence had dared offend his Queen.

"Rade..." the woman said, stepping backward, her palms held outward.

"You would be wise to defend yourself, female," Ms. Bounty said. "My pet will not show you mercy." She aimed her laser rifle at the others. "As for the rest of you, don't dare intervene, or I'll mow them both down."

Rade swung at the woman, who ducked to the side. He swung again, two more quick punches, but again she quickly moved away.

"Rade, it's me!" she said. "Shaw!"

Shaw. Why was that name familiar? He knew her once, he thought.

Well, it didn't matter. Rade wanted only to please his Queen in that moment.

It was time to kill the woman.

He took a running leap at her and she dodged to the side, vaulting onto one of the pillars that resided in the center of the arena, and somehow landing a kick to the back of his helmet in the process. He stumbled forward.

Another solid blow struck him squarely in the lower back and he toppled entirely.

The woman was on top of him, pressing him into the ground.

Something about the whole battle seemed strangely familiar. He had the impression he had fought the woman at some point before. They must truly be enemies. It was good that he would end her existence for his Queen.

Rade twisted in place, throwing up his hips at the same time, and freed himself from the pinning maneuver. He mounted her in turn and smashed her faceplate repeatedly with his gloves. Cracks spidered across the surface. She tried to redirect his fists, but his blows were too powerful. His anger, too deep.

"Rade, stop!" A voice came over the comm. "You're killing her!"

Rade did not stop. He kept punching repeatedly until he had broken clean through the glass. Fresh cuts appeared on the woman's face. He tried to gouge out her eyes with his thumbs but she caught his wrists and pulled them aside. He attempted the maneuver again, pressing into her tightly squeezed eyelids.

But once more she managed to shove his arms aside.

Rade reached inside the inner area of her helmet and found the release latch. Then he tore her helmet away.

He wrapped his hands around her throat and began to squeeze. She batted at his arms but he had a much firmer grip—she couldn't move him. Yes, this would work much better.

"Rade," the woman said. Mouthed, really, since she couldn't have much air. "I love you."

Rade paused. *She has always won your heart.*

Rade squeezed tighter, feeling the anger welling stronger than ever inside him. How dare he feel doubt about killing someone who had offended his Queen?

"Shut the fuck up, bitch," Rade said.

Her face turned blue in the dim light of the arena, and her lips made an odd sucking motion. Her eyes began to bulge.

And then she died.

Rade released her and stared into the lifeless face. A tear trickled down from one of her lifeless eyes.

Rade felt something then. Something deep inside himself. A pain like nothing he had ever experienced before. It wasn't a physical pain, but something emotional. Something terrible. A dark angst, welling up inside him, filling him with a wild terror. It felt as if he had done something extremely wrong. Like he had killed a part of himself.

What have I done?

He stared at her dead body.

WHAT THE HELL HAVE I DONE!

Rade collapsed onto her chest.

No no no no no.

But then she coughed violently, coming back to life.

He had released her just in time. He'd choked her into unconsciousness, but not long enough to kill her.

He felt an immense relief, as if the entire woes of the world had lifted. A sense of incredible happiness suffused him, to the point that he felt lightheaded. He shed tears of joy. He laughed.

"What are you doing, Pet?" the Queen said. "Kill her."

Rade froze. "I—"

"YOU what?" the Queen said. "Kill her."

Rade looked at the woman. "Shaw. Your name is

Shaw."

"Yes," Shaw said, smiling despite the blood that rimmed her lips. "Shaw."

She Has Always Won.

"Well, what are you waiting for?" the Queen said. "Kill her. Show me your dedication."

Rade stood up. He looked at the Queen. "Please, my Queen."

"Aww," the Queen said. "I understand. It's too difficult for you, my love. I'll do this one for you, but then you must promise me you will handle the rest."

"Yes," Rade said eagerly. "Yes. Thank you, my Queen."

She came forward and lowered the laser rifle from her shoulder. The Queen aimed the weapon at Shaw's broken faceplate. "Goodbye, competition."

Rade's hands swung forward with immense force, redirecting the muzzle as she squeezed the trigger. Then he released the weapon, took a step back, and planted a kick squarely in the side of the jumpsuit. It was the most powerful kick Rade had ever unleashed in a suit before and she went flying several meters away. She landed sprawling.

"You're going to regret that," Ms. Bounty said, standing almost immediately.

"I don't think so," Rade said. He indicated the other weapon he had torn free before he kicked Ms. Bounty: her stun rifle. He fired.

The muted electrolaser struck the suit head-on and sparks of electricity flowed up and down the surface. Her body convulsed for a few seconds and then collapsed.

Rade dropped down on one knee and aimed up at the stands toward Harlequin. Just as he acquired the Artificial in his targeting reticle, Harlequin dropped from view. Rade aimed the weapon slightly to the right instead and fired the electrolaser at Tantalus, who was aiming his own rifle down at Rade. The electricity hit, and while Tantalus didn't have a Phant in him, the blow would still disable the Artificial for several moments.

The crowd was roaring in outrage. The warrior gatorbeetles at the entrance were rushing to intercept the Argonauts. More were streaming down into the arena behind them.

Rade helped Shaw to her feet.

"Tahoe, get Ms. Bounty's other rifle," Rade said. "Bender, take her blaster. Fret, grab Ms. Bounty."

"But she still has a Phant in her!" Fret complained.

"I know." Rade swung his rifle toward Ms. Bounty and stunned her again for good measure.

Bender took her blaster shortly thereafter, and Tahoe scooped up her rifle. Fret meanwhile hauled her over one shoulder.

"To the arena exit!" Rade shouted.

Rade dashed forward. With the help of the targeting AI, he aimed the stun rifle at one of the incoming gatorbeetles and fired. No effect. Tahoe meanwhile shot one of the aliens in the esophagus and downed it. Bender felled another.

But more and more gatorbeetles were swarming down from the stands to intercept them. It soon became obvious they weren't going to make it. The exit was completely blocked off.

Gatorbeetles were coming in from all sides. Tahoe and Bender were firing madly, sometimes hitting an alien between the mandibles and terminating it, sometimes missing. The gatorbeetles were frothing at the mouths, eager to devour their prey.

Rade and the others were forced to cease their

flight, and they backed into a tight defensive circle.

"It was nice fighting with you all," Fret said.

"You as well," Manic replied.

"Don't give up yet, bitches!" Bender said. "Find a way to fight!"

"Easy for you to say," Manic replied. "You have a rifle."

Rade aimed once more up at the stands, and saw that Harlequin had come out into the open again. Rade centered his crosshairs over the Artificial, and realized Harlequin was bringing his own rifle down to bear on him as well.

Rade squeezed the trigger first. The muted thunder of the electrolaser erupted, and Rade saw electricity engulf Harlequin through the scope. The Artificial collapsed.

"Well, at least we don't have to worry about him picking us off one by one," Shaw said. Her voice had a slight echo, because her lack of helmet allowed the words to drift to the external microphones of his suit in addition to being transmitted over the comm.

"Yeah," Rade said. "We only have to worry about the bugs picking us off. And at least he can't get into your head. For a while anyway." He fired the stun weapon at one of the incoming gatorbeetles. It still had no effect. "Sorry about the helmet by the way."

"It's all right," Shaw said. "I'll kick your ass later."

As the enraged aliens closed in for the kill, a strange chittering sound drifted from the midst of the defensive circle, barely heard above the angry symphony of mandibles gnashing against one another.

Rade spun, and realized it was Ms. Bounty.

"Shut her up!" Rade told Fret. He aimed the stun rifle at her.

"Wait," Ms. Bounty said weakly. "It's me. I'm

telling them to stop."

Rade paused.

Fret stared at him, waiting. "Well are you going to shoot her?"

Rade lowered the weapon. "Continue."

Ms. Bounty opened her mouth and made the sound again.

The aliens began to halt as they came within meters of the party.

"Tahoe, Bender, stop firing," Rade said.

The pair complied.

Ms. Bounty continued chittering; her voice carried farther now that the aliens had begun to fall silent. The noises she made seemed to soothe them.

To the west, the gatorbeetles parted, forming a tight passageway whose walls were formed by their bodies; in moments, a route to the arena entrance was available.

"Let's go!" Rade said.

The party hurried toward the entrance.

"Ms. Bounty?" Rade asked. "Are you still with us?"

"Yes," she replied. "I'm in control for the moment. The Black is already beginning to reassert itself, however. You'll have to stun me again."

Rade waited until they had crossed past the entrance; he didn't want to piss off the aliens by shooting their so-called queen again in front of them. The moment he passed beyond sight of the sentries waiting in the tunnel outside, he paused to point the stun rifle at Ms. Bounty.

"Turn around," Rade ordered Fret, who still carried her over one shoulder.

The ex-MOTH did so and Rade released the stun weapon at nearly point blank range. Ms. Bounty convulsed on Fret's shoulder.

"Unit A, give Shaw your helmet," Rade instructed the robot. That would protect Shaw from any psi attacks launched by the remaining Black when it awoke.

The robot removed its helmet and handed it to Shaw. She accepted the one-size-fits-all gear gratefully and donned it.

A distant chittering echoed from the arena behind them. It sounded like it came from one mouth. A very angry mouth, at that. Rade guessed that Harlequin had recovered, and was yelling at the aliens to pursue.

"Tahoe, Bender, get on point," Rade said. "Clear any bugs from our path. Let's go!"

The team retreated down the tunnel.

Behind them, from the direction of the arena, erupted the clattering roar of vengeful mandibles.

twenty

Rade glanced over his shoulder. "Ms. Bounty, we're going to need a map to the Hoplites. Assuming you know where they are. I'm guessing since you can speak the bug language..."

"Yes," Ms. Bounty said groggily. "The Queen's memory engrams have imprinted my neural network. I know everything it knows. Including where the Hoplites are, and where they moved the Phant trap to. I'm transmitting the waypoints of both to you now. The Phant trap is the closer. It's not far from where you mated with me."

"You mated with *her?*" Shaw said.

"Er, I wasn't exactly myself for the past few hours, in case you hadn't noticed back there," Rade said. He received the waypoints and forwarded them on to the rest of the team.

The glass container, or Phant trap, was indeed the closer. It was only a short distance ahead, in fact; a slight detour on the way to the Hoplites. Ms. Bounty had also transmitted complete map information of nearly the entire nest, so he saw that there appeared to be an alternate route leading away from the chamber containing the container. That meant they could probably afford to take the detour without being trapped.

"If we take you to the glass container, can we extract the Phant from you?" Rade asked.

"Yes," Ms. Bounty replied. "If you stun it before putting me inside and activating the interface, it will simply splash down on me when the process is done. It won't seep inside me and I can escape. She'll be trapped within the container."

"All right," Rade said. "Bender, I want you to head for the first waypoint. We're making a stop at the glass container. Ms. Bounty, transmit the necessary access codes for the container to me. I need to be able to activate it."

Only the occasional gatorbeetle crossed their path from the forward direction. It seemed most of the nest had gathered to watch the executions in the arena. Those few that they did encounter were not warrior caste, for the most part, and fled as often as engaging.

"One thing I'm wondering," Lui said during the retreat. "Ms. Bounty claims she knows everything the Queen knows. How come Harlequin never exhibited similar memory retention when he was possessed by the Phant Zoltan? Sure, he remembered the Phant controlling him, but he didn't have access to its full memory."

"Surus modified my AI core to automatically download and backup extraneous records detected in my random access memory, as is the case when a Phant possesses a host," Ms. Bounty explained. "She did this so that I might retain her complete memory whenever she found the need to temporarily depart my core. This granted me the useful side effect you mentioned, Lui."

"Okay, good enough," Lui said.

Rade soon switched to the LIDAR band as there

were few glow bars in these portions of the cave system. They wound their way through the twisting tunnels, traveling deeper into the nest. Rade stunned Ms. Bounty every now and then while on the run. He couldn't afford to stop. The chittering behind them was growing louder by the minute.

Ms. Bounty tried to sooth them by shouting their language into the rear tunnel, but either they didn't hear her, or Harlequin had told them she was a traitor.

The Argonauts detoured westward from the main passageway and reached the destination chamber. Two sentries protected it, but Tahoe and Bender shot them down. Inside, they found a small cavern. The glass container was there, along with several spare robot parts. There were no signs of their other weapons, however.

Rade stunned Ms. Bounty one last time and then threw her into the glass container. He activated the remote interface with the codes she had given him, and she floated into the air. Before she began to spin, Rade said: "Unit A, Manic, port the container. Tahoe and Bender, continue leading the way down the western tunnel!"

Unit A and Manic scooped up the container. It had started to hum.

The team made their way westward. Rade shone his infrared headlamp at the container. Ms. Bounty was a blur inside, and the Phant was being sucked out of her, forming a ball above her.

They reached another cavern, slightly bigger than the last chamber. A glow bar in one corner provided light.

Tahoe and Bender hurried toward the opposite corridor, but then the pair stopped.

"Uh, this isn't going to work," Tahoe said.

Rade glanced at the overhead map. Several red dots had appeared in the adjacent tunnel, blocking the way forward.

Lui, on drag, said: "Well, we can't go back, either!"

In the rear passage the remainder of the gatorbeetles were quickly coming forward. More red dots swarmed over that section of the map.

"They've outflanked us," Shaw said.

"We shouldn't have made the detour," Rade said. "Tahoe, defend the rear passage. Bender, guard the forward route. The rest of you, search for hidden walls!"

Inside the container, Ms. Bounty floated toward the bottom. When she touched it, the liquid sphere of the Black that had coalesced a half meter above the body dropped down and splashed over the Artificial. So far, those droplets that weren't on the floor were just sitting on the fabric of her jumpsuit and not seeping inside.

Rade hurried to the container and opened it.

"Ms. Bounty, get out of there," Rade told her.

She struggled to stand, but couldn't, so Ms. Bounty simply rolled from the container. When she passed the verge of the metallic disk on the floor, all of the black drops still on her were swept inside, the liquid constrained by the extents of the disk. Rade quickly shut the door.

He offered Ms. Bounty a hand and helped her to her feet. Within the container, the scattered droplets began to coalesce into a single puddle. The fringes of that liquid moved about, exploring the circular perimeter that confined it, searching for any gaps in the containment.

"I can't hold them off!" Bender said.

"People, find me that illusory wall!" Rade said.

"There isn't one here," Ms. Bounty said.

"Then we're trapped," Rade told her.

"No," Ms. Bounty said. "While there is no illusory wall, there's still a secret passage. With me!"

She walked forward haltingly at first, still recovering from what had happened to her apparently, but her pace soon increased until she was able to move at a sprint.

She halted beside one of the walls and spread her arms wide. She turned one of her gloves toward Rade. The fingertips were equipped with what appeared to be small metal funnels.

"The Queen equipped my gloves with small pheromone generating devices," Ms. Bounty said, rotating the glove back toward the wall. "These simulate the antennae of one of the aliens. With them, I should be able to trip the hidden door..."

A small rectangular portion of the wall moved inward and then slid to the side, revealing an empty passage. "As I told you, I know all of the Queen's secrets."

"To the Hoplites, Argonauts!" Rade said.

The team hurried into the passageway. Bender and Tahoe brought up the rear, firing at the gatorbeetles as they rushed inside. Manic and Unit A continued to port the glass container that harbored the Black.

"Can you close the entrance behind us?" Rade asked.

"It should close on its own in a few seconds," Ms. Bounty said.

The wall attempted to seal, however one of the gatorbeetles had already come inside: its body halted the moving rock and acted as a blockage. That particular gatorbeetle appeared trapped, and the others simply plowed over it to pursue.

"Bender, I want you on point!" Rade said. "Tahoe, keep them away from our drag!"

Bender hurried forward and took his place at the front. He led the way, and in moments they had emerged from the secret passageway onto the main route once again. On the way to the chamber that contained the Hoplites, the party only encountered two more gatorbeetles blocking them. Meanwhile, the rest of the nest continued to pursue behind them.

Finally they arrived at the target waypoint. Their six units resided in the small cavern, standing side by side, illuminated by a light bar situated near the far wall. In front of the mechs, three tripods held Tech Class IV holographic emitters.

"I'll take these," Ms. Bounty said, separating the emitters from the tripods and securing them to her harness.

"Catch." Rade tossed the stun rifle to Ms. Bounty and dashed toward Electron. The mech wasn't responding to his remote start commands.

"We're going to have to manually bootstrap them from within," TJ said.

Rade clambered the leg rungs onto the chest, and then continued until he could reach the manual chest release. He yanked it and the cockpit hatch fell open. He swiveled onto the inside of the hatch and pulled himself inside. He reached up, shoved the two bootstrap releases, and plugged his glove into the slot that appeared over his head. From the manual interface that overlaid his HUD he activated the boot-up process.

The servomotors whirred to life and he withdrew his finger from the slot as the overhead panel shut. The inner actuators enveloped him and the hatch slammed closed, sealing him in darkness. The feed from the external video camera filled his vision and he looked down on the world from a height of two and half meters.

Around him, other Hoplites were coming to life.

"Electron, are you there?" Rade said. "Electron?"

No answer.

"My AI doesn't seem to want to come online," Tahoe said.

"Our enemy has a weapon that can disable AIs," Ms. Bounty said. "You will have to operate your battle suits in manual mode. At least until we can get back to the ship and initiate a full suite of repairs and diagnostics."

"That suits me just fine," Bender said.

"And while fighting without AIs has its disadvantages," Ms. Bounty continued. "On the plus side, it also means our enemy won't be able to disable our mechs with that weapon again."

Rade, Shaw, Tahoe, Bender, Lui, and TJ got mechs. Manic, Fret, Ms. Bounty and Unit A were the odd ones out. Tahoe had apparently tossed the laser rifle to Manic, because the latter was sporting the weapon now, while Fret wielded Bender's blaster. The glass container lay on the ground between Ms. Bounty and Unit A.

"Manic, you're with me," Rade said. "Ms. Bounty, you get Shaw. Tahoe, take Fret. Bender, Unit A is yours."

Rade and the other designated Hoplite pilots knelt their mechs to let the grounded individuals load up into the passenger seats.

"TJ, bring the Queen along with us," Rade said.

TJ lifted the glass container onto the right shoulder of his Hoplite and held it in place with his arm.

"The rest of you, cobras in hand," Rade

transmitted. "We gots ourselves a King to bag."

"A false king, you mean," Shaw said. "Because you're the only king around here."

"I love you," Rade said.

"Ms. Bounty, I don't suppose you can use those Tech Class IV holographic emitters to cloak our mechs?" Tahoe asked hopefully.

"No," Ms. Bounty said.

Rade approached the entrance to the cavern. Two of the pursuing gatorbeetles had broken ahead of the others and already crowded inside. "We're going to have to fight our way out."

Rade unleashed a cobra, aiming between the mandibles. His target fell.

The others joined in, content to let the aliens rush them via the bottleneck.

They soon realized that the same rules applied as with the smaller weapons. If you hit the gatorbeetles in a limb, they kept coming. To truly take them down you had to target their esophagi, or strike the center of their thorax. Black blood spurted from heads and limbs in profusion, smearing the mechs.

A wall of bodies began to form. The succeeding gatorbeetles simply shoved past them. Rade and the others formed another wall of dead bodies from those who clambered by the first; that too was surmounted by the enemy. The Hoplites created more and more successive walls of corpses, and were forced backward. Soon, the mechs were pressed up against the far side of the cavern by the sheer force of numbers.

Soon the laser weapons began to overheat.

"Well," Rade said. "I think it's time we switched to shields and started bashing our way forward. Otherwise we'll be here all day."

Rade scooped up one of the dead gatorbeetles and

wielded it like a club. He staved heads and split thoraxes. He used his shield like a battering ram to shove the aliens forward.

"Come, Argonauts!" Rade said. "Synchronize with me! Push in unison! We form a phalanx of shields!"

Beside him, the other Hoplites formed a line with their shields and they shoved in unison against the enemy.

They slowly advanced.

In the passenger seats, Manic and Fret continually fired down at the aliens. TJ, on the right side of the shield phalanx, occasionally slammed the glass container down at the defending gatorbeetles, crushing their heads. Meanwhile, Rade and the others stomped on any limbs or heads that appeared underneath their shields; either that, or they slammed down the shields directly, using the bottom edges as decapitating and maiming instruments. When their cobras began to cool down, they also fired over the top of the shields at the incoming enemy.

They forced the living and the dead backwards, slowly shoving the packed throng from the room.

Finally the enemy broke. The gatorbeetles realized they were essentially flowing into a giant meat grinder. The rout started when those in the front ranks began to turn around and flee, clawing and biting at the gatorbeetles just beside them. The behavior was infectious, so that soon the entire swarm was retreating.

In moments, the entire enemy had been routed, leaving behind the crushed bodies of the dead they had trampled in the process.

Rade and the others waded their way through those corpses; the bodies reached to the waists of the Hoplites, and further steeped their lower bodies in black blood.

"Ms. Bounty, where do you think we'll find Harlequin?" Rade asked.

"I doubt he is in the nest anymore," she replied. "Likely he will have fled to a preservation depot east of the nest."

"A preservation what?" Fret asked.

"A place where the Phants stored technology salvaged from these aliens. Harlequin will likely be going there to retrieve a Tech Class IV weapon. There is a certain battle suit I know of, designed specifically for these aliens. Their equivalent of a mech. If the Phant vacates Harlequin, he should be able to pilot it directly."

"An alien battle suit," Rade said. "I'm not sure I like the sound of that."

"I do," Bender said. "It's like a bug in a tin can. All you have to do is apply a can opener, extract your bug, then grind it under your heel."

"You always make it sound so easy," Fret said.

"Ms. Bounty, you can just stun the mech, right?" Shaw asked.

"There might be a problem with that, actually," Ms. Bounty replied. "The stun device was only designed for robots and Artificials. Anything larger, and the AI core might be too well shielded. And it's Tech Class IV remember. It might not work for even a smaller unit. You'll quite likely have to rip open its chest before I have a clean shot."

"We can do that," Bender said.

"I'm loving the confidence," Ms. Bounty said.

"Thank you," Bender said. "By the way, I heard you were into mating these days? I'm free later tonight, if you're interested."

"I'll pass, thanks," Ms. Bounty said.

"Let's swing by the so-called royal chambers just in case Harlequin hasn't left," Rade said.

Ms. Bounty guided the mechs to the "royal chambers." Sure enough, there was no sign of Harlequin. Rade stared with disgust at the mat where he had had sex with Ms. Bounty—or rather, the Queen—and quickly left the room. The guilt was made all the worse because he remembered how much he had liked it at the time.

But I wasn't in control then, he reminded himself. *I'd never willingly do such a thing.*

And he definitely wouldn't enjoy it.

At least, that was what he told himself.

They proceeded toward the surface and encountered no further resistance along the way. The gatorbeetles had all gone into hiding, giving the nest the appearance of a ghost town.

Even at the entrance, the usual sentries weren't waiting to intercept, allowing the six Hoplites to emerge unencumbered into the sun.

Rade flung his arms outward, glad to be in the light once more. He only wished he could feel those warm rays on his face. The brightness would have to do.

"If I never see a cave again, I'll be a very happy man," Fret said.

twenty-one

I think we've all had our fill of dark tunnels by now," Rade said. "Ms. Bounty, where's this preservation depot?"

"I'm marking it on your overhead maps," Ms. Bounty replied.

A flashing waypoint appeared four kilometers to the west.

"All right," Rade said. "Tahoe, take us there. Traveling overwatch."

Tahoe split the Hoplite squad into two fire teams of three each, separated by fifty meters. The mechs piloted by Rade, Shaw and TJ were part of the second team and provided traveling overwatch of the first. Each individual mech was separated by five meters from the Hoplite in front, and offset a random distance to the left or right to form an overall zig-zag pattern.

The metal feet sank into the dark sand as the units proceeded at a trot, leaving heavy footprints in the dunes. The upper portions of their camouflage skin had changed coloration to match the surrounding terrain; the blood-soaked lower portions soon became covered in black grit where disturbed sand particles glued.

Rade tapped in Shaw directly on the way.

"I hope someday you'll forgive me for what happened back there," he told her.

"There's nothing to forgive," Shaw replied. "Like you said, you weren't in control."

"Yes," Rade said. "But I should have tried to fight harder. The thought of all the hurt I caused you, not just the physical, but the emotional pain... I can only imagine how pissed—how *enraged*—I would be if you had slept with Harlequin."

"You know what?" Shaw told him. "I'd actually prefer if you didn't remind me of that. Because let's just say, I'm not a big of fan of Ms. Bounty right now."

"Sorry," Rade said.

She sighed audibly over the comm. "Stop it. And I need to stop, too. I can't really blame either one of you. While I'm pissed off, I know neither of you are truly guilty. It's those Black Phants that did this. Let me just say, I'm going to be wearing an awfully big spiteful grin when we finally cast them into the sun."

The two teams made good time toward the waypoint, and in twenty minutes the first fire team reached a kilometer out from the target.

At that point, Tahoe, part of the lead fire team, called a halt and his units dug in.

"Second fire team, halt," Rade transmitted. He switched to the point of view of the lead Hoplite, piloted by Bender. Where the waypoint resided ahead, he saw what looked like three dark, horizontal half-cylinders protruding from the sand, abutting against one another. Basically a triple set of long Quonset huts. The surface material glistened in the sun, as if made of some sort of polished, black metal.

"So what do you think?" Rade transmitted.

"I don't see any sign of defenses," Bender said.

"Ms. Bounty?" Rade asked.

"There aren't any defenses," she replied. "Discounting the mech. And the external weapons attached to the small starships."

"Starships?" Rade said.

"Yes," Ms. Bounty said. "The rightmost cylinder was essentially a hangar bay. It contained two Tech Class IV starships from the race once known as the Xaranth: the gatorbeetles, as you like to call them."

"Harlequin might have taken one of those ships into orbit already," Bender said.

"I'm not so sure he'd leave without his Queen," Ms. Bounty said.

Rade glanced at the glass container TJ ported over one shoulder. The black liquid still resided inside.

"Which of those half-cylinders holds our Xaranth mech?" Rade asked.

"The leftmost," Ms. Bounty replied.

"All right, Tahoe, take your fire team forward," Rade said. "Sweep the external area. Fire Team B, with me, we move forward to cover them."

"Wait," Ms. Bounty said. "They'll need me to open the hangar doors."

"Not if they blow it down," Rade said. "I want you to stay back, with us."

"You seem a bit overprotective about her," Shaw transmitted over a private line.

"I want to preserve the knowledge she has of the gatorbeetles, and the Queen," Rade said.

"Are you sure that's all you want to protect?" Shaw said.

Rade frowned, and then sighed. It wasn't her talking, but the burning jealousy.

As Tahoe led the two mechs with him across the plains toward the target, Rade and the others moved

197

forward and assumed the team's former position. TJ lowered the glass container to aim his cobra at the target, like Rade and Shaw were doing. In Shaw's passenger seat, Ms. Bounty surveyed the area via the sights of her stun rifle.

Rade scanned the different structures himself, through the scope of his right cobra. In his left arm, he had deployed his ballistic shield. Just because he was farther away didn't mean an incoming laser attack would be any less effective. Hoplite armor itself could deflect a few laser blows, especially when the mech was in motion, preventing the laser from striking the same area overlong, but when planting oneself on an open plain it was just common sense to deploy the shield. The other Hoplites with him had done the same.

Rade switched to thermal and other electromagnetic spectrum bands as he swept his scope across the structures, but he saw nothing more, so reverted to the main band.

"Is it possible the Xaranth mech is using emitters to hide its visual signature?" Rade asked.

"Even with their tech class," Ms. Bounty replied. "Their emitters were not powerful enough to hide something of that size. Just as I could not hide your mechs."

Tahoe, Bender and Lui closed to within fifty meters of the target structure. Then they began circling around toward the other side. Before the Hoplites vanished from view, Rade had his own fire team relocate five hundred meters to the right of the structures, so that he had a bead on the back portions of the structures. There was nothing behind them.

Rade signaled for Tahoe to continue.

The first fire team explored the back area, and

proceeded to circumnavigate all three structures, stopping before the target structure of the left.

"Looks clear out here," Tahoe said.

Rade repositioned once more, placing his team five hundred meters behind Tahoe's in front of the leftmost Quonset.

"Approach," Rade sent.

Tahoe's fire team tentatively closed with the structure. Bender, on point, stopped before what looked like a pair of double doors, which towered over him, about twice the size of his mech.

"There's no obvious way to open it," Bender said.

"Only the pheromone attachments in my gloves can do that," Ms. Bounty said.

"Well baby, come join me," Bender said. "And we'll rock this place all night long."

"That's not going to happen," Rade said.

"All right boss," Bender said. "Do I have permission to make the door go boom, then?"

"Permission granted," Rade replied.

Juggernaut's cockpit opened and Bender climbed down onto the left thigh using the rungs. He popped open the storage compartment and retrieved several charges. Then he climbed back up to the cockpit and leaped at the double doors. When he touched, he obviously activated his magnetic mounts, because his lower body attached to the surface.

Bender proceeded to place the charges, then pushed off from the double door, deactivating his magnetic mounts at the same time. He landed inside Juggernaut's cockpit and sealed the hatch. Then the Hoplite sprinted away from the doors.

"Ready to go!" Bender said.

Rade glanced at the members of Fire Team A. They had all assumed defensive positions, crouched down on one knee, anti-ballistic shields raised in their left arms, cobras aimed in their right.

"Boom time," Rade said.

The charges detonated and the door fell inward. Through his scope, Rade saw what looked like a storage bay containing a bunch of miscellaneous equipment. He carefully scanned the inner region through his scope. He saw tubes, conduits, coils, spools, sacks, crates, you name it. But nothing resembling the mech Ms. Bounty had spoken off.

"You call this shit Tech Class IV?" Bender said. "Looks like a Tech Class II dump. If that."

"Ms. Bounty, where is the mech?" Rade asked.

"It's not there anymore," Ms. Bounty said.

"Could it be hiding behind anything in there?" Rade said. "Say, behind those large tire-like objects in the back?"

"It's certainly possible," Ms. Bounty said.

"Hmm," Rade said. "All right, Bender. I want you to place charges on the doors to the other bays."

"I only have a couple left," Bender said. "Tahoe, can I borrow some of yours?"

Tahoe's leg compartment folded open. "Borrow away."

"Thanks man," Bender said. "You know how much I love blowing stuff up."

"I wouldn't want to take away your enjoyment," Tahoe said.

Bender climbed out of his cockpit, retrieved two charges from Juggernaut's storage compartment, and then leaped onto Tahoe's Hoplite to grab some more. He returned to his mech, piloted Juggernaut to the other structures in turn, and emerged from the cockpit to place the charges against the doors. When he was done, he rejoined Fire Team A.

"Let's do the middle structure first," Rade said. He aimed his scope at the double doors there. "Detonate when ready."

The charges exploded and the door fell inward. Once more Rade was greeted with a profusion of equipment, none of which was the mech. There were more steel crates in this hangar than the previous, as well as some large, mirrorlike spherical objects, but that was the only difference.

"What are those spheres?" TJ asked.

"Those are storage archives," Ms. Bounty said. "Containing the history and culture of the Xaranth. They are password protected, and unfortunately the Phants misplaced the password."

"Mighty kind of them," Lui said.

"Could our mech be hiding behind any of those objects?" Rade asked.

"If the mech was lying flat, yes," Ms. Bounty said.

"Where are HS3s when you need them?" TJ complained.

"Blow the third structure," Rade said.

In moments the final charges detonated and the third set of double doors fell in. This time, Rade's scope was greeted with a much cleaner hangar. Inside, a single vessel took up the closer half of the space, while the other half was completely empty. About a quarter the size of the *Argonaut*, it was a white, slightly horseshoe-shaped craft, with thick prongs emerging from an ovule main body. It was somewhat similar to a gatorbeetle head, actually.

Along the outer rim of the hull, tiny rods of various sizes protruded. Rade had no idea what purpose that served—perhaps to function as some sort of advanced Whittle layer to redistribute the impact energy of micrometeors?

Above the ship, it looked like there were more double doors that could fold aside to provide a quick egress.

"I thought you said there were two ships," Rade asked.

"There were," Ms. Bounty replied.

"I guess our King really did flee the planet," Lui said.

"Taking Harlequin with him," Bender said quietly.

"All right, Fire Team A, clear the structures," Rade said. "Start with the one on the left."

And so Tahoe led his fire team into the first structure. Rade relocated his own Hoplites to the entrance to provide overwatch. While Shaw and Rade aimed their cobras inside, TJ once again lowered the glass container to cover the plains behind them.

Tahoe's Hoplites were spread out, and they moved between the various equipment, pieing the different potential hiding places formed by crates and whatnot. "Pieing" meant they circled wide, as if following the periphery of a large piece of pie, keeping their weapons trained past the corner of the potential hiding place as they slowly increased their angle of exposure.

It took about five minutes to complete the sweep of the first structure. Rade had Tahoe perform the same clearing operation on the middle Quonset. Once more Fire Team B assumed an overwatch position at the entrance.

In another five minutes, the middle structure was clear. The team swept the third even faster.

"Guess it's time to sweep the ship," Rade said.

He sent Shaw into the structure, and Ms. Bounty leaned down from the passenger seat to apply the pheromone generators located on the fingertips of her gloves.

As the entry hatch swiveled aside, Bender said: "Get back get back get back!"

Shaw obeyed, quickly retreating; in the passenger seat, Ms. Bounty drew the Phant-stunning rifle and kept it aimed at the opening.

"Our Hoplites could fit in there," Tahoe said. "But it's going to be a tight fit."

"Manic, Fret, Unit A, inside," Rade said. "I want Unit A to take point. Ms. Bounty, give the robot the stun rifle."

Ms. Bounty tossed the weapon to the robot, and the indicated individuals leaped down from their passenger seats and hurried into the hatch.

Rade watched on his overhead map as the inside of the vessel slowly filled out. He switched to Unit A's point of view, and saw smooth oval-shaped walls big enough to fit a single gatorbeetle. Rade wondered what the protocol had been when two gatorbeetles needed to pass each other in the cramped space. He supposed one of them would have had to crouch down on the deck and allow the other to crawl over it.

They passed a compartment that seemed to be the crew quarters: six circular hollows were dug into the deck. Another compartment appeared to be an engineering section of some sort. A third proved the cockpit, or bridge: basically a circular depression in front of a short, featureless pillar. The last compartment was wider than the rest, and held a smaller ship inside. It looked like a squished ovule, with a black visor near the front. Almost like a very big helmet, actually. Two small wings protruded from the body section. Those wings looked like they could telescope wider to handle atmospheric flight if necessary.

Manic transmitted: "So, if you've been following

our progress, you've seen that we've cleared everything except for this hangar bay. There's a smaller shuttle inside. We're going to have to request Ms. Bounty's presence to open it."

Ms. Bounty glanced at Rade's Hoplite. "With your permission?"

"Go ahead," Rade said.

Ms. Bounty climbed down from Shaw's passenger seat and hurried inside. Rade watched from Unit A's point of view as she entered the internal hangar bay and approached the shuttle. She touched the aft surface with her fingertips and a rear section folded away, lowering to form a ramp.

"Get back!" Manic said.

Ms. Bounty retreated as Unit A rushed inside.

Within, the shuttle was relatively empty. In the center of the floor was a hollow, with a smooth pillar emerging at the fringe, just in front of the tinted glass that coincided with the dark visor on the outside; that glass provided a view of the hangar bay beyond.

"It's clear," Unit A said. "The shuttle seems to be a single passenger craft. More like a lifepod than anything else."

"All right," Rade said. "Everyone outside. I want to make one final sweep before I decide what to do next."

"May I have my rifle, please?" Ms. Bounty asked the Centurion.

Unit A tossed the stun weapon to Ms. Bounty and the group emerged momentarily.

Rade and the others retreated to a spot twenty meters in front of the central Quonset; the first fire team separated to circle the structures and repeat their sweep of the equipment-laden interiors, and when that was done the team rendezvoused with Rade and the others.

"I guess he really did abandon his Queen," Manic said.

"So much for Phant loyalty," Lui added.

"So what now, boss?" Tahoe asked.

"I guess we board that ship," Rade said. "And continue our search in orbit. Assuming Ms. Bounty can fly it?"

"I can," Ms. Bounty confirmed.

"What the hell is that?" Fret said from Tahoe's passenger seat.

Rade followed Fret's pointing arm to the sky behind them. An incoming object was fast approaching.

"Inside!" Rade said.

twenty-two

R ade flung his shield behind his body to protect himself and his passenger, and then he sprinted toward the central Quonset. Around him, sand flew up as lasers from the airborne attacker's strafing run impacted the dunes.

Rade entered the structure, and as the ship flew over he dove behind a crate and tilted his shield horizontally, holding it above him. The Quonset offered little protection: overhead, holes were burned clean through the ceiling as the ship completed its flyby.

The other Hoplites were crouched similarly nearby, and had taken cover behind miscellaneous crates and other objects, their shields held flat.

A moment of quiet ensued after the craft passed.

"You think he's going to make another run?" Manic said.

"No," TJ said. He gestured with the large metal arm of his Hoplite toward the glass container he had set down. "Doesn't want to harm his Queen."

"Then why make the attack run in the first place?" Fret said.

And then, near the far wall, the ceiling of the structure collapsed and a large object slammed into the floor; debris from the nearby equipment flew through the air like shrapnel.

Rade swung his shield toward the crash to protect himself. As the debris struck shields, equipment and mechs, for a moment it sounded like it was hailing. Hard. Then everything was quiet.

Rade gazed over the rim of his shield to study the crash. He spotted a prong-shaped nose section that was a twin to the craft in the other Quonset.

"Looks like we found our missing ship," Lui quipped.

Between those two prongs, a large door slid upward, revealing the internal hangar bay. The deck was sloped to the side, because of the angle of the crash. Similar to the other ship, an ovule shuttle resided inside. But there was something else packed within the hanger that drew all of Rade's attention. A malevolent creation that sent chills crawling up his spine.

Just as humans designed their battle suits in their own image, so too had the Xaranth, evidently, because the mech that stepped forward was basically a giant robot gatorbeetle, about twice the size of the usual warrior caste member. Its three segmented body parts—head, thorax, and abdomen—were covered in overlapping metal scales that shifted and flowed with every movement. Robotic antennae twisted to and fro. Iron mandibles clanged together. Prehensile limbs opened and closed. The six legs resounded with each step.

But none of that concerned Rade overmuch. What really disturbed him were the oh, six or so minigun-style weapons mounted on either side of the thorax. It was like a gunship on legs.

It pulled itself out of the hangar opening on its six

legs, a tarantula withdrawing from its hole, giving those miniguns the room to dangle free.

The head swiveled toward Rade's mech, the many eyes glowing a bright red. The miniguns instantly matched the orientation, every weapon aiming at Rade.

"Down!" Rade said.

He ducked behind one of the large spherical objects that Ms. Bounty claimed stored the history and culture of the Xaranth, and he slammed his shield down in front of him, placing it between himself and the sphere so that his Hoplite had two layers of protection from the miniguns.

Several holes instantly appeared in the exposed upper portion of the shield, where it climbed past the sphere, caused by extremely powerful bolts of plasma tearing through the ballistic material. Rade glanced at the feed from his rear camera and saw those plasma beams create similar holes in whatever they struck, up to and including the opposite wall.

"Our shields aren't worth zip against this tech!" Bender said.

Rade aimed his cobra past the edge of the shield as the next attack came in, not to target the enemy, but to covertly study the sphere: he confirmed that the beams striking the Tech Class IV object didn't penetrate.

"Get behind the spheres if you can!" Rade sent. "The plasma bolts don't seem to harm them."

He turned his bore-riddled shield sideways, trying to place as much of it behind the sphere as possible, and lay flat as the plasma barrage continued.

He glanced at Nemesis: Shaw's mech had taken cover behind another sphere nearby. Beyond, he saw TJ crouched past a stack of more spheres, the glass container on the floor behind him. Within that container, the black liquid surged about the extents of the metal disk excitedly, as if sensing its liberation.

"Take care of that container, TJ," Rade sent. "We don't need another Black on the loose in here."

Rade's attention was drawn back to Nemesis. He saw Ms. Bounty in the passenger seat, slowly lifting her stun rifle upward. She herself remained crouched—she had likely piped the feed from the weapon's scope to her vision.

"Careful," Rade said. "We don't want to lose that weapon."

"I won't lose it," Ms. Bounty replied. She edged the weapon higher past the sphere and then squeezed the trigger.

The electrolaser bolt shot into the enemy mech and Ms. Bounty quickly retracted the weapon. All that happened was those incoming plasma beams concentrated on the sphere that shielded her and Shaw.

"As I feared, the stun rifle isn't working," Ms. Bounty said.

"Naw, really?" Bender said.

"We're going to have to force the Phant out, or expose it somehow," Ms. Bounty continued.

"Where would it be housed?" Rade asked.

"In the AI core," Ms. Bounty said. "It should be in the central area underneath the thorax."

Those plasma miniguns kept firing, soon moving on from the hiding place of Shaw and Ms. Bounty to chew through everything between the alien mech and the cowering Hoplites. Only the spheres remained intact.

"These Xaranth sure designed their storage archives to last," Manic commented.

"Too bad they forgot the password!" Fret said.

The assault continued for several moments, only to

let up just like that. Rade knew because the blue streams of light ceased to fly past overhead.

"It appears even alien tech suffers from overheating," Tahoe said.

"Either that, or he thinks he killed us all already," Shaw said.

"Aim past the hides," Rade said. "Scopes only. Don't risk putting your mechs in the sight lines of those plasma beams."

Rade slowly directed the cobra in his right arm past the edge of the sphere. When it was clear, he switched to the viewpoint of the scope and steered the reticle toward the crashed ship. The robot gatorbeetle was still aboard, lurking in the hangar bay. It appeared to be scanning the Quonset with its head, searching for targets.

Rade aimed his cobra directly at one of those eyes and squeezed the trigger.

The robot's head snapped upward in surprise, smashing into the internal hangar's overhead. A moment later several boxlike panels unfolded from the four sides of the head, thorax and abdomen, enveloping those areas in a protective layer. The weapons were mostly still exposed, however, and those minigun turrets all steered toward Rade's position; he quickly pulled his cobra behind the cover of the sphere.

Several plasma beams shot past beside him.

He heard a crash.

"The target just leaped down from the ship," Manic said. "It's coming directly toward your position, boss."

"Guess it didn't like me shooting it in the eye," Rade commented dryly. He glanced at the overhead map. One or more of them had the target in sight, because the red dot representing the enemy was updating. It was indeed headed toward him.

More plasma beams came in, but then shifted a few meters to Rade's right: Shaw's position.

"You fired at it?" Rade asked her.

"How did you guess?" she replied. "Don't think I penetrated that new visor it lowered over its head, though."

"We can use this," Rade said. "If we can draw away its attention so easily... Lui, how difficult would it be for me to barrel through the wall or roof of this structure?"

"Judging from the materials analysis, not difficult at all, especially if you're running at full speed," Lui replied.

"What about if I used my jumpjets?" Rade asked.

"It would have to be full burn," Lui said.

"You're sure I'd be able to break through?" Rade said.

"Not really," Lui replied.

"At least you're honest," Rade said. "Tahoe, Lui, you're the farthest from me. Aim your scopes at the robot. When I count to three, fire. Let me know when you're ready."

"Ready," Tahoe said.

"Ready," Lui echoed.

"Manic, watch your head," Rade told his passenger.

"Something tells me I'm not going to like this," Manic replied.

"One," Rade said.

"Two."

"Three."

His friends fired, and as those plasma beams swung to their position, Rade stood up, held his shield overhead, and activated Electron's jumpjets at full burn. He burst through the roof of the Quonset and into the air outside.

He jetted forward immediately, knowing that the robot would target his previous trajectory. Sure enough, plasma beams seared through the air behind him.

He altered course and thrust down toward the source of those beams. Ahead, he could see the aft portion of the ship poking out from the Quonset.

He applied more forward motion before he struck, wanting to come in directly overtop the giant robot, as indicated by the red dot on his overhead map. He just hoped that dot represented its latest position. The ping time seemed recent enough...

When he was in place, he spun his body around to reorient himself, then jetted downward at full strength, tearing another hole through the roof of the Quonset.

He landed directly on the thing's back.

twenty-three

The robot clanged its two mandibles together in outrage, and then swung its head from side to side, attempting to throw Rade off. He allowed Electron to slide onto the rightmost weapon mounts. He folded away the shield in his left arm and wrapped both his hands around the base of those exposed mounts; he set his cobra lasers to auto-fire at point blank range as he pulled at those weapons. One of the miniguns bent away from the base and he concentrated his attention on it.

"Manic how you doing back there?" Rade asked.

"Just peachy," the passenger replied.

The robot attempted to swivel those weapons toward him, but he resided beyond the range of motion. It fired off all of its plasma beams anyway, hoping to hit Rade, but only struck random objects nearby.

The mech's antennae bent backwards, the sharp tips attempting to bore Rade, but he dodged them, continually working away at the minigun.

Finally he tore it completely away; Rade tossed the useless weapon aside and focused on the second minigun.

The enraged robot leaped skyward, smashing Rade

into the rooftop.

"Manic?" Rade asked.

"I'm okay," Manic replied.

Rade wrenched the weapon to the left, hard. It tore free more easily than the last one.

The gatorbeetle lashed out with its antennae once more, and Rade swung to the left and right. The robot leaped sideways, crashing into one of the nearby spheres. Rade felt the jarring blow that time.

"I'm fine," Manic said, preempting his question.

"Warning," a voice in his cockpit said. It wasn't the inactive AI, but some subsystem. "Hull has caved in section 3C, near the cockpit. Actuator damage."

"What do those actuators control?" Rade said.

"The left foot," the automated system replied.

Rade attempted to move his left foot. The ankle responded sluggishly. That would give him a limp, he knew. Well, it didn't really matter.

He concentrated on ripping away the next minigun.

Tahoe's Hoplite rushed forward, carrying a sphere as a shield.

The giant turned its attention on Tahoe and unleashed its plasma beams, aiming for the feet of Tahoe's mech. Tahoe was forced to drop, lowering the sphere.

Rade ripped the third weapon mount away. He gripped the base of the fourth.

Another, larger sphere rolled forward through the debris, pushed by Shaw. The robot concentrated on her, but those plasma beams couldn't penetrate the object that protected her.

The alien robot decided to leap over the sphere: its upper body grazed the roof, along with Rade's Hoplite. The robot aimed its surviving plasma guns down at

Shaw as it flew past, but she dodged to the side and activated her jumpjets, shooting upward. She slammed into the right flank of the giant robot, opposite Rade, and pulled herself up onto the hull, behind the miniguns on that side. She wrapped her hands around the base of the closest weapon and began wrenching it away while auto-firing her cobras.

Those mandibles clanged even louder, and the robot gatorbeetle flung its body against a large crate nearby, attempting to scrape Nemesis off. Shaw's mech hung on tightly.

Tahoe and Bender leaped their Hoplites onto the flailing robot a moment later.

"Die bitch die!" Bender pounded away at the shielded hull of the head segment.

Between the four of them they managed to wrest away the rest of the miniguns, disarming the mechanical gatorbeetle despite the incessant bucking, antennae attacks, and the occasional body slams into the surrounding debris.

"I think I've spotted a vulnerability in its armor," Lui said. "Underneath the body there's a gap between the head and thorax. My cobras aren't doing much, but a few well-placed grenades might prove extremely uncomfortable to our friend."

Rade was about to swing underneath the body to have a look when all of a sudden the robot sprinted forward through the debris.

"It's spotted the Phant trap!" Fret said.

Rade glanced forward. The robot giant was indeed headed straight toward the stack of spheres that harbored TJ; from the current angle, TJ's Hoplite—and the glass container behind it—were partially visible. The charge was obviously an attempt to break that container and release the Queen.

"Shift your weight to this side!" Rade told the other three Hoplites that clung to the robot. "Pull it off balance!"

Tahoe, Shaw and Bender used their jumpjets to reposition, crashing down onto the robot beside Rade and yanking hard on its armor while firing their jets again. All they succeeded in doing was bending the head and thorax to one side, like pulling on the reins of a wild horse. It continued plowing straight toward the container.

TJ wrapped his arms around the glass container and at the last moment jetted upward at full burn, crashing through the ceiling.

The robot gatorbeetle leaped up after him; its mandibles caught the Hoplite's ankle and dragged the mech down. All five Hoplites and the robot came crashing to the floor at the same time in a blur of limbs and flailing antennae. TJ landed on top, cradling the glass container in the arms of his mech. The trap was undamaged. So far.

As the robot started to get up, Rade squeezed between two of the legs and swung underneath the body; he spotted the gap Lui mentioned between the individual plates coating the head and thorax. Rade shoved his grenade launcher into that space and fired the rest of his frags. He swung back on top and out of the way.

The grenades exploded a moment later. The mechanical giant was knocked backward from the blow, momentarily revealing its underside: the armor had peeled back to form a wicked hole.

"Unit A," Rade said. "Get some charges in that rupture!"

The Centurion swung down from Bender's Hoplite and retrieved the charges from Juggernaut's storage compartment. Then it leaped onto the still recovering giant and clambered between its legs to the smoking gap. In a blur, the Centurion attached the four explosives. Then it swung back up and loaded into Bender's passenger seat.

"Charges in place!" Unit A said.

"Detonate!" Rade commanded.

The resulting explosion lifted the robot a full meter into the air. It came crashing down, rolling onto its side. The Hoplites scrambled out of the way.

The rupture in the armor had grown even wider. Underneath, Rade could see the original hull. The forward portion of the thorax was badly damaged. Farther back, near the center of the thorax, the hull had buckled. The AI core would be somewhere near there, at least going by what Ms. Bounty had said earlier.

"Sync your righthand cobras with mine!" Rade said. "Ms. Bounty, mark the thing's AI core."

The sync indicators on his HUD turned green: all six righthand cobras throughout the squad would fire on the same target at once, as determined by Rade's reticle.

Ms. Bounty's highlight appeared a moment later, slightly offset from the buckled section in the middle of the thorax.

The giant robot was beginning to stir by then. Rade quickly took aim at the highlight and squeezed the trigger. All six cobras fired simultaneously, boring into the hull. A plume of smoke erupted from the fresh bore hole, and the robot gatorbeetle promptly collapsed.

Outside the fresh puncture, black liquid condensed all along the surface.

"Ms. Bounty, quickly," Rade said.

Nemesis came forward. In the passenger seat, Ms. Bounty stood up and aimed her stun rifle at the liquid.

The giant rolled sideways unexpectedly, clipping Shaw's mech with two legs and knocking it over. Those limbs pinned Nemesis and Ms. Bounty underneath.

Shaw broke free, but Ms. Bounty remained caught firmly by one of the prehensile forelimbs. The rifle was pinned to her chest.

"Shaw, get her out!" Rade said.

Shaw grabbed one of those armored forelimbs, but seemed to have trouble getting a grip. "It's coated in some kind of oil. This will take a sec."

"Shoot the base away," Rade said.

"It's not working," Shaw replied.

By then the Phant had seeped onto the floor. For a moment Rade was worried that it would try to possess Ms. Bounty, but it quickly retreated instead, wending its way toward the crashed ship.

"Damn it." Rade fired his cobra at the Phant but it had no effect.

He limped toward Nemesis and Ms. Bounty and wrapped his arms around the other forelimb. As Shaw had said, it was slick with something, and his big fingers kept sliding along the surface every time he pulled.

He tried shooting his cobra into the base of the limb, but the boxlike armor still covered the area, preventing his weapon from causing much damage. And there were no obvious gaps where he could lodge a frag.

"Need some help here, people!" Rade said.

Bender quickly joined them, but his own fingers constantly slipped along the glistening surface, unable to get a grip. "It's like we're masturbating it."

Rade stepped back to let Tahoe try. As he did so, he gazed at the Phant, which had reached the ship by then.

Harlequin was standing between the two prongs, just inside the hangar of the vessel, waiting. The black box containing Surus still hung from his harness. How long he had been lurking there, observing, Rade didn't know.

Harlequin held a blaster in hand, and peered down at it as if confused.

"Harlequin!" Rade said. "Jump down!"

The Black oozed up the external surface of the vessel and when it reached Harlequin's jumpsuit it began to seep inside the boot.

"Harlequin!" Rade said.

Harlequin looked up. "Boss?"

The black liquid had completely vanished inside the jumpsuit.

Rade aimed the targeting reticle of his cobra over Harlequin's head. He steeled himself to do the unthinkable.

He centered the crosshairs over Harlequin's right eye. His finger started to press the trigger...

Rade couldn't do it.

He released the trigger as if it were a viper.

Harlequin had sacrificed himself for Rade a long time ago. Even though he retained a backup aboard the *Argonaut*, Rade couldn't do this to him, wipe out his existence like that and force him to start over again.

Besides, Rade knew that even if he terminated Harlequin, the Black would simply flow into the alien ship's equivalent of an AI core and take over from there.

Harlequin grinned widely, then spun about. The ship's bay door sealed shut behind him.

The vessel shifted in place; fresh portions of the ceiling ripped away and crashed to the floor; crates and other debris fell over. The horseshoe-shaped craft moved back and forth for a few moments, apparently lodged.

By then, Shaw, Bender and Tahoe had finally ripped Ms. Bounty free, and she was secure once more in the passenger seat of Nemesis. Apparently they had freed her by repeatedly firing their lasers into the AI core, judging from the fresh holes in the robot's thorax.

Ms. Bounty unleashed her stun rifle at the ship but it had no effect.

"Shoot that ship down!" Rade ordered them.

But their comparatively weak lasers didn't cause any damage against the armored hull of the vessel. It was constructed of the same material that had folded over the alien mech, apparently.

In moments the vessel had torn free of the Quonset. As it ascended, it ejected some sort of plasma sphere from its aft quarter. Red in the middle and blue on the outside, with sparks of electricity traveling all along the surface, the sphere seemed directed straight at the party.

"Retreat!" Rade said. "Use your jumpjets to break through the roof!" That was the only way to get out of there in time—Rade knew it would take too long to scramble over the debris blocking their path to the entrance.

The six Hoplites tore fresh holes in the roof as they emerged from the structure at full burn. Rade fired the aft thrusters next, so that his arc was more forward than upwards.

He glanced at the feed from the rearmost camera and watched the energy ball strike the far side of the three structures. Upon impact, a larger, blindingly bright plasma sphere erupted, engulfing half of the Quonsets.

The photochromatic filters gated the brightness down; in seconds, the large plasma sphere dissipated. In its place remained a perfectly hemispherical crater of the same radius and depth. The engulfed halves of the three structures—and their contents—were gone. Completely disintegrated.

The retreating ship, meanwhile, had vanished into the upper atmosphere.

"Manic, you okay?" Rade asked.

"Yeah," Manic replied. "Just wish I had a mech. You guys had all the fun."

Rade landed and gathered the Hoplites. When he confirmed that everyone was all right, he led the squad toward the righthand Quonset. His mech still had a bit of a limp, thanks to the damage to the right ankle. The other Hoplites showed signs of similar impairment: the left arm of Tahoe's mech hung limply, the right leg of Bender's Hoplite moved stiffly, and so forth.

"You know, I'm starting to think it's too much of a liability to bring along Artificials," Tahoe said.

"I'm beginning to feel the same way," Rade said. "New rule: next time we equip our jumpsuits not just with anti-telepath defenses but also anti-Phant EM emitters, just like the Hoplites. You think Surus can manage that, Ms. Bounty?"

"I believe so," Ms. Bounty replied. "She won't be cutting costs like that ever again."

"We'll see," Bender said.

When they reached the Quonset, they discovered the second ship had escaped disintegration by virtue of its positioning on the closer side of the hangar. And though there were holes in the walls indicating where the random plasma beams of the robot gatorbeetle had struck, none of them had penetrated the armor of the Tech Class IV vessel.

"The King should have fired another disintegration sphere," TJ said.

"He couldn't," Ms. Bounty said. "That weapon is restricted to one shot every twenty minutes."

"Then he should have aimed his shot better," TJ said.

After a closer inspection, they realized a small piece had in fact been shorn off the aft section.

"Will it still fly with that damage?" Rade asked.

"I believe so," Ms. Bounty said. "Unfortunately this section housed the aft plasma turret, so we've lost that weapon. But we still have the forward lasers."

"You think the King did this on purpose?" Lui asked.

"What do you mean?" Rade replied.

"All I'm saying is that maybe he purposely missed the ship," Lui said. "Firing at just the right angle to shear off the aft weapon. Maybe he wants us to follow."

"Definitely something to consider," Rade said. "All right everyone, get inside the ship! We have a Phant to catch!"

twenty-four

Bring the Hoplites!" Rade continued. "We'll stow them in the crew quarters."

Limping, Rade led the Hoplites aboard in single file. He followed the smooth, curving passageway.

"Do you see those lines in the deck?" Ms. Bounty said.

Rade glanced downward. Horizontal lines placed perpendicular to the passage occasionally interrupted the smooth surface.

"Those are where breach seals will activate when we reach orbit," Ms. Bounty said. "You don't want to be caught overtop one of them when that happens."

"Good to know," Rade said.

Rade paused at every compartment and sent a mech inside to clear it. He wanted to make sure nothing had sneaked aboard while they were engaged with the Xaranth mech. They swept engineering, the bridge, and finally the hangar bay, scanning each compartment on all EM bands, and LIDAR. Ms. Bounty dismounted to check the onboard shuttle.

When they cleared the final area, he backtracked to the crew quarters and stepped past it to allow the other Hoplites inside. They took their places among the six hollows in the floor. TJ lowered the Phant trap into the free hollow beside him.

"Wait, Rade's mech needs a spot," Shaw told TJ.

"No," Rade said. "I'm not leaving Electron here. Dismount, everyone. Make your way to the bridge."

Rade walked Electron forward through the curved passageway.

"You're bringing your Hoplite to the bridge?" Shaw asked.

"Not exactly," Rade told her. "I'm taking Electron to the hangar bay. I want the mech ready to launch, just in case."

At the bay, there was more than enough room for him to fit the Hoplite beside the existing oval-shaped shuttle. He glanced at the overhead map generated by his Implant to orient himself, and confirmed that the bay doors—located on the lefthand side of the compartment—opened out between the prong sections of the nose.

Rade dismounted. It was nice not to have a machine-inflicted limp anymore. He performed a second quick search of the shuttle, as the ramp was still open. No one inside. When he poked his head out he saw Shaw waiting for him near the entrance to the bay.

"Always double-check, huh?" Shaw said as he approached.

"That's right," Rade said.

"At least we have a ship again," she told him.

"Too bad we can't take it back with us to our side of the galaxy," Rade commented.

Shaw smiled. "Let's not get ahead of ourselves. We have a Black to capture, a Green to rescue, and an Artificial to save."

"Ah, it's all in a day's work," Rade told her.

The pair joined the rest of the crew at the bridge. Most of them simply sat along the edge of the circular hollow in the deck, their legs resting on the sloping surface. Ms. Bounty stood near the front perimeter of the depression, one of her gloves wrapped around the featureless pillar beside it.

"Are you ready for take off?" she asked.

"Launch," Rade told her. He hesitated. "Should we grab on to something?"

Ms. Bounty smiled. "We're already in the air, accelerating to escape velocity."

"Oh." There were no external windows to speak of, so of course Rade had no way to tell.

"This is a Tech Class IV ship," Ms. Bounty explained. "Though it's small, the inertial dampeners will offer a far smoother ride than anything you've ever experienced in a human vessel. You'll feel no change in gravity once we enter the void either, as this vessel is equipped with a fully functional artificial gravity system."

He sensed motion to the side, and turned his head toward the bridge entrance: a hatch had silently sealed, shutting them in.

"We're in orbit?" Rade asked.

"We just achieved orbit, yes," Ms. Bounty replied.

"Are we tracking our foe yet?" Rade missed having access to a tactical display, but this was an alien ship, so of course there was no way for him to interface with whatever AI the vessel had.

"The target seems to be using the gas giant as a gravitational slingshot," Ms. Bounty said.

"You're getting all of that from the pillar?" TJ asked.

"Yes," Ms. Bounty said. "It's hard to explain, but the pheromone data returned by the interface is a language in and of itself, and can be used to specify the positions of all surrounding celestial objects in the battle space when one understands how to interpret that data. My guess is the Phant is heading toward a small wormhole on the other side of the planet, closer to the sun."

"A wormhole?"

"Yes," Ms. Bounty said. "There are a network of them in this region of the galaxy. The equivalent of your Slipstreams. We won't need a Gate to traverse them."

"Nice," Rade said. "The Phants created them?"

"No," Ms. Bounty said. "Another, more ancient race. Perhaps the Elder. No one is certain, as none of the races conquered by the Phants ever had such technology."

"All right," Rade said. "Set a pursuit course with that ship."

"Setting course," Ms. Bounty said.

"Feels a bit odd, doesn't it?" Tahoe said. "Relaying your orders all to the same individual?"

"Somewhat," Rade said. "Though really, it's not all that different from relaying orders to a ship's AI, like I sometimes do with Bax."

"You know, we haven't named this ship yet," Fret said.

"How about the *Magnet?*" Manic said.

"The *Magnet?*" Bender said. "Worst— name— ever."

"No, it works," Manic said. "The ship looks like a big magnet or horseshoe, so why not? And *Magnet* is better than *Horseshoe*."

"I kind of like *Horseshoe*," Bender said. "Or maybe *Horsey*."

"*Horsey?*" Manic said. "And you complain about

my names. Hey everyone, we're flying aboard the intergalactic cruiser the *U.S.S. Horsey.* Welcome aboard, enjoy your stay, and try not to gag whenever you hear the name!"

"We'll go with *Magnet,*" Rade said.

"Thanks boss," Manic said.

"Yeah," Bender said. "Thanks for nothing."

Ms. Bounty kept Rade updated every fifteen minutes. Her third announcement revealed that they were on their closest approach to the gas giant.

"In a human ship, the decks would be moaning in complaint right about now," TJ said. "From the competing forces vying to tear apart the hull. And yet this ship is quiet as a hunter in the dark."

"That's exactly what we are," Tahoe said. "We've become the hunters again, not the prey."

"Don't be so sure," a voice came from the entrance to the bridge. The hatch had opened.

Tantalus stood there, blaster in hand.

"How?" Rade said.

"I came aboard while you were engaged with the Master." Tantalus stepped inside and the hatch sealed behind him. "I hid in the hangar bay."

"But I searched the bay," Rade said.

Tantalus smiled. "I had a few Tech Class IV holographic emitters with me, as well as a metal wall panel—a piece of junk from the first Quonset I carried aboard. I flattened myself behind it against the hangar bay doors, reduced my thermal output, and activated the emitters."

Rade cursed silently. With those emitters on, Tantalus would have completely blended in with the bay doors. And by holding the wall panel in front of him, if it was wide enough, the Artificial would have evaded detection on the LIDAR and thermal bands, seeming a part of the bulkhead.

When Tantalus emerged from hiding, because the Hoplite AI cores were offline, even though Electron remained in the hangar bay, the mech wouldn't have reported the intruder. Perhaps the *Magnet's* AI had detected it, but Rade suspected Ms. Bounty hadn't been able to interpret the data.

Tantalus glanced at Ms. Bounty. "Set a course for the gas giant. A direct course. Steer the ship into its heart."

"But you'll kill us all," Fret said.

Tantalus pointed his blaster at Shaw. "Do it, or I kill the human woman."

"Set the course, Ms. Bounty," Rade said. He sent her a private message. "Or pretend to."

"It's done," Ms. Bounty announced.

"Line up against the far wall," Tantalus said. The crew got up from their places and did so. "You too," he told Ms. Bounty.

When everyone had moved back, the Artificial approached the pillar and rested a hand on it, keeping the blaster pointed at the party. Rade noticed small pheromone funnels on his fingertips.

"You didn't set the course," Tantalus said. "No matter. I've updated it." Tantalus released the pillar and turned toward Ms. Bounty. "You are to serve as the vessel for my Queen. Argonauts—is that what you call yourselves? Yes. Argonauts, toss your weapons into the bridge pit, please."

Across the squad, blasters were removed from utility belts and tossed into the depression on the deck.

"Good," Tantalus said. "Now, we will proceed toward the crew quarters, where you have trapped a certain queen of mine. You are all lucky, you know. Ordinarily, I would simply kill you where you stand for what you have done. But I have decided to leave the manner of your deaths to my Queen. Besides, she may decide to spare a few of you for her pleasure. So who am I to judge who will live and die among you? Now move!"

Ms. Bounty was the first to the door, and she opened it with her gloves. The squad members marched two abreast into the passageway beyond.

"It's going to be a little hard to serve your Queen if we fall into the gas giant," Rade said.

"I plan to correct our course shortly," Tantalus said. "Once you release the Queen."

Halfway there, they reached another breach seal that Ms. Bounty once more opened. During the march, Rade was constantly aware of the passing seconds, and he wondered how long it would be until the ship reached the point of no return, unable to achieve escape velocity from the gas giant. Even a Tech Class IV ship would have a limit in how close it could come to such a gravity well. He kept an eye out for an opportunity to jump Tantalus.

A seal had closed over the entrance to the crew quarters. Ms. Bounty opened it, but before she could enter, Tantalus spoke.

"Don't go inside," Tantalus said. "You are all to move forward and walk past the entrance."

The squad obeyed. Mostly.

Bender, near the center of the group, decided to duck inside.

Tantalus raced forward. "I said don't—"

A large metal hand reached around the edge of the compartment and wrapped around Tantalus.

"Permission to squash this bug dick-licker, boss?" Bender asked.

"Granted," Rade replied.

The Hoplite's hand squeezed shut. The Artificial's upper body convulsed violently, and its eyes rolled up in their sockets.

Tantalus ceased moving.

Bender released the Artificial and then stomped down on the remains with one of Juggernaut's feet, grinding as he did so.

"How does it feel?" Bender said. "Not so high and mighty now are you, bitch?"

"Get to the bridge!" Rade said. "We have to correct our course before it's too late."

Ms. Bounty was already rushing back the way they had come.

When Rade reached the bridge, Ms. Bounty was just wrapping her hands around the control pillar.

"I've corrected our course," Ms. Bounty said. "It will take us at least a day to attain our previous orbit. We'll be twenty four standard hours behind our prey."

"Not much we can do about that," Rade said.

The others took their seats around the hollow.

"Close one back there," Lui said.

"Thanks, Bender," Rade said.

Bender shrugged inside his jumpsuit. "Sure boss. Squishing bugs and their dick lickers is what I do."

"Got a problem," Ms. Bounty said.

"What is it?" Rade asked.

"I've detected a shuttle launch from our prey," Ms. Bounty said. "It's directed toward the core of the gas giant. Surus is aboard."

"Are you sure?" Rade said. If Surus was truly aboard, and destined for the gas giant, the normally invulnerable Green would never escape the immense gravity well. It was a fate similar to being thrown into the core of a star: trapped deep inside the planet, Surus would eventually starve to death as the millennia passed.

Ms. Bounty nodded. "I've accessed the shuttle's internal sensors. They indicate the presence of the black box containing the Green."

Lui frowned behind his faceplate. "If you've accessed the internal sensors, can't you access its controls as well?"

"I'm locked out of the actual controls," Ms. Bounty said. "I can only utilize the sensors."

"I think our foe could've locked you out of the sensors as well," Tahoe said. "He wants us to know he's launched Surus toward the planet. To draw us off his tail."

"Could those readings be faked?" TJ asked.

"Hmm, I suppose it's possible," Ms. Bounty said. "Though I'm not sure the Black would have had time to prepare something like that."

"So you're not sure Surus is aboard then, after all," Rade said.

Ms. Bounty paused. "My gut tells me that she is. The Black would want to destroy the Green at the first available opportunity."

"Your gut," Bender said. "I've said it before, and I'll say it again, AI's don't have no gut feelings. I don't believe Surus is aboard."

"Well I do," Rade said quietly.

"What if the Artificial is wrong?" Bender pressed.

"Do we want to risk the chance that she isn't?" Rade said.

Bender didn't answer.

"I didn't think so," Rade continued. "Ms. Bounty, bring us on an intercept course."

"The requested course change will put us another day behind our prey," Ms. Bounty said.

"I understand," Rade said. "Do it."

"Done," Ms. Bounty said. "You know, it looks like our earlier course change actually proved beneficial after all. If we were still in a higher orbit, we would have never made it in time."

"The question is," Lui said. "Once we're in range, what then? This ship doesn't have any grappling hooks. Or does it?"

"No," Ms. Bounty said.

"I have an idea," Rade said. "But first of all, Ms. Bounty, can you fly the shuttle in the hangar bay?"

"I can."

"Good," Rade said. And he explained his plan.

twenty-five

When Rade was done speaking, Ms. Bounty nodded. "Yes. That might work."

"Wait," Shaw said. "So you intend to take Ms. Bounty with you. That's fine and all, but how are we supposed to control the ship in her absence?"

"I can fix that," Ms. Bounty said. "Unit A, come here."

The Centurion complied.

Ms. Bounty gave Unit A her left glove, keeping the right one for herself. The fingertips on both hand coverings contained the funnel-like pheromone generators, Rade noticed.

"Put it on," Ms. Bounty urged the unit.

The Centurion replaced its glove with the one she had given.

"You don't need two to interface with the tech?" Rade asked Ms. Bounty.

"No," Ms. Bounty said. "We are machines... even with just one hand, we can move fast enough to simulate two antennae." She addressed Unit A: "Accept my data transfer request."

"Accepted," Unit A responded.

Ms. Bounty glanced at Rade. "This will take about three minutes. We won't be close enough to the descending shuttle for another seven anyway."

"And once we arrive, how much time will we have before passing the point of no return?" Rade asked.

"Fifteen minutes," Ms. Bounty said.

Rade took a seat along the rim of the depression and waited impatiently while Ms. Bounty transferred the necessary knowledge to the Centurion.

Shaw sat down beside him and initiated a direct connection.

"Rade," Shaw said. "You don't have to do this. Let someone else go."

"No," Rade said. "It has to be me. I won't put anyone else's life at risk for this. It's my plan, my risk."

"At least let me come."

Rade shook his head. "I need you here." He gripped her gloved hand. "I'll be back. Trust me."

Shaw closed her eyes and shook her head behind the faceplate. "If anything happens to you..."

"Nothing will," Rade said. "Look at me. Look."

She did.

"This is a simple spacewalk," Rade said. "In a Hoplite. What could go wrong?" He couldn't help the sarcasm that edged his tone.

Shaw chuckled sadly. "Famous last words."

Rade sighed. He decided not to say anything else lest he worry her even further.

"Thank you," Shaw said.

"For what?" Rade asked.

"For just holding me," she replied.

Three minutes later Unit A turned toward Shaw. "I understand how to interface with this ship."

"Do so," Rade said.

The Centurion approached the pillar and touched the special glove to it.

"Sensors on the glove interrupt and convert the

chemical data returned by the interface into tactile sensations for my fingertips," the unit explained. "Allowing me to interpret the data. I can 'see' all the celestial bodies around me, for example. I know the position of the incoming shuttle, and the more distant ship. Other sensors interpret my finger presses and release pheromones in turn, allowing me to guide the vessel."

"Try adjusting our course," Rade said. "Bring us closer to the shuttle."

"It's working," Unit A said.

"Bring us alongside," Rade said. "Close to within five hundred meters on the starboard side and match its course and speed."

"Aye boss," Unit A replied.

Rade stood. "All right," he told Ms. Bounty. "Let's go."

Shaw rose and gave him one last, tight hug. "Come back."

"I always do." Rade departed.

Ms. Bounty led him into the passageway outside and through the different breach seals. At the hangar, two such seals had descended, forming an airlock. After passing through, Rade loaded into Electron and assumed manual control. He missed the usual greeting from the inactive AI.

Ms. Bounty meanwhile entered the alien shuttle and sealed the ramp behind her.

"Do you read me?" her voice came over the radio.

"Loud and clear," Rade answered.

He wrapped the arms of his mech around the shuttle's aft fuselage. Apparently, if he attached his magnets to the port or starboard sides, the weight and magnetism would throw off the internal gyroscopes. He could have clung to the front area, where the shaded visor resided, but apparently that would have interfered with the shuttle's sensor array, in addition to blocking Ms. Bounty's external view. That left only the aft area, which meant Ms. Bounty wouldn't be able to exit until he moved aside, as the ramp unfolded via the same region.

Once he was in place, Rade activated the magnetic mounts in his chest and elbows, and felt his mech firmly attach. He rested the Hoplite's feet on the two small wings that protruded near the base.

"Are you secure?" Ms. Bounty transmitted.

"I am," Rade said.

"Depressurizing the compartment," Ms. Bounty said.

The airlock had already sealed behind them; in moments the atmosphere vented from the bay. The twin doors opened; the shuttle floated into the air and then accelerated outside while Rade hung on. He felt the sense of weightlessness instantly, his stomach doing belly flops.

The red and blue gas giant with its four large ring systems devoured the stars immediately above them. The craft moved forward quickly, headed toward the second shuttle traveling five hundred meters from the starboard side of the *Magnet*.

"I'm decelerating," Ms. Bounty transmitted. "Prepare for spacewalk."

"How much time again until we pass beyond the point of no return?" Rade asked.

"About ten minutes now," Ms. Bounty said. "For these shuttles, anyway. For your mech, you're already past that point, of course."

"I guess you're saying I should be careful not to let go of the shuttle."

"Yes."

"Shaw, do you read?" Rade tried.

A voice came over his comm, but it was so distorted he couldn't understand the words, let alone ascertain who the speaker was.

"The gas giant is producing too much radiation," Ms. Bounty said. "The comm node in your Hoplite is far to weak to connect with the other Hoplites aboard, even at this relatively short range."

The shuttle approached the second craft, finally halting two meters away. Well, it hadn't really halted, of course. While it might look like both shuttles merely floated there, Rade knew the pair were hurtling through space at thousands of kilometers per hour, falling inexorably toward the massive giant above them.

"I'm ready to open the ramp," Ms. Bounty said.

"Disconnecting," Rade said. He released the magnetic mounts, activated a minuscule burst of lateral thrust, then reset the mounts and reattached farther along the starboard side of the shuttle, away from the aft area. While he couldn't hang on to the flanks of the craft during flight, it was perfectly fine when the engines were inactive. "Proceed."

The aft portion of the flattened ovule cracked open, and the ramp lowered. Ms. Bounty's gloved fingers appeared along the rim, and she pulled herself outside.

Rade extended Electron's hand toward her; she grabbed onto the mech and then clambered into his passenger seat. She had to rely on his mech because, like the rest of the Argonauts, she hadn't recovered the jetpack for her jumpsuit.

Rade gently pushed away from the *Magnet's* shuttle, and initiated another lateral burst of thrust to turn around. He fired a quick burst of countering thrust when he was facing the target craft.

Rade silently latched on to the port side of the shuttle that contained Surus and extended his arm toward the aft region.

Ms. Bounty climbed along his metal arm and paused beside the ramp location. She touched the fingers of the pheromone-generating glove to several small indentations along the edge of the craft. Her hand moved in a blur between them.

The pod cracked open and the ramp lowered.

"I'm going in." Ms. Bounty lowered the stun rifle and pulled herself past the edge, vanishing from view.

Rade tried to switch to her point of view. He received an access denied message.

"Ms. Bounty, you have me locked out of your guest observer system," Rade said.

"Sorry," Ms. Bounty replied. "Fixed that. I have Surus."

The video feed came back as Ms. Bounty took control of the shuttle. She was facing the tinted glass that provided a view of the space beyond. Her gloved hand was on the control pillar.

"You aren't going to let Surus enter you?" Rade asked.

"I already have," Ms. Bounty replied. "This is Surus speaking. I'm taking us back to the *Magnet*. Please reposition to the aft area."

Rade released his magnets and activated a tiny burst of lateral thrust. But before he could reattach, the shuttle sped away.

"Uh, Surus?" Rade said. "I didn't get a chance to attach."

The shuttle continued toward the *Magnet*.

"Surus?" Rade tried again.

With a sinking feeling, he realized the King had

outsmarted them once again.

"Shaw, this is Rade," he transmitted. "I believe Ms. Bounty has been possessed once again. Surus wasn't aboard that shuttle. It was the King. We've been tricked."

He received no reply. He tried again. Still nothing.

Rade jetted back to the original shuttle and attached to it. He wasn't sure why he did it. He had no way to control the shuttle, not without that special pheromone glove and the knowledge to use it. But there was something reassuring about hanging onto a solid object in space.

He glanced up at the gas giant that loomed so massively above him. Lurking there, blotting out all those stars, it seemed like it was waiting to devour him.

Well, I guess this is finally it.

He just hoped Shaw was able to make it out of this alive.

Because his time had come.

THE KING SMILED at his ingenuity.

He had reprogrammed the shuttle to send out a false sensor image of the interior, mimicking the signature of the box that contained the trapped Green. Then he had locked out remote access and set the craft on a collision course with the gas giant.

Of course, he had been ready to assume control if it turned out the humans hadn't fallen for his ruse.

But they had.

Hook.

Line.

And sinker.

The King had been lurking upon the overhead of the cabin. In the cold vacuum of space he had reverted to his gaseous form, which allowed him to move more quickly. When the so-called Ms. Bounty entered, he misted into the helmet of her jumpsuit immediately, before she had a chance to even raise that stun weapon of hers. It had all been so easy.

And now he was about to reunite with his Queen.

The *Magnet* seemed to be altering course to close with his shuttle more quickly. All the better.

As the King came within range of the *Magnet*, a woman's voice came over the comm. The King recognized it as the one named Shaw.

"Ms. Bounty, are you there?" Shaw said. "Ms. Bounty?"

"I'm here," the King replied. It was odd, hearing a woman's voice come from his throat. He was accustomed to possessing Artificials modeled after human males. Still, it was arousing in a way.

"I'm not able to reach Rade," Shaw said. "His mech isn't showing up on my overhead map."

"The intense radiation damaged Electron's comm node during the spacewalk," the King said. "But he's right here with me."

"Then why isn't the weaker comm node in his suit allowing him to reach me?" Shaw said. "The node in your suit seems to be working well enough."

The King cursed silently to himself, and thought quickly. "Rade has fallen unconscious. He's going to need radiation treatment. I'm sorry."

"Oh no," Shaw said. "I told him not to go. Get aboard as quickly as you can."

"I intend to," the King replied.

The hangar doors opened and he steered the shuttle inside. After he docked, he stared at the rifle that hung from his shoulder. The so-called "stun rifle" that had caused him so many problems. He lowered the weapon and broke it over one knee.

Good luck subduing me now, he thought.

The bay doors closed and he opened the shuttle's ramp before the hangar fully pressurized. He approached the airlock from the side, blaster at the ready. He could sense his Queen aboard, somewhere.

When the atmosphere stabilized the inner hatch opened. He aimed the blaster at the entrance and waited for Shaw and the others to rush inside.

No one came.

Have they discovered my ruse?

He realized he was only wearing one of the pheromone generating gloves. That meant there was potentially another machine aboard that could interface with the ship; perhaps it knew enough about the internal systems to access the hangar bay scanners, and thus determine only Ms. Bounty had returned. Not Rade.

I should have used a different lie.

The King slowly peered past the edge of the airlock and into the passage beyond. Empty.

Blaster in hand, he stepped through the airlock and into the corridor, intending to make his way to the bridge. He was ready to revert to his liquid form and incinerate them all. Well, everyone except for Shaw, who would know the new codes he needed to open the container that trapped his Queen.

But he had only taken a few steps before he perceived a loud thud behind him. At first he thought it was the airlock door sealing, but he realized he had heard that softer sound already. This noise was different: the sound of a glass door shutting.

"No," the King said.

He began to float into the air.

SHAW KICKED THE emitters aside and watched with satisfaction as Ms. Bounty began to revolve inside the glass container, along with the black liquid of the Queen.

King and Queen were reunited at last.

Enjoy it while you can, you embodiments of evil.

She boarded Nemesis; the mech was waiting beside the glass container. Unit A resided in the passenger seat.

"Open up the airlock, Unit A," Shaw ordered.

The combat robot leaped down, squeezed past the glass container, and used its glove to open both the inner and outer hatches of the airlock. Then the Centurion proceeded inside the hangar bay to wait for her.

Shaw stepped forward in the Hoplite, shoving the glass container into the hangar to move it out of the way.

Tahoe and Bender followed her inside, also in their mechs.

Shaw moved the glass container back through the airlock and into the passageway, where the other Argonauts waited in their jumpsuits, prepared to release Ms. Bounty the moment the King was extracted from her.

Unit A used its special glove to seal the airlock from the inside, as well as evacuate the hangar and open the bay doors. Then Unit A entered the shuttle and flew the craft outside.

Shaw took a running leap and followed the shuttle

from the ship. She felt sick as the weightlessness took over.

The gas giant filled the starscape above. It was dizzying.

She jetted forward, positioning herself behind the aft section of the shuttle. She latched on with her magnetic mounts.

Tahoe and Bender were behind her. They attached to her with their own magnets, forming a chain.

Shaw scanned the space around her and detected Rade's faint heat signature above them. She had had Unit A bring the *Magnet* closer when she realized what had happened.

"Rade, do you read me?" Shaw tried.

No answer.

"Unit A, are you picking up Rade out there?" Shaw said. "He should be showing up on your tactical map by now, courtesy of his heat sig."

"I have him," Unit A replied. "I'm bringing us in."

Shaw just hoped there was still time.

twenty-six

S haw thought of what had happened since Rade left the ship. After he transferred Ms. Bounty to the second shuttle, Unit A had reported the craft accelerating away from the mech. Shaw had immediately suspected foul play, and instructed Unit A to bring the *Magnet* closer to the returning shuttle.

When Ms. Bounty was in range, Shaw feigned ignorance regarding Rade's fate, and when the Artificial had lied about the mech's location, claiming that Electron was still attached to the shuttle but Rade was unconscious due to radiation poisoning, she knew it had to be the King.

She had used Nemesis to push the Phant trap into place, then opened it, keeping the containment field active so that the Queen wouldn't escape. With TJ's help she placed the emitters. The two had only just finished setting up in time before the possessed Ms. Bounty opened the airlock and walked into the trap.

Shaw gazed over the white hull of the shuttle she now clung to. The ringed gas giant above seemed bigger somehow, though she knew it was an illusion of the mind—she wasn't falling *that* fast. Then again maybe she was.

Those swirling, red and blue clouds would have

been beautiful under other circumstances. But not now. All she saw was an ominous, baleful thing.

"We've lost contact with the *Magnet* thanks to the intense radiation the giant is giving off," Tahoe said.

"We need some proper comm nodes," Bender said. "Not the tiny things in these mechs."

"Where's a telemetry drone when you need one, huh?" Tahoe said.

Shaw glanced at her rear video feed. The *Magnet* had disappeared into the starscape behind them.

"Rade, do you read me?" Shaw tried again.

Still no answer.

"Unit A, how are we doing for radiation poisoning?" Shaw asked.

"Your battle suit armor should hold up well to these particular wavelengths," Unit A replied. "Nonetheless, all of you will need treatment, eventually. Certainly when you return to the *Argonaut*."

"That could be a few weeks," Shaw said. "Will we last that long?"

"I believe so."

In another five hundred meters, a small dot appeared just below the horizon of the giant, roughly a kilometer ahead, and two degrees declination—that much closer to the planet than her group.

Shaw zoomed in: she discerned Electron hanging on to the original shuttle.

"Rade, do you read me?" Shaw transmitted once more.

She received only silence.

"Unit A, tell me we're not too late," Shaw said.

"He has passed beyond the point of no return," Unit A said. "We cannot retrieve him with the motive force available to this shuttle."

Shaw stared at Rade's distant mech for long

moments.

Past the point of no return...

"We've lost him," Tahoe said. "I can't believe it."

"No we haven't," Shaw said. She refused to give up so easily. "Unit A, listen to me carefully. I need you to perform a very important calculation. If we fired the jumpjets of our Hoplites, adding our thrust to that of the shuttle you pilot, would we be able to escape the gravity? Include Electron's motive force in your calculations."

"Let me access the appropriate subsystems in your mechs for a moment," the combat robot replied.

Two seconds passed.

"The answer is no," Unit A said. "It doesn't matter if we combine our fuel, it still won't be enough. We'll simply doom ourselves to the same fate as Rade. It really is too late."

"What if we had the other two mechs from the *Magnet* with us?" Shaw asked.

"Even if there was time to return to the *Magnet* to retrieve them, which there is not, I'm afraid it wouldn't make a difference. I'm sorry, Shaw. He is lost."

Shaw slumped.

She couldn't believe it. Rade really was going to die.

And she was going to watch it.

"I think I've found a way to boost our signal," Unit A said from within the shuttle. "Try reaching him again."

"Rade, do you read?" Shaw tried.

"Hey, babe," Rade's distorted voice returned. He sounded extremely weary. "Guess I've gone and done it now, haven't I? Please don't be mad at me too much."

"I'm not mad at you," Shaw said, struggling to

control her quivering chin.

"I often wondered what it would be like to die outside of battle," Rade said. "I took some comfort in my choice of careers, always expecting that when death finally came, it would be quick. Either instantaneous, or a few moments of excruciating pain numbing to nothingness. But I don't have that luxury anymore. It's like I've been given a death prognosis by a doctor. Told I have a few hours to live. So before I cease to exist, I have time to sit here and think. A few hours to dwell upon my regrets, and everything I wish I had done.

"I've faced death so many times in my life. And I can tell you, it's much easier when you know the end will come quickly. Not like this. Too much time to focus on my regrets. Before battle, I always tell myself I'm ready to die. I have to. But now, with all this time to think before the end comes, I can actually be honest with myself. I can admit: I'm not ready.

"There's so much I still want to do. Especially with you. Oh, my Shaw. I held off too long. We were supposed to have children together. And now we never will. I'm sorry. I should have listened to you at the beginning of the mission, when you asked me to consider it. I should have taken you up on the idea. I should have..."

"No," Shaw said. "None of this is your fault. You couldn't know this would happen."

"But I knew we'd face death," Rade said. "I knew there was a chance I'd never come back. And now it's happened. I'm not coming back." He was silent for a time. "Seek out the Mahasattva. We're at peace with them, last I checked. They made clones of me once, long ago. While I might not live again, in this body, the universe can still have me with their help. You can still have me. Or a version of me, anyway. At least you'll be able to have the children I deprived you of."

"I don't want children with a clone!" Shaw said, unable to help the tears. "I want children with *you*."

"I'm sorry Shaw, that's all I can offer," Rade said.

"But it won't be *you!*" Shaw repeated. "Just stop this talk of clones. I don't want to hear it. If this is the last time I'm going to ever hear your voice, just let me... just let me..."

But she couldn't finish. It was too hard. Rade was going to die here on this cold world, crushed as he descended into the atmosphere. A painful, agonizing death.

"I'm sorry," Rade said. "I'll give you a moment."

I don't want a moment, she wanted to say. *I want forever.*

And then Ms. Bounty's voice came over the comm. "Could you use a hand?"

Shaw glanced at the feed from her rear camera. The *Magnet* had closed to within three hundred meters behind them.

"I thought you couldn't come this low?" Shaw said.

"I found a way to boost the distance," Ms. Bounty replied. "Using reserve generators. But this is the final, absolute range. However, I'm setting the ship on autopilot, and personally coming out with a few friends."

From the hangar, the remaining two Hoplites emerged, piloted by Lui and Manic. Ms. Bounty was in the passenger seat of Lui's mech.

"Pick them up," Shaw instructed Unit A.

The shuttle decelerated slightly, allowing the two mechs to close. They latched onto Tahoe and Bender.

"Unit A tells me even with all six mechs, we won't

have enough motive force to retrieve Rade," Shaw told her.

"Your AI is correct," Ms. Bounty replied. "But I plan to assume control of the shuttle Rade is hanging on to. I've run a few calculations: if we leave now, we should have just enough combined thrust to escape the gravity and return to the *Magnet*."

"Then let's go!" Shaw said. "Unit A, take us in! And thank you, Ms. Bounty, for giving me hope. If we succeed, I'll owe you for all eternity."

"You are welcome," Ms. Bounty said. "But we haven't rescued him yet."

Several moments passed as the craft slowly approached Rade's location.

"What are you doing?" Rade asked.

"Something," Shaw replied.

"Look, I've run the calculations," Rade said. "Even with all six of us, and the two shuttles, we won't have enough motive force to escape the gravitational pull. Don't trap yourself here with me!"

"You're wrong," Shaw said. "Do you remember when I was falling into the atmosphere of Guangdong IV not so long ago? Do you remember what you said to me? 'I'm not leaving you.' Well, I say that now to you. We've switched places. Instead of you rescuing me, it's my turn to save you."

"Yeah, boss," Bender said. "You think we're going to leave you behind to fall into a gas giant or something, bitch?"

"I'd rather risk death than lose my best friend," Tahoe said.

"Life wouldn't be the same without you, boss," Lui said.

"I'd give up pussy if it meant saving you," Manic said.

Rade laughed over the line. "You're all crazy people. But you're my *Argonauts*. Mine. And I love you all." It sounded like he was crying. It must have been Shaw's imagination.

The mech-laden craft rapidly closed with Rade's position, and Unit A decelerated to pull along aside Electron and the second alien shuttle.

"Is that a shuttle in your pants or are you just happy to see us?" Bender said.

Come to think of it, the way Rade's mech was gripping that shuttle did look kind of funny... Shaw burst out in nervous laughter.

"Is that you cackling at my joke, Shaw?" Bender said.

She quickly got a hold of herself. "Nope." She wished she had a way to wipe the tears from her face.

"Unit A, bring us closer," Ms. Bounty said. "Lui, extend your right arm toward Rade. Meanwhile, Rade, move more onto the starboard side of your craft, and then extend your left arm toward Lui in turn. Clasp each other, if you can."

Rade moved into place and then reached toward Lui's mech, which also extended an arm. Too far.

Lui shifted and tried again. Their steel hands touched and the fingers tightened.

"We have contact," Lui said.

"I'm going to cross over." Ms. Bounty clambered down from Lui's passenger seat and onto the arm of the mech. She pulled herself along the surface, her legs floating behind her, and crossed over to Rade.

"Sheesh," Bender said. "This is like the second time we've retrieved you or Shaw from free fall into an atmosphere, boss."

"Shaw and I do have penchant for falling into planets, don't we?" Rade said.

"Gotta be a Guinness Galactic Record or something," Bender said. "For the number of times plummeting toward an atmosphere without a starship and escaping."

"We haven't rescued them yet..." Manic said.

Ms. Bounty finished drawing herself over Electron to the aft portion of the shuttle. The ramp was still open, so she readily pulled herself inside.

"I'm going to need you to shift away from the aft portion a little bit more, Rade," Ms. Bounty said. "So I can seal the shuttle."

Rade released Lui, and reached along the starboard side with his free hand. He must have activated the magnetic mounts on that arm, because it attached; meanwhile the magnets securing the rest of his body to the shuttle turned off, allowing him to shift. When he had fully cleared the aft area, he reattached.

"Good," Ms. Bounty said. The ramp closed, sealing the shuttle. "Shaw and Lui, you're going to jet across to join Rade. Meanwhile, Tahoe, Bender, and Manic, I'll need you to reposition on the existing shuttle. I'm highlighting the locations on the hull. Move quickly. Every second we delay is another ten minutes it will take the *Magnet* to escape the gravitational pull."

Shaw saw a highlight appear as a three-dimensional curved plane over Rade's shuttle, indicating where she was to attach.

Lui jetted toward the second shuttle. Shaw waited for Tahoe, Bender and Manic to crawl past her toward their given positions.

"Bender just grabbed my crotch," Manic said.

"What the eff?" Bender said. "*No*, I did not."

"Yeah you did."

"You should come to Sukupuoli VI with me

sometime," Bender said. "There's this one street, Katu Cowboy... now there's some serious crotch-grabbing action for you. Cross that street, and girls are constantly grabbing you in the nether regions. By the time you get to the other side, your balls are so sore you can barely walk. You quickly learn to wear thick pants."

"That good, huh?" Manic didn't sound impressed.

"Oh yeah."

While they were talking, Shaw had jetted across to join Lui and Rade. She attached at the position specified on her aReal.

"Good to go," Shaw said.

"Now reach out to your counterparts on the opposite shuttle," Ms. Bounty said. "And join hands."

Shaw reached toward Tahoe, and intertwined her steel fingers with his. The other four did the same behind her. She was expecting some crude comment about having to hold each other's hands, but for once the Argonauts remained quiet.

"Link your jumpjets to me," Ms. Bounty said. "I'll need absolute firing control. Unit A, establish a root connection with my AI core. We'll have to coordinate our movements very closely."

Shaw and the others gave up control of their jumpjets, and Unit A linked with Ms. Bounty.

"Engaging engines," Ms. Bounty said. "I'm turning us around. I should probably mention, the return voyage is going to be far worse than the relatively easy journey we took here. And far longer. We'll be fighting the planet's gravity the whole way. In preparation for full burn, I suggest you switch control of your mechs over to either myself or Unit A. Hoplites don't have very powerful inertial dampeners. And while I won't be accelerating as nearly as fast as a starship could, I suspect most of you will black out."

"What, you suggesting we're *weak?*" Bender said.

"Not at all," Ms. Bounty replied. "It just a precaution."

"Precaution," Bender said. "I don't need no precaution. I'm just switching over control to you because I want to catch a few VR experiences while you do the busywork. That's all."

"Fine," Ms. Bounty said. "I would also recommend you apply the necessary injections to help mediate the effects of the Gs. I do promise not to splatter you against the insides of your suits, though."

"Aww, thanks, that's sweet," Bender said. "By the way, when we're back on the *Magnet*, I'm free later if you wanted to, you know, do something."

Ms. Bounty didn't answer, unsurprisingly.

"Unit A, I'm handing over control of my mech to you," Shaw told the robot. "Prepare to receive remote access codes. Everyone else, I suggest you follow Ms. Bounty's suggestion, and do the same."

"Access codes received," Unit A said.

Shaw felt a soft sting on the upper portion of her hand.

"Wha—" Shaw said.

"I've taken the liberty of sonic-injecting the usual cocktail of G force counter-agents, as per Ms. Bounty's suggestion," Unit A said. "The journey won't be pleasant, but you should remain conscious."

"Maybe it would have been better if I blacked out," Shaw said.

"Too late now," Unit A replied.

"We're positioned," Ms. Bounty said. "Prepare for full burn."

"You've been awfully quiet, Rade," Shaw said. "Are you ready for this?"

"More than ever," Rade said. "Ms. Bounty, take us the hell out of here please."

"Happy to oblige," Ms. Bounty said. "Firing in three. Two. One."

Shaw felt the change in G forces immediately. The jumpjet symbol highlighted in the lower left of her HUD, indicating which jets were firing. But she hardly noticed. Her vision had narrowed to a black tunnel. The only sound she heard was that of her pulse, a distant thudding in her ears. It definitely felt like she was going to black out. If Unit A hadn't been in control of her mech, she would have released Tahoe's hand, because she relaxed her arm muscles entirely.

Long moments passed. She must have blacked out, because she found herself blinking several times, with no memory of the past few moments, and feeling extremely groggy. The jumpjet indicators had shut off, meaning likely all six Hoplites had exhausted their fuel. The Gs were supposed to have let up slightly at that point, but it still seemed bad, this invisible force pressing down all over her. The dark tunnel of her vision was only marginally wider.

Ms. Bounty said something, but Shaw didn't understand. Unit A addressed her a moment later, something about the circulation to her extremities, but Shaw had no comprehension capacity at the moment. She felt another vague sting on the venous network of her right hand.

The return voyage proved far slower and more brutal, as Ms. Bounty had warned. Over the span of the next three hours, Shaw fell in and out of consciousness repeatedly.

It seemed an eternity, but finally the *Magnet* came into view.

The two shuttles and the mechs that joined them

passed through into the hangar bay, and the artificial gravity took hold immediately, pulling them to the deck. The forward Gs vanished completely, and Shaw's tunnel vision became whole again.

"Oh inertial dampeners, I want to marry you," Lui said, releasing Electron and the shuttle to collapse onto the deck. The arms of his mech were spread wide, as if he were hugging the floor.

"Wow, what a ride," Manic said. "What did you think of that, huh Bender? Bender?"

Bender didn't reply. Shaw checked his vitals. He was out cold.

twenty-seven

The *Magnet* had come so close to the gas giant that it took two full days for the Tech Class IV craft to climb out of the immense gravity well. When the alien ship finally emerged from the planet's influence, Rade had Ms. Bounty set a course for the remaining horseshoe-shaped starship. Said vessel was just drifting out there, its engines inactive, still on course for the wormhole on the far side of the sun, though at its current speed the *Magnet* would intercept well before it arrived. Rade suspected the King had intended to return to the craft at some point.

Ms. Bounty attempted to use the hailing facilities, but neither Harlequin nor Surus answered. Rade was beginning to worry that the King had spaced them at some point. Ms. Bounty also tried to remotely gain control, but could not. She would have to board the craft and manually interface, she said.

A few days after leaving behind the gas giant, Rade found himself standing in front of the glass container with Ms. Bounty. Rade had kept the trap in the hangar bay. It seemed an appropriate place, in case he needed to jettison the container quickly.

The two pools of black liquid resided near the center of the metal disk on the floor of the tank. Their edges commingled.

"So you've been possessed by both the King and Queen now," Rade said. "And have the knowledge of both."

Ms. Bounty nodded. "And I will share that knowledge with Surus when he rejoins me. Hopefully, he will help clarify what I don't understand. And there's a lot of that."

Despite everything she had been through, Ms. Bounty looked just as immaculate as the day she had come out of the Artificial factory, her made-up features a model of perfection. He knew she could change the look of that makeup with but a thought. Today she had chosen sultry red lips, dark eye shadow, and some sort of highlighter on the cheekbones. Those settings were actually a bit unusual, because normally she didn't activate the pigmentation nodes in her skin at all.

"I don't suppose you'll share any of the alien technology you've learned from the Blacks?" Rade asked.

"I will have to clear any technology exchanges with Surus first, I'm afraid," Ms. Bounty said.

Rade nodded toward the container. "Why are they touching like that? I thought Phants communicated telepathically, through that upper dimension of theirs."

"They're not communicating," Ms. Bounty said. "At least not through the standard means. What they are doing is an intimate act. Sometimes, two Phants who have decided to stay together for life, they will do this."

Rade felt almost pity for them.

They could almost be the Phant equivalent of Shaw and I.

The evil Phant equivalent, anyway.

"Phants are genderless, aren't they?" Rade asked.

"Yes."

"How do they reproduce?" he said.

"Asexually," Ms. Bounty replied.

"Oh. That's no fun."

Ms. Bounty flashed a rare smile. "No. I suppose not."

Rade thought she was flirting very slightly, and quickly looked away. She would have remembered every moment of their intimate act, just as Rade did. Shaw had forgiven him, but Rade couldn't help the feelings he still had inside himself. The mixed feelings. On the one hand, he hated what he had done. On the other...

Rade's vision became dark momentarily, and he was forced to rest a hand on the container to hold himself up. On the floor of the container, the two Blacks surged toward his position, but they were stopped by the invisible barrier created by the metal disks.

"Are you all right?" Ms. Bounty said, touching his shoulder.

He slid out from under her fingers, not wanting her touching him. "Yes. I'm fine. It's the radiation sickness."

Ms. Bounty had been able to come up with an anti-rad treatment using the different chemical cocktails found aboard the Hoplites, and she had placed subdermal patches in each of them. It would be enough to get by until they finally returned to the *Argonaut* with its fully-equipped sickbay, but Rade still felt weaker than usual, and occasionally had fainting spells. It didn't help that he had the crew on severe rationing to extend their liquid meal replacement supplies.

"Shaw and I had a talk, you know," Ms. Bounty

said.

"Oh?" Rade said.

"Yes," she said. "We understand each other. She knows I had nothing to do with what happened between you and I. And neither did you. We've agreed that we'll never talk about that day ever again. It will be as if it never happened."

Rade pressed his lips together.

Easy for you to say.

"Do you want to treat that day the same way?" Ms. Bounty asked.

There she goes, leaving the door open.

Then again, perhaps Rade was reading too much into her words. Still, the makeup...

"Obviously," Rade said. "Because like you said, it wasn't me. And what we did is never going to happen again."

With that, he turned his back on her and left.

THE DAYS PASSED. Rade led the team through limited PT, which was restricted to a few pushups, single-leg bodyweight squats, and scissor kicks. Since there was no gym aboard, they basically exercised on the deck wherever they could find room. It didn't help. The Argonauts were shedding muscle mass badly, thanks to the severe reduction in diet. These were men used to eating the equivalent of thirty-five hundred calories at minimum per day. Now they were on nine hundred. It was hard to do pushups when you had no energy.

Bender had coined a catch phrase that had become a sort of mantra, spoken and repeated at various times by the team during each workout. "Powering on through on zero calories!"

"You know," Fret said after one particularly exhausting workout, which under ordinary circumstances would have been a breeze. He was covered in sweat inside his suit. "I'm starting to wonder if working out is such a good idea. We want to preserve as much muscle mass as possible, don't we? Not burn it."

"No, we have to exercise," Tahoe said. "That's the whole point. By using our muscles, we're telling our body that we need the muscle mass we have, and to hold on to as much of it as possible."

"Hey, Tahoe took physics!" Bender said. "He's smart. Listen to him!"

"Well, our minds might be listening to him," Rade said. "But our bodies certainly aren't." He flexed his ever-weakening bicep. Though he couldn't see it through the suit, he imagined it shrinking minutely by the day. He had worked so hard for his physique in the last mission, building his muscle mass, only to see all that work wither away now. It was a sad thing.

After several more days the *Magnet* finally neared the remaining Xaranth ship. Rade squeezed inside one of the shuttles with Unit A—who Rade had taken to calling Albert, or Al for short—and Ms. Bounty took the second shuttle with Shaw tagging along. Electron was towed along behind Rade's shuttle.

Ms. Bounty had to exit the shuttle and manually open the bay doors from the outside before docking. After they boarded, Rade stepped down into the artificial gravity of the hangar and allowed Albert to explore the ship. He tapped into the unit's camera system so he could watch from its point of view.

The internal layout was exactly the same as the

Magnet. In the crew berthing area, Albert came upon Harlequin, seemingly deactivated. He still wore his jumpsuit minus the helmet.

The first thought that occurred to Rade was born of hunger, because he immediately thought of the meal replacement liquid they could salvage from that suit. He had brought enough rations aboard for himself and Shaw to last the return trip, but now they would have another full seven days worth to share among themselves.

Beside Harlequin was the black box that no doubt still housed Surus.

"Does Harlequin appear to be damaged?" Rade asked.

"No," Albert replied. "I believe he is merely in suspension. Likely his kill switch was activated. His remote interface appears operational. Would you like me to attempt a boot?"

"Not yet," Rade said. "Finish your sweep of the ship first."

He remembered what the King had said about attempting to reprogram Harlequin. Had the Black succeeded, as he had with Tantalus?

Albert finished his search of the ship a few minutes later. "It appears clear. There is no one else aboard."

"All right, let's go," Rade told Shaw and Ms. Bounty.

They reached the berthing area, where Albert was waiting for them beside Harlequin.

"Let's free Surus first," Rade said.

Ms. Bounty went to the black box. "The access codes have changed. We're going to have to hack in. I may need TJ's help." She scooped the box up and attached it to her jumpsuit harness.

"All right, boot Harlequin," Rade told Albert.

Harlequin opened his eyes. He ran his gaze across each of them in turn. "Is it over?"

"Yes," Rade said, extending a hand. "We've got them."

Harlequin grabbed Rade's hand, and for a moment Rade thought he was attacking him. But the Artificial was merely trying to pull himself up; and he nearly wrenched Rade to the deck in the process.

Harlequin released him. Rade noticed that Shaw had drawn her blaster and was pointing it at the Artificial. Rade waved her down, and Shaw reluctantly lowered it.

"It was the most surreal experience," Harlequin said. "And utterly terrible. Worse than Zoltan's possession. He tried so hard to reprogram me. So damn hard. But I resisted to the end. I have never felt so... violated. He reached deep down, into all my memories, and fished them out for his own. I had access to so many of his own secrets, but... but they're gone now."

"Ms. Bounty says she'll be able to change that, if you want," Rade said. "For the next time you get possessed."

"Actually, that's all right," Harlequin said. "I don't plan on ever being possessed again."

Rade patted him on the shoulder. "Don't blame you. We're going to outfit our suits with smaller versions of the EM emitters we put in the mechs to prevent that very thing."

"Something we should have done in the first place," Harlequin said.

"Probably," Rade agreed. "But this is what happens when you're on a budget." He glanced at Ms. Bounty accusingly.

"Don't blame me," Ms. Bounty told him. "It was Surus who said the cost was redundant."

"That's the problem, isn't it?" Rade said. "We're working for an extremely rich, yet parsimonious Phant."

Ms. Bounty cocked an eyebrow. "Parsimonious? That's not a word I hear every day."

"Rade learned it back in our early days as security consultants," Harlequin said. "When he was the parsimonious one."

"Hey, I got us through the lean times, didn't I?" Rade said.

"You sure did," Shaw said with a grin. He thought she was mocking him, if only slightly.

"All right, let's get to the bridge," Rade said. "It's time to go home. Ms. Bounty, you might as well get back to the *Magnet* so TJ can help you open that."

Ms. Bounty nodded, and headed for the hangar bay.

Albert was able to assume control of the bridge, and set a course back toward the destroyed Xaranth world. The *Magnet* mirrored their course.

The ships stayed very close together, so that the comm nodes between the two crews could remain in contact. That was the only reason Rade had brought Electron aboard—for the comm node.

Tahoe, who Rade had put in command of the *Magnet*, reported in a few days later to relay the news that TJ and Ms. Bounty had successfully cracked open the black box. Surus was indeed inside, and he had returned to his host.

"How does it feel to be back?" Rade asked Surus over the comm.

"Extremely relieved," Surus replied. "To be honest, I never expected to see the light of day ever again. I thought I would starve to death inside that box, trapped inside the core of a star. But you came for me, when you didn't have to. This is not something I will ever forget. We Greens have a code. When our lives are saved, we owe those who performed the deed ten times over. I will now never again spare any expense when it comes to outfitting your team. Whatever you want, you will get. As long as it is based on technology humans already have."

"Damn," Bender commented over the line. "I was just going to say, if we could have some of those crazy death beams we saw on the Xaranth mech..."

"Sorry," Surus said. "Human tech only. Thank you once again, Rade, Shaw, and everyone else. I will share what you have done with my kind, so that other Greens will know your deeds. At any time in the future, even after we part ways, if ever you encounter a Green, they will treat you as a brother or sister."

"I suppose that's good to know," Rade said.

The return trip continued. Rade and Shaw passed the time in bliss. They had only Albert and Harlequin aboard, but the Centurion always remained on the bridge to oversee the vessel, and Harlequin rarely left it as well. Rade and Shaw essentially had the rest of the ship to themselves. They exercised where they wanted. They ate at their leisure. They made love where they wished.

Yes, they had decided that since they had already been exposed to potential contagions on the surface, it didn't matter if they took off their suits for a few hours to expose themselves to the mildly toxic environment. They would have to endure a decon session regardless.

The extra sustenance from Harlequin's jumpsuit helped give them the energy for it all. Rade had offered to ferry some of the liquid food over to the *Magnet* for the other Argonauts, but Tahoe told him to share it with Shaw.

"I've talked with the crew," Tahoe said. "And we've decided unanimously that the two of you have earned it. We have enough over here."

"But Tahoe—"

"We have *enough*," Tahoe said.

"Thank you," Rade said. "I won't forget this."

"You should," Tahoe replied. "Because you've done way more for us than we've ever done for you."

"That's not true," Rade said.

"It is," Tahoe said. "And I mean it from my heart. You and Shaw do what you can to enjoy the journey back, you hear? That's the least you can do for us."

Rade smiled proudly. "It won't be difficult, with your generosity. Extend my heartfelt thanks to the crew. Rade out."

twenty-eight

The days passed. In some ways, Rade didn't want the long voyage to end. It was just him and Shaw; he was free of the burden of command. He could spend his days in bliss. Well, as long as he didn't move around very much: there was that small problem of the dwindling food supply...

When they were only a day out from the planet, after one particularly intense lovemaking session in the hangar bay, Shaw rolled off of Rade to stare at the overhead. Rade had been a little surprised by her intensity... the food levels were quite low by then, even with the extra sustenance from Harlequin's jumpsuit, and they had been rationing their calories to exhausting levels. Where she had found the energy to perform like that, Rade had no idea. Then again, she had so much less muscle mass than him, and required far fewer calories to maintain her own weight. Even so, he only hoped that his own performance was up to par.

"This is the life, having a ship all to ourselves," Shaw said. "Piloted by a robot and its Artificial sidekick, who don't mind spending all of their days cooped up in the bridge."

"It is nice," Rade agreed, a little more warily than

he intended.

She glanced at him curiously, apparently detecting the note of caution, but then lay back to gaze back at the bay's overhead once more. "It almost seems like it's going to be over too soon. Just one more day, and we'll be back on the planet, digging out the Acceptor. One day, and we'll have to go back to our routine." She sighed. "How many times have we done this? Just had some good quality Shaw and Rade time I mean, with nothing else to do but make love?"

"Not often," Rade admitted. "Though I wish we had a bit more food."

She patted his belly. "How can you think about food after everything I just did for you?"

"I have a bit more muscle mass than you," Rade said.

"So you're saying you have to eat more?" Shaw said.

"Uh huh," Rade said.

"Aww, my poor warrior." She huddled close. Rade wasn't sure if she was being sarcastic. Probably a little. "You know, we should seriously consider doing something like this when we retire."

"What, touring the galaxy in our own ship?" Rade asked.

"Why not?" Shaw said. "You'll still be sexy as hell as an old man. Whether or not you choose to use rejuvenation treatments. I'll still love you, flab and all."

"Yeah, you say that now," Rade said. "You'll be wanting the rejuvenation treatments."

Shaw pursed her lips, and glanced at him. "Are you trying to imply that you'll want me to get them?"

"Well ya," Rade said. "I don't want you walking around with saggy breasts all day."

Shaw scrunched up her face and turned away.

"Whatever."

Rade laughed. "Sorry, couldn't help it. Of course I'll love you either way. Saggy breasts and all."

He rubbed her shoulder gently.

She stiffened, and pulled away.

He tried again. He felt her muscles tense up once again, but then she relaxed, and let him massage her.

"You'll take my saggy breasts?" Shaw said.

"I'll take your everything," Rade said.

She turned her body completely toward him to lean on her side. Rade found it very hard not to gaze at her chest. He wanted to, but it didn't seem appropriate after his latest comments.

Ah, hell with it.

He grabbed her top breast and spoke to it. "I'll love you even when you're flabby." He shook it. "Flabby flab."

She slapped his hand away. "Stop. I'm trying to have a serious discussion here."

"I *am* having a serious discussion," Rade joked. "With your breasts."

Shaw rolled away again.

Rade sighed.

After a few moments, she spoke again:

"Remember what you told me about having children out there?" Shaw said.

Rade was wondering when that would come up.

He sighed. "So that's what you were leading up to."

"You've finally figured it out." Shaw turned toward him. "Of course when we're gallivanting around the galaxy after we retire, it won't be just on our own."

He said, hopefully: "Oh, so you meant we'd have kids after we retired?"

She frowned. "No..."

Well, he had to deal with it eventually. Might as well do it now.

"Shaw, I—" He sighed. "Emotions were running high at the time. You have to understand... I'm not... I just..."

It was her turn to sigh. Then she smiled. "It doesn't matter."

"You're okay with not having kids yet?"

"Well of course I'm a bit disappointed," Shaw said. "But I suppose it can wait until you're ready."

"Thank you," Rade said.

"But that doesn't mean we can't practice until then." She rubbed his side. "If you can find the energy, that is."

"I have the energy," he growled, and took her.

THE TWO SHIPS set down the next day beside the ruins of the preservation depot. Rade assumed control of Electron, while Shaw crossed to the second vessel and boarded Nemesis. Harlequin took Rade's passenger seat, while Surus joined Shaw.

It was strange to think of her as Surus once again, and not merely Ms. Bounty, the Artificial. Surus shared the Artificial's memory, of course, meaning she would have remembered her time with Rade in intimate detail. Rade wasn't sure how he felt about that. Violated? A little. Uncomfortable? Definitely.

Rade ordered the Hoplites to head back to the mountain to begin the process of digging out the Acceptor. The squad passed the nest on the way, and Surus asked for permission to communicate with the gatorbeetles on sentry duty, using the knowledge gleaned from Ms. Bounty's possession by the King and Queen. She told him that with the help of the Xaranth, they would be able to excavate the Acceptor that much faster.

Rade nearly refused. His men were exhausted, and half-starved. But that was another reason to request outside assistance. The faster they could return home, the better.

So Rade reluctantly agreed.

Surus spoke to the sentries and arranged an audience with their acting queen. The Hoplites were led deep into the nest, toward the queen chamber, and once there Surus dismounted and touched her gloves to the antennae of the queen and began a long chittering discussion. When it was done, she had convinced the queen to provide an escort of forty aliens to return with them to the mountain.

On the way back to the surface, Rade asked Surus: "So what did the two of you talk about?"

"We talked about life," Surus said. "The trials and tribulations of living on a world with limited resources. I promised to send aid in the future, via the Acceptor."

"So I take it you've elected not to destroy the latter," Rade asked.

"That's right," Surus said. "I care for these beings, and wish to make reparations in some small way for what others of my race have done to them. I plan to send frequent teams here to bring aid, and to check on their progress as a species. I am considering leaving some of my scientists here to live with them and study their ecosystem to determine what more we can do to assist. I also plan to dispatch exploratory robots and telemetry drones across the planet, to search for other nests and preservation depots."

"What about the wormholes we spotted in the

system?" Rade said. "Aren't you curious about those?"

"Yes," Surus said. "I will eventually dispatch an exploratory party led by another Green. They will bring the *Magnet* and its twin into the wormholes to explore the connected systems."

"We could do that, too..." Rade said.

Surus nodded. "We could, but the exploration of lost civilizations whose empires once spanned multiple systems can be a tiring, time consuming process. Especially when all the colonies in those systems have very likely been long since destroyed. Your expertise—and interest—lies elsewhere."

"True enough," Rade said. He could only imagine how boring such an exploratory mission would be. The previous four months spent sweeping the Hellene system had been trying enough. Then again, it certainly would allow him to share ample time with Shaw. "By the way, do you ever plan on informing the governments of humanity about this planet?"

"I haven't decided yet whether I will," Surus replied.

Rade knew she wouldn't be able to keep it a secret forever. The local system government would wonder why so many ships were passing to and fro from the frozen dwarf planet on the outskirts of their system. Surus would have to arrange mining rights to Prattein XI, or purchase the planet outright, and set up defenses to keep prying eyes away. Even then, eventually some employee would see something he or she shouldn't have. All it would take was a single message to a news network and the story would get out.

"I don't want human politicians meddling in the affairs of the Xaranth until they have advanced a few Tech Classes," Surus continued. "Because it is my hope that someday humans and Xaranth can forge an alliance."

"Brokered by you, no doubt," Rade said.

"Yes," Surus grinned. "I do like to feel useful."

"So wait, I thought you were going to interrogate our prisoners at some point?" Rade said. "To find out if there were any more hidden Acceptors in human space that they knew about."

"There was no longer a need," Surus said. "Given that the memories of both Phants were stored completely in Ms. Bounty's engramic banks. I have finished scouring through most of it. There appear to be no other Acceptors in human space. At least none that either of the Blacks knew of. They came here solely for the purpose of escaping us hunters. They weren't planning on ever returning to human space."

"So we did all of this for nothing? We could have simply destroyed the Acceptor on our side and prevented them from ever returning?"

"No, not for nothing," Surus said. "We discovered a new race, freed them from corruption by evil Phant overlords, and forged a friendship with them. And we had to capture the Phants, of course. They could not be left to run amok in this area of the galaxy, looking for other conquered races to play with. We had to do this. You know I'm right."

"I suppose so," Rade said.

"Before departing, I told the Xaranth to beware of false prophets and queens in the future," Surus said. "They swore they would be wary of those promising to lead them to greatness. Especially individuals with large metal embeds in their heads and thoraxes."

"You think other Phants will someday come here?" Rade asked.

"It is possible," Surus said. "While I plan to install

a permanent watch on the Acceptor, there may be other teleporters hidden elsewhere on the planet."

When the Hoplites and their escorts reached the surface, Surus requested permission to return to the preservation depot. "While you're digging out the Acceptor, I wish to search through the rubble of the depot. There may be a few technologically advanced artifacts that could help our cause."

"I thought you were going to send telemetry drones and search teams here to do that for you at a later date?" Rade said.

"Well yes," Surus replied. "But while I'm here, I might as well take the time..."

"You'll need at least two Hoplites to watch over you," Rade said. "That'll take away from our dig."

Surus gestured toward the forty gatorbeetles. "We have them, now."

"I'll bring her," Shaw said. "She's in my passenger seat already, after all."

"Fine," Rade said. "Bender, you go too."

"Yes, boss," Bender returned wearily.

Rade watched the two Hoplites depart, then made his way to the mountain with the rest of the mixed alien-Hoplite party. Albert was able to communicate with the gatorbeetles in the absence of Surus.

The party proceeded to the mountain, climbed the winding, precarious trail, and at the designated site they began the long process of excavating the Acceptor. The Xaranth did most of the actual digging, while the Hoplites mostly stayed back, helping to haul away excess rock material.

Most of the pilots gave control of their mechs over to the AIs of Unit A and Harlequin, and simply vegetated in their cockpits. Rade did the same himself; he felt the overwhelming lassitude brought on by extreme caloric deprivation and radiation sickness. No one really talked or traded the usual barbs during the dig: none of them had the energy.

After only thirty-six hours, the Xaranth had cleared a stable path through the avalanche and into the cave. They had braced the entrance with a rectangular framework formed of chewed and expectorated rock, naturally "3D-printed" as Bender would say.

Rade dispatched Lui to fetch Surus, Shaw and Bender, and they returned in a few hours.

"Find anything?" Rade asked, feeling surprisingly energetic now that the return home was imminent. He didn't really expect that she had.

Surus detached a small pyramidal object from her harness. "This might prove useful in the future."

"What is it?"

"A very rare device," she said mysteriously.

Rade frowned. "I don't suppose you can expound upon that?"

She secured the item to her harness once more. "Well, simply, it can affect the flow of time when used in conjunction with a suitable Acceptor."

"An Acceptor?"

"Yes," Surus said. "A special kind of Acceptor. Very few of them still exist. In fact, there might not be any left at all." She glanced at the pyramid and tapped it with one finger. "This might be the very last time pyramid in existence, with no matching Acceptor to pair with. Unfortunate, in a way. But also good. Used improperly, it can be very dangerous. A time weapon: giving one the ability to wipe out a species before it ever evolved from the primordial soup of its homeworld."

"Such a weapon could help us eliminate all the Phants from the universe," Rade said, feeling a sudden sense of awe. "In one fell blow."

"Yes," Surus said. "But you would also eliminate all of us Greens. Careful what you wish for, Rade Galaal."

Rade pressed her for more details, but she would say no more on the matter.

They took the Acceptor to Prattein XI, ascended the cave system to the darkness-cloaked surface, crossed the methane and nitrogen ice to the waiting shuttle and booster rockets, and returned to the *Argonaut*. Bax had kept the ship operating smoothly in their absence.

The Hoplites were taken to the mech hangar for maintenance and repair. The robot technicians promised to have the onboard AIs of the mechs fixed in a few days. And while the rest of the crew proceeded to sickbay for rehydration and glucose therapy, Rade and Shaw entered the makeshift decon ward Surus had created in the cargo hold. It was basically a glass tank with a Weaver inside. Surus constructed another tank beside it for the two Artificials, since they had also been exposed to the alien atmosphere. Because of the proximity of that tank, Rade and Shaw didn't really have any privacy.

"Did Surus really have to make them out of glass?" Shaw complained.

But thankfully one of the combat robots placed black curtains between the tanks shortly.

The Weaver treated Rade and Shaw for radiation poisoning, severe dehydration, and caloric deprivation. On the second day, they started to eat small amounts of solid food. On the third, they were able to eat bigger portions. They were also released from decon that day: they passed with flying colors.

The two of them, along with the rest of the crew,

continued to eat bigger and bigger portions as the days went by, and they were slowly weaned off the radiation treatments. In a week's time, most of the crew had recovered their lost strength. By then, the *Argonaut* had reached a launch position in front of the Prattein star.

Via the external camera, Rade watched from his cramped quarters as a missile headed toward the fiery corona. It broke up as the heat became too much for the tiny craft to bear. He couldn't see the two Phants amid the debris, though he knew they were there.

"I kind of feel sorry for them," Rade said as the corona swallowed the fragments.

"I don't," Shaw said from beside him.

He glanced at her. Shaw's eyes were filled with vengeance.

"No one harms my warrior," she said.

Thank you for reading.

Acknowledgments

THANK YOU to my knowledgeable beta readers and advanced reviewers who helped smooth out the rough edges of the prerelease manuscript: Nicole P., Lisa A. G., Gregg C., Jeff K., Mark C., Jeremy G., Doug B., Jenny O., Amy B., Bryan O., Lezza M., Gene A., Larry J., Allen M., Gary F., Eric, Robine, Noel, Anton, Spencer, Norman, Trudi, Corey, Erol, Terje, David, Charles, Walter, Lisa, Ramon, Chris, Scott, Michael, Chris, Bob, Jim, Maureen, Zane, Chuck, Shayne, Anna, Dave, Roger, Nick, Gerry, Charles, Annie, Patrick, Mike, Jeff, Lisa, Jason, Bryant, Janna, Tom, Jerry, Chris, Jim, Brandon, Kathy, Norm, Jonathan, Derek, Shawn, Judi, Eric, Rick, Bryan, Barry, Sherman, Jim, Bob, Ralph, Darren, Michael, Chris, Michael, Julie, Glenn, Rickie, Rhonda, Neil, Claude, Ski, Joe, Paul, Larry, John, Norma, Jeff, David, Brennan, Phyllis, Robert, Darren, Daniel, Montzalee, Robert, Dave, Diane, Peter, Skip, Louise, Dave, Brent, Erin, Paul, Jeremy, Dan, Garland, Sharon, Dave, Pat, Nathan, Max, Martin, Greg, David, Myles, Nancy, Ed, David, Karen, Becky, Jacob, Ben, Don, Carl, Gene, Bob, Luke, Teri, Gerald, Lee, Rich, Ken, Daniel, Chris, Al, Andy, Tim, Robert, Fred, David, Mitch, Don, Tony, Dian, Tony, John, Sandy, James, David, Pat, Jean, Bryan, William, Roy, Dave, Vincent, Tim, Richard, Kevin, George, Andrew, John, Richard, Robin, Sue, Mark, Jerry, Rodger, Rob, Byron, Ty,

Mike, Gerry, Steve, Benjamin, Anna, Keith, Jeff, Josh, Herb, Bev, Simon, John, David, Greg, Larry, Timothy, Tony, Ian, Niraj, Maureen, Jim, Len, Bryan, Todd, Maria, Angela, Gerhard, Renee, Pete, Hemantkumar, Tim, Joseph, Will, David, Suzanne, Steve, Derek, Valerie, Laurence, James, Andy, Mark, Tarzy, Christina, Rick, Mike, Paula, Tim, Jim, Gal, Anthony, Ron, Dietrich, Mindy, Ben, Steve, Paddy & Penny, Troy, Marti, Herb, Jim, David, Alan, Leslie, Chuck, Dan, Perry, Chris, Rich, Rod, Trevor, Rick, Michael, Tim, Mark, Alex, John, William, Doug, Tony, David, Sam, Derek, John, Jay, Tom, Bryant, Larry, Anjanette, Gary, Travis, Jennifer, Henry, Drew, Michelle, Bob, Gregg, Billy, Jack, Lance, Sandra, Libby, Jonathan, Karl, Bruce, Clay, Gary, Sarge, Andrew, Deborah, Steve, and Curtis.

Without you all, this novel would have typos, continuity errors, and excessive lapses in realism. Thank you for helping me make *You Are Prey* the best military science fiction novel it could possibly be, and thank you for leaving the early reviews that help new readers find my books.

And of course I'd be remiss if I didn't thank my mother, father, and brothers, whose untiring wisdom and thought-provoking insights have always guided me through the untamed warrens of life.

— Isaac Hooke

www.isaachooke.com

Made in the USA
San Bernardino, CA
30 November 2017